WICKED IN WINTER

JENNIFER BERNARD

CHAPTER ONE

"You have one job," Gretel Morrison told herself as she walked down the snowy path to the Noonans' woodshed. "Don't end up in the snowbank. That's it. You can do this."

She pulled up her zipper the last inch so the fleece-lined hood of her parka snapped into place. It felt like wearing a biohazard suit. But the only hazard in this ice-pure Alaskan air was the snow.

Well...and hazards like loading firewood onto the sled. The last time she'd attempted this task, she'd wound up face down in the snow while the sled headed down the path like a magic carpet on the run.

She flat-out refused to let a sled of firewood defeat her. She was trying to turn a corner in her life, after all.

She confronted the woodshed, a sturdy structure about fifty yards from the main house of Abby and Earl Noonan's homestead. Apparently the family spent much of the fall chopping down dead trees and chain-sawing them into rounds to stack inside the woodshed. On one of his two weeks off from his job on the North Slope, Earl had given her a tour of the shed—green wood in the back, seasoned wood in the front, cut logs to the right, kindling to the left.

He'd shown her the stump that served as a chopping block and the maul used for cutting the rounds into more burnable "splits."

"Next time I'm here I'll show you how to split wood," he'd offered.

She'd laughed out loud, until she realized he was serious. "Oh, um...yeah, sure...that would be—"

"You're right. It's not hard. Anyone can show you, Abby or even Eli."

Eli was their seven-year-old son. Granted, he was tall for his age and had grown up on this homestead. But still.

At that moment, Gretel had vowed to teach *herself* how to chop wood. Maybe after she managed to fill a sled without diving into a snowbank.

She could do this. She *had* to do this.

The whole purpose of her living here on this remote homestead was to help Abby through her recovery from brain surgery and a C-section, and right now, the household needed firewood. The Noonans had been so kind to her—she loved them dearly—and she couldn't let them freeze to death because she was afraid of a sled.

Straightening her spine, she trudged through the snow to her nemesis, which was propped inside the woodshed.

"Let's talk, shall we?" she said to the sled, a long orange molded-plastic monstrosity. "This isn't about me. This is about Abby and the kids and the new baby. Whatever your beef is with me, can you just put it aside and think about the Noonans? They're counting on us here. Do we understand each other?"

A tiny creature darted from inside the woodshed and scurried across the snow. She gave a shriek and staggered a step backwards. The vole or ermine—she didn't yet know how to distinguish them—disappeared under one of the Noonans' ancient trucks.

After she caught her balance, Gretel balled up her fists inside her gloves and marched toward the sled. "Oh ho. That's how you're going to play it? Calling in your little *friends* for backup? That ain't going to fly, mister. Big mistake. Now I'm really fired up."

She grabbed hold of the sled and lifted it away from the stack of wood it was leaning against. Even though she dislodged some kindling and nearly tripped over the chopping stump in the process, she managed to wrangle it out of the woodshed. When it was entirely clear, she let it slide onto the snow-packed ground, where she quickly placed one foot on it.

"Gotcha," she told it. "Now just...chill there for a minute while I get the wood. We cool?"

Oh my God, she was talking to a sled. Had she totally lost it? Had the last couple of months in Alaska caused her to completely lose her mind?

Shaking her head at her own absurdity, she lifted her foot off the sled. It didn't move—*whew*—so she headed into the woodshed to fill her arms with logs. Earl had taught her to start by anchoring the load with a couple of the rounds—which were unfortunately the heaviest of all. With the near-zero temperature, they sometimes got iced together by bits of frozen sap.

Of course. Because nothing could be easy here in Alaska.

It took her a moment to pry a round off the top of the stack. "If you fall on my toe, you're dead to me," she warned it as she settled it into her arms like a baby.

Carrying her prize, she ducked out of the woodshed and blinked in the pearly morning light. The sled was gone. The sneaky bastard had slid down the path and was now pinned under the ski-booted foot of Zander Ross.

Zander could definitely be considered another Alaska hazard. The rugged and smolderingly sexy male kind.

He'd stuck his skis in the snowbank next to the path. He must have skied over from his own place about half a mile away.

"So..." Zander called to her as he did some kind of flippy move with his boot that sent the sled flying from the ground into the secure grip of his right hand. "I'm trying to figure out if you're talking to the wood or to the vole or just to the world in general."

"You left out imaginary friend." She lifted her chin in defiance. With his height and physique, Zander was one of those men who reminded her of her small size. "Probably because the concept of friend eludes you."

"Now that's funny, because if I were your friend I might offer to help you out."

"I don't need your help. But I do need my sled back." Pointedly, she gestured with her head for him to bring it her way.

"Your sled just made a run for it." Nevertheless, he walked toward her with the sled slung behind his shoulder, its tether hooked by one finger.

She clenched her teeth together. Did he have to be so fricking attractive while he was teasing her? He had the body of an outdoorsman and super-fit former Marine, which Abby had told her he was. His hair was very dark, almost black, in a cut no actual barber would take credit for. He wore Carhartts—the standard outdoor work gear in Alaska—but he somehow made them look mouthwatering.

The closer he came, the more she could make out the hazel green in his eyes and the stubble on his jaw. Like many men here, he kept a short beard to fend off the winter rawness. Unlike some of those men, Zander maintained his facial hair properly.

She'd noticed because one of her talents was cutting hair— not because she'd been closely assessing him. Not at all.

He dropped the sled on the ground at her feet and angled it so that it couldn't go anywhere.

"Thank you," she said with dignity. "You can go now. You must have important things to do over at your own place."

Zander and his younger brothers were the Noonans' closest neighbors. That didn't mean much; their house was down the road, with a thick growth of spruce forest between them. But still, they saw more of the Ross family than anyone else.

"I came to see if Abby needs anything from town. Couldn't reach anyone by phone and I got worried."

"Ugh. The kids keep unplugging it by mistake. Sorry to make you ski all the way over here."

"No problem." Still, he lingered. "Sure you don't need any help? It'd take about a minute to load this up between the two of us."

"I'm sure," she said firmly.

Zander didn't understand; how could he? Her entire life, things had been made easy for her. Money did that. With enough money, you could pay anyone to do anything for you. She hadn't become fully aware of this reality until she'd come to Alaska—and until her father had cut her off.

Which was painful, but probably the best thing that could have happened to her. She'd jumped on the opportunity to try something different. To become someone different.

He was still watching her, a perplexed frown on his face. It wasn't exactly a handsome face—his eyebrows were too strong, his cheekbones too prominent, jaw too stubborn. But it was hard to look away from. He wasn't a big talker, in her experience, and his face reflected that with a kind of banked intensity. He looked like someone who kept things inside. Maybe not handsome—but definitely smoldering.

Silence always made her nervous—as if it was her job to fill it. And so she added, "I'm on a mission to do things for myself."

Right away, she regretted telling him that. One of his eyebrows lifted. "Oh yeah? How's that going?"

Maybe he wasn't being sarcastic, but it sure felt that way.

"Super," she said firmly as she placed the log in the sled exactly as Earl had instructed. "Everything's great. But you'd better check with Abby about town. The only thing I need is eyeshadow, maybe in a sapphire-blue shade?"

He cocked his head at her. "Nah. I'd go for more of a light brown to set off the turquoise."

As she gaped at him, a smile quirked one corner of his mouth. "YouTube makeup tutorial. Don't ask."

A wisp of wind brushed against her cheeks and drew her attention to the fact that her face was growing numb. She turned away to stack more firewood.

"So you're serious about this," he said.

"About not needing your help? A thousand and twenty-eight percent."

"Very specific. That's not what I mean. I mean you're serious about staying here?"

She dislodged another round from the pile and hauled it to the sled. She saw his gloved hands twitch, as if he could barely stop himself from helping.

"Staying with Abby? Sure, as long as she needs me. She's not supposed to lift her arms above her head for like, another month, poor thing."

"Okay, so another month. And then?"

She scrunched her forehead at him, then turned away to fill her arms with cut logs. "Our arrangement is open-ended. We're going to see how it goes. Why, are you trying to get rid of me?"

But she'd loaded her arms with too much wood, and one of the logs went rogue and slid off the stack. It bounced on the ground, then landed on her foot. "Ow."

He made a move toward her, as if to help—but she made a snarly face at him. "Don't you dare. This is a minor setback."

With a snort, he shook his head. A puff of condensation curled through the air. His mouth must be so...warm. "It's not my job to get rid of you. Alaska's going to do that all on its own."

"Excuse me?" She dumped the rest of her armful of logs onto the sled with a satisfying clunk. A raven cawed from the woods, as if she'd surprised him.

"You'll never make it through the winter."

Gretel bent over to pick up the runaway log. She could have simply knelt, but that wouldn't have been nearly as provocative a move. Hopefully, even in her snow pants and parka, Zander would take notice. Just because she was trying to do things for herself didn't mean she was giving up flirting—even with cocky, annoying neighbors. "Is that a challenge?"

She peered through her eyelashes at him. He flicked his eyes away from her ass just in time. Oh yes, he'd noticed her. Good. *Busted, Zander Ross.*

"It's more of a prediction, but sure," he said coolly. As if she hadn't just caught him checking her out. "You can call it a challenge. Do you know how many people think a winter in Alaska would be a fun adventure? And how many take off for Hawaii come March?"

"Care to put your money where your mouth is?"

"Never understood that phrase. Am I supposed to smear dollar bills on my face?"

She laughed despite herself as she fetched another armload of firewood. "Nice image. Very creative. I was thinking more of a bet."

"What are the terms?" he asked promptly. That was one thing she liked about Zander. He picked up on things quickly and he didn't beat around the bush.

"If I make it through the winter, you have to go on KLSW

and make a public proclamation that you underestimated me."

"Done."

He was so quick to say it that she had to add on a little more. Blame the deal-making gene she'd inherited from her father. "On the Bush Lines."

The Bush Lines were a way for people out in Lost Souls Wilderness who could only communicate by radio to get messages to people in Lost Harbor or elsewhere around Misty Bay. Birthday wishes, love notes, requests for ride shares, items for sale—all kinds of things found their way into the Bush Lines.

"On the Bush Lines," he agreed. "And if you ditch before the winter is over, then you will...do something. To be named later."

"Oh no. I'm not committing to anything that vague."

"What does it matter, since you're going to make it through the winter anyway?" He pulled off his glove, preparing for a handshake.

"Schoolboy taunts are not going to work on me. Come on. Be specific."

He scratched at the underside of his jaw with his bared hand. It was so large, that hand, and looked so capable. Zander was the surrogate parent of his two brothers, and he had a lot of responsibility loaded onto him. But with those wide shoulders and big hands, he looked like he could handle it.

"You'll sing something. Abby said you're a good singer."

Oh ho, so Abby had been talking about her to Zander? She'd very much like to know more about that conversation.

"Sing what?"

"Whatever. Something about the Alaska winter. About how great it is."

"I don't know any songs about how great the Alaska winter is. They probably don't exist."

"So write one. Whatever. That's the bet. If you can't handle the winter in Alaska, you'll perform a song in praise of our great state. If you do make it through the winter, I'll go on the Bush Lines and talk about how stupid I was to underestimate you like that."

She stuck out her hand. "I like the sound of that. You have a deal." They moved to shake hands, but she whipped hers away at the last second.

He squinted at her. "What are you, twelve?"

"I thought of something else. Define winter. Is it the first day of spring? Is it when the temperature stays above freezing for a week? Is it when girls start wearing sundresses?"

First he laughed. Then he sobered quickly and his expression went back to its usual reserve. "Everyone knows the winter isn't over until the snow melts."

"*All* of the snow?" She looked around at the Noonans' homestead. It was composed of a house, a barn, the woodshed, an outhouse, a well house, a spacious hooped plastic tunnel for early planting, a shop, and acres of land—all of which was tucked under at least two feet of snow.

And it was still only early January. People were predicting many more feet of snow to come.

"When does that usually happen?"

"It's different every winter. Hard to say."

Gretel considered that, then shrugged. She didn't actually know if she would stay for the entire winter. She wasn't really planning that far ahead. She might leave, she might not. But she intended to leave on her own terms.

Besides, she loved to sing.

"Okay, it's a deal. We can work out the rest of the details later."

Almost formally, she drew off her glove and stuck out her hand. He wrapped his big palm around hers. The flood of warmth from his hand made her a little dizzy. A big guy like Zander really put out some body heat.

He looked down at their joined hands with a funny expression, as if almost incredulous that her hand had disappeared so completely within his. "May the odds be ever in your favor," he said solemnly.

"I feel like it's a bad sign to quote *Hunger Games* at me."

"Too late now. Deal's a deal."

She pulled her hand away and tugged her glove back on. One more handful of kindling and her sled would be full and she could get her ass inside the house. She grabbed some branches from the kindling stack and added them to the sled. "Excuse me."

Zander stepped out of her way and edged down the path toward his skis.

She took hold of the tether with both hands. Facing the sled, with her back toward the house, she leaned backwards and tried to make it move across the snow. But the weight of the wood pinned it in place. Once again she'd piled it too high.

She tried again, jerking the line. This time it moved, practically leaping toward her. Yes! She had forward motion. That was the first step. She backed toward the house, digging her cleats into the hard-packed snow. Now all she had to do was turn around and pull it behind her the rest of the way.

The fact that Zander was watching made it extra sweet.

As gracefully as possible, she turned around, switched her hands on the tether. But she pulled too hard on one side of the strap and caused the sled to tilt up.

Before she knew it, she lost her balance and about half the firewood spilled into the snow. She windmilled her arms—*don't end up in the snow. Don't end up in the snow.* It worked, but in the process, the tether strap got wrapped around her glove. Somehow it got ripped off her hand and flung toward Zander.

He caught it just before it landed on the snow.

"So...uh...need a little—"

"No!"

He snapped his mouth shut.

"I don't need help," she added stubbornly.

"Fine. At least take this." He tossed her the glove. "I draw the line at frostbite."

She caught the glove and quickly pulled it on. In that short time, the chill had already reddened her skin. By now, her face was practically numb. She clapped her hands together, then bent to load the firewood back onto the sled. The raven cawed from a closer perch, almost as if mocking her. She glanced up to locate the bird, and caught one of those dazzling moments that sometimes came her way here at the Noonans'.

The raven launched itself off the branch, dislodging a cloud of snow. The movement of the branch let the morning sun shine through. For a quiet moment, the myriad of snow crystals hung suspended in the air, vibrating with golden light. The snow cloud gently wafted to the ground, where she noticed the tiny snow tracks of the creature who'd fled the woodshed.

She caught her breath in wonder at the perfect serendipity of the moment—the raven, the snow, the ray of sun, the tracks. The fact that she was here in the cold and the snow to witness it.

"Did you see that?" she said softly after all the snow crystals had settled onto the ground. "The raven and the..." She trailed off as she glanced in Zander's direction. He was already gone, skiing toward the big house to consult with Abby.

She was talking to herself again.

"Anyway, it was beautiful. Totally worth nearly freezing my ass off while I reload this mother-forking sled. You orange beast, I'm going to take you to an incinerator one of these days. I thought we had a deal. But no, you had to betray me in front of Zander Ross, of all people."

Muttering to herself, she set to work reloading the sled. No way was she going to give Zander the satisfaction of seeing her give up.

CHAPTER TWO

"Is she okay out there?" At the window, Abby Noonan, holding her newborn in a sling that kept the baby above the level of her incision, rocked from one stockinged foot to another. Their dog, a rambunctious mutt named Groovy, snoozed by the woodstove.

"So she says." Zander stayed in the arctic entry so he didn't have to take off his snow boots. "Believe me, I tried. She doesn't want help. My help, anyway. I don't think she likes me much."

"Oh, don't be silly. She likes you just fine."

Zander grunted. He completely disagreed with that assessment. But it didn't matter anyway. He gave Gretel another month, at the most. A girl like her, so beautiful, so coddled, so magnetic, could go anywhere she wanted. Why would she choose to be here, twelve miles outside of Lost Harbor, at the end of the road that hugged Misty Bay, a seven-hour winter drive from anything resembling a city?

"I think she's talking to herself again," said Abby, peering out the triple-paned glass.

"Not exactly. She might be talking to the sled."

Abby laughed, then halted the sound. "Can't laugh yet.

Stitches. It's kind of a problem because Gretel is really very funny."

"That is one way to describe her," Zander said as diplomatically as he could. He still didn't understand how Gretel had ended up here. He might never understand.

Again, not that it mattered. He had enough other things to worry about. "I'm headed into town, need anything?"

"Did the kids unplug the phone again? Damn it. I'd yell at them but they're napping and I need those nap times more than oxygen. Did you hear that they might put another cell tower up and we might actually get real service out here?"

"I'll believe it when I see it."

"Right? Anyway, sorry to make you ski all the way over here."

"It was no problem," he assured her. "It gave me a chance to set the trail." Several times each winter, he had to set down new tracks for skiing between their properties. His brother Jason didn't know it, but he was about to get assigned that task. Jason was thirteen now and a ski nut, so why not?

"Well, let me think." Abby adjusted the hand-woven sling and glanced toward her kitchen. She and Earl had a passion for living off the land. They fished, hunted, canned vegetables from their summer gardens, picked berries in the fall, made jam, knitted their own sweaters. For a few years they'd made it all work, but once they'd reached three kids, Earl had taken a job on the North Slope to earn extra income. Two weeks away, two weeks helping Abby with the kids and doing what he could around the property.

Even though Zander had his hands full with Jason and Petey, he'd gotten in the habit of stopping by to see if Abby and her kids needed anything. This close to the edge of the wild, people had to stick together.

"We can always use more milk. But make sure it's the hormone-free kind. Some toilet paper. The biggest case you can find. Unsalted butter. And Gretel has a thing for those shelled pistachios, so can you grab a bag of those?"

"Pistachios? Really?"

"Hey." She frowned at him. "*Anything* to keep her here, you hear me? She can have pistachios day and night. Actually, get some pistachio ice cream too. Anything in the entire store that has pistachios in it. If that girl leaves me, I can't be held responsible for my mental breakdown."

Zander shook his head as he made a note in his phone. "Is she really that helpful? Has she made it back with the firewood yet?"

Abby glanced out the window. "She's getting there. And you really need to open your eyes, kid. Considering she was raised with a silver spoon, she's doing pretty well. Imagine if you were plopped into a situation that was completely new and strange and zero degrees on top of that? Think you'd do half as well?"

Zander gave her a hard stare, until she blinked in recognition.

"Right. You did that when your parents died. Sorry."

He shrugged, not wanting to make a big deal out of it.

"The main point is, all my babies love her and she's great with them. So be nice to her. You don't have to be all grumpy-pants around her. And get her the damn pistachios."

"Yes, ma'am."

The baby was stirring, so he made his escape.

On his way out of the arctic entry, which was lined with coatracks holding winter gear from toddler size to adult, he passed Gretel. Her cheeks were flushed from the cold and she held a full armload of firewood. She lifted her chin as they squeezed past each other. The scent of fresh snow and lavender swirled around her—along with a touch of spruce pitch. Carrying the firewood like that, she was going to get it all over her coat and that shit never came off.

But she didn't want advice from him.

"Zander," she said, with a formal nod.

"Gretel," he responded. He liked how her name felt in his mouth—like the sugar glass his mother used to make.

"Let the games begin."

"Make it so."

Her eyelids fluttered. God, those eyes—they were flat-out dazzling. Sparkling aqua, like sunlight on a tropical sea.

"I'll see you in court," she added.

He forgot about her eyes and frowned down at her. "In court?"

"Sorry. I like having the last word. Learn it, live with it." She pushed open the door that separated the arctic entry from the rest of the house and disappeared inside.

He shook his head and stepped outside, where his skis were propped next to the door. Spoiled princess, that girl. And there was no frickin' way she'd last through the winter.

Too bad—she definitely brightened things up around here. *Oh well.* He shrugged and snapped on his skis. She was a short-timer. Learn it, live with it.

CHAPTER THREE

Both the Noonan and the Ross homesteads were carved out of the vast spruce forests that covered the hills and valleys east of Lost Harbor. Previous generations had cleared the land and put up the first buildings from fallen trees.

Zander's grandfather had purchased their fifty-acre lot, worked it, then willed it to Zander's mother. She'd married an airline pilot; they'd lived in Colorado until Zander was about fourteen.

When Brenda Ross got pregnant again, they'd all moved onto the Lost Harbor property. His father had flown for the National Park Service and his mother had worked on the house. She was the one with the hands-on skills and artistic eye. Jason was born and three years later, Petey.

Zander had graduated from Lost Harbor High, then joined the military. That life hadn't suited him much—he'd chafed under all the rules—but it had given him a sense of purpose. After a freak boating accident had killed his parents, he hadn't hesitated to resign from the Marines and come home to raise his younger brothers. They were ten and seven at that point. He'd been twenty-four.

How was a twenty-four-year-old former Marine supposed to know how to raise two wild and grieving boys?

Three words. Chain of command.

Thank God for his military experience, because that was the structure he'd relied on for the past three years. Rules, consequences, order, accountability. Those were the pillars that kept the teetering Ross household from falling apart.

But being the stern platoon leader could get exhausting, so he cherished moments like this when he was all alone in the peaceful woods, skiing between snow-laden spruce with the wind against his face.

The hissing strokes of his skis were the only sounds—at first. But as he skied, he caught more. The curious chirping of a flock of waxwings wheeling high above. The croak of a raven. The distant whine of a twin-engine plane.

Those few sounds only emphasized how quiet these woods were in winter. The snow absorbed sound, almost like a layer of insulation.

Which reminded him that he needed to patch up the hole that Jason had made in the wall of the weight room during a freak free weight incident. He'd have to pick up some spackle when he was in town.

He checked his watch—set to military time—and picked up the pace. Today was his day for the carpool, which meant he had to pick up his brothers, Abby's oldest son, and Chloeann, another neighbor girl, from the school bus drop-off about three miles down the road. He and Chloeann's parents did most of the driving except when Earl Noonan was in town.

So far, no one had suggested that Gretel Morrison take a shift. Winter driving was too sketchy to take that kind of chance.

Abby's words came back to him—*don't be such a grumpy-pants around her.*

Was he? He didn't intend to be. It wasn't personal. Maybe he was just that kind of guy. The grumpy kind with a lot of responsibilities.

When he reached his house, he ditched his skis, hanging them on their assigned hook under the overhang. The house that his grandfather had begun was still under construction—and probably always would be. It had a steep metal roof to shed the snow and cedar siding most of the way around. The fourth side still had patches of Tyvek showing.

He really needed to get to that. And to the floors, which were still bare plywood. And a million other things.

But the boys were weirdly sentimental about the house and didn't like big changes. They staged a rebellion every time he talked about putting down flooring.

Inside, he added a log to the fire in the woodstove and damped it down.

A smile flitted across his face as he remembered Gretel and her firewood struggles. He had to give her credit—she was persistent. And that kind of determination went a long way in a place like this.

He did a quick whirlwind cleanup of the kitchen, putting away the dishes Jason had washed that morning and wiping off the counter Petey had forgotten. Niko, their Alaskan Malamute, followed him as he worked. Even though he was getting on, he still loved to be part of whatever was happening.

He checked the giant chore chart that lived on an erasable easel he'd found at the dump. Yup, Petey had also neglected to take out his choice of frozen meat from the freezer. He added a red dot to that box. *Uncompleted chore.*

Petey had three red dots already this week. Five red dots and he'd get assigned a much bigger chore, a really no-fun task like scrubbing the bathroom floor.

Oh well—those were the rules. Created by him, the leader of the family, and handed down the chain of command. The only nod to democracy that he offered was a monthly family meeting during which changes to the rules could be discussed. Occasionally—very occasionally—he agreed to revise a rule. But nothing changed unless he said so.

Sometimes one of his brothers would have a meltdown and yell at him that he was being a dictator. He didn't disagree. His usual answer was something about "power" and "responsibility" and "do you want to be in charge for a day? Be my guest." That usually worked. Because they could see for themselves that being in charge mostly sucked.

He stepped outside and jogged through the cold to his workshop, which had been the original barn on the homestead. He was repairing an antique chair for one of the wealthy retirees who'd moved to Lost Harbor. His woodworking skills were paying the bills until the life insurance came through. *If* it ever came through; after three years of angry phone calls, sometimes he wondered if it was a lost cause.

Luckily, his father had taught him woodworking and he'd always loved it. Best of all, it allowed him to stay close to home. It still amazed him that people were willing to pay for simple things like regluing a chair leg. But if someone was willing to pay him to take care of easy shit, why not take the job?

Once again, he thought about Gretel. She came from a rich family. Word around town was that both Gretel and her sister Bethany had grown up with plenty of money to spare. Bethany was now a doctor at the hospital, and had recently gotten engaged to Nate Prudhoe, the firefighter.

He knew that Gretel had come to Lost Harbor because of Bethany, but he wasn't clear on how she'd ended up living at the Noonans'. He was definitely curious about that, and about most things related to Gretel. He wanted to know more about her.

But what was the point, when she'd be gone before he could blink twice, like some kind of fairy flitting through the woods?

He shook off that ridiculous thought and focused on his handiwork. The glue was dry, so he loosened the clamp that had been holding the broken pieces together. Great. He could deliver this baby and collect a check.

After securing the chair in the back of the big Suburban he used for deliveries and carpooling, he let Niko hop in the back and headed into town. The gravel road had been plowed just this morning; he could still see the ridges of dirty ice left by the blade. The plow truck driver who had the contract for this area had recently asked Zander if he wanted to take over.

He was still wrestling with that decision. Yes, it would be another source of income. But it would also be another layer of responsibility. It would mean early mornings and possibly long hours. It meant more time for Jason and Petey to tear the house apart in his absence.

He let out a sigh as he reached the start of the wider paved road that led to town. Sometimes he felt more like forty-seven than twenty-seven.

His last girlfriend had flung that insult at him. "You're like an old man, except you still like to fuck."

She wasn't wrong.

He stopped at the cluster of mailboxes that served their road —Wolf Ridge Road. Among the bills and circulars, the return address on one piece of mail sent a bolt of fear right to his gut.

The Alaska Department of Health, Office of Children's Services.

Fuck. He hated hearing from them. Even though he'd been successfully caring for his brothers for three years, they still watched over his shoulder like a set of vultures ready to swoop down if he screwed something up.

Or at least that was how it felt.

He pulled forward and took a moment to scan the letter.

This is to inform you that a new caseworker has been assigned to Jason and Peter Ross. Susan Baker will be contacting you within the next few weeks to arrange a home visit.

A home visit? What the hell? That didn't happen very often because the department was located in Juneau and extremely understaffed. Alaska was a big territory to cover. Usually the caseworkers only made home visits when there was a good reason —like when he'd first assumed guardianship of his brothers. A caseworker had shown up after Jason had gotten into a few fights at school. Trouble like that could inspire a home visit.

But things were fine at the moment. Jason was pulling a solid B average in eighth grade, which wasn't bad considering he spent all his time either skiing or thinking about skiing. His main goal in life was making the ski team once he got to high school.

Petey was...Petey. A stubborn little ball of energy who did things his own particular way. Sometimes the other kids thought he was weird, but so what? They just didn't know him the way his family did.

Maybe there was nothing to worry about. Maybe this was a routine visit from a dedicated new caseworker. Maybe the only problem was how clean they'd have to keep the house until she'd come and gone.

AN HOUR LATER—CHAIR delivered, groceries and spackle acquired—Zander pulled up at the turnaround where the school bus dropped the kids. The spot happened to offer an incredible view of Misty Bay and the snow-covered mountain range on the other side. Clouds hovered over Zertuche glacier, which was wedged between steep slopes. More clouds were stacked behind those, as if a storm was flowing from the ice fields into Lost Souls Wilderness.

He turned on the radio to listen to the forecast. Ironically, the announcer was reading out the Bush Lines. "To the fishing boat that stopped at Ninlik Cove two days ago, please come back for your cooler. It's becoming litter, and that's rude. Ride needed from Lost Harbor to Anchorage on January 13, willing to share the usuals."

He smiled at the thought of submitting a Bush Line praising Gretel Morrison. "When pigs fly, Niko. That ain't happening."

Niko had nothing to say.

The bus pulled up a few minutes later. It was already mostly empty, since their stop was the last on the route.

Jason, Petey, Chloeann and Eli came spilling out in a flurry of parkas and backpacks. The driver gave Zander a salute, performed a complicated five-point turn, and steered the bus toward town. It made a splash of yellow against the backdrop of snowy peaks across the bay.

The Suburban filled up with kids and chatter.

"I need new ski poles, I snapped one of mine in half," Jason announced. "On accident," he added quickly.

"I'm going to need a complete incident report," said Zander. "Filed in triplicate."

"Can Petey come over to play?" asked Eli hopefully from the passenger seat. "We got a new trampoline."

"After his chores and depending on his homework."

Zander glanced at Petey in the rearview mirror. He was listening to Chloeann whisper something in his ear and had missed the request from Eli. Being three years older than Eli, he wasn't always interested in playing with him.

"A trampoline, huh? When did that happen?"

"Gretel got it. It's a little one and it's only in my room and I'm the only one allowed to jump on it. Except her, since she got it for me. And Petey if he comes over."

Gretel got him a trampoline? Interesting. It made sense because Eli had a lot of energy to burn off, especially in the winter. And he would love having something that was just for him, since the twin toddlers got so much attention.

It was thoughtful.

Another surprise from the pretty girl next door.

"What if I come over? Can I try it?"

Eli shot him a dubious glance. "You might break it. No way."

Zander hid a laugh. That was the thing about this whole surrogate parenting gig. The kids could really crack you up. Especially the ones you weren't directly responsible for.

"Moose!" shouted Chloeann, pointing to the trees off the road. He located it—a spindly-legged youngster who swung his big head toward them and watched as they passed.

"Thanks for watching my six," he told Chloeann.

"What?"

Jason rolled his eyes. "He means thanks for watching his back. That's how they say it in the military. Like how he always says that he'll pick us up at sixteen-thirty. Sixteen is four o'clock in normal people language."

"But why does six mean the same thing as your back?"

"Imagine a clock face, and you're looking toward the twelve. The six is at your back."

"No, it isn't. It's by my feet."

Zander laughed along with the other kids. She had a point, he couldn't deny that.

Petey spoke up for the first time. "Zander, can I go to Chloeann's and do homework?"

"Sorry, kid. You have chores to do."

Storm clouds gathered on Petey's face. "I always have chores. Life doesn't stop because of chores. I'm not your prisoner."

"Don't be so dramatic. If you finish your chores quickly, I'll drive you over to Chloeann's."

Petey subsided, though he still looked furious. Too bad— Zander took chores seriously, because if he didn't, no one else would, that was for sure.

Just wait until Petey heard about the red dot on the chart.

They reached the mailbox that marked the end of Chloeann's driveway. Zander pulled over and let her out. Out of habit, he watched her until she was safely at the door of her house.

"Come on, Z," said Jason impatiently. "I'm already behind on my miles."

Jason had set himself a goal of skiing twenty-five miles a week. That was a lot, but Zander approved of the goal-setting part.

He wasn't so sure about the nickname.

"Since when do you call me Z?"

"Out loud? Just since today."

Zander hid another laugh. These kids. They truly cracked him up. "Well, I'm not sure I like it."

"There's no rule about nicknames. Petey, is there a rule about nicknames?"

"Prisoners have numbers, not nicknames," Petey said morosely.

"Good God, how'd I turn into a prison warden named Z? Sounds like a character in a movie."

That lightened up the mood, and they spent the rest of the drive tossing out ideas for this hypothetical movie. The prison warden was also a bandit who went only by the letter Z. He jailed people by day, robbed people by night. He had an accomplice known only as X, who was a master swordsman, while Z specialized in archery.

"What about Y?" Zander asked.

"Y is their nemesis, he wants to kill everyone. Why, Y? Why?" Petey clutched his hands at his heart. The kid was such a natural when it came to drama.

When they dropped off Eli at the Noonans' place, Zander got out to hand him the box of groceries. "Is that too much for you to carry? Want me to bring it in?"

"Course not. Jeez." The boy shifted the box in his grip as he peered inside. "Pistachios?"

"They're for Gretel. Hey, can you pass on a message to her?"

Eli nodded. His hat had gotten displaced during his exit from the van; Zander reached out and adjusted it for him.

"Tell her pistachios grow best in warm climates. Can you remember that?"

"Pistachios grow best in warm climates," Eli repeated obediently, with little puffs of breath accenting every word.

"Good. Thanks, dude. And hey—Petey will come over and jump on your trampoline soon, okay?"

Eli nodded and marched toward the house with his bulky load.

On his way back to the driver's seat, Zander noticed a piece of firewood in the culvert by the driveway. It must have rolled out of Gretel's sight when the sled spilled over.

Should he pick it up despite all her instructions about not helping her?

Screw that. Firewood was valuable. And she didn't even know it was there.

Quickly, he snatched it up and whisked it into the woodshed, then hurried back to the van.

"Why were you running?" Jason frowned at him from the backseat, where he was slouching with his iPhone. Service was very spotty in their area, but there were a few hot spots. The Noonans' driveway occasionally got one bar.

"Exercise." He didn't feel like explaining anything related to Gretel. Maybe because he couldn't really explain it to himself. Why did he think about her as much as he did?

Well, there was the obvious explanation—she was new around here.

And so beautiful.

And fun to talk to.

When she wasn't actively trying to piss him off.

He took one last lingering look around the property, but she was nowhere to be seen. No flash of hair with magenta streaks or tasseled snow boots or sparkling blue-lagoon eyes.

He slowly backed out of the driveway. With his head turned to look behind him, he caught sight of a figure in the woods. Someone small, wearing a snowsuit, using snowshoes to wend their way through the woods. He couldn't really get a good look, so he checked the rearview mirror, angling it to get a better view.

It was Gretel.

If he had to guess, this was her first time on snowshoes. She was exaggerating each step, making sure she didn't catch the snowshoe on any stray brush. She wasn't looking where she was going, at all. The contraptions on her feet drew all her attention.

The hood of her parka had blown back and her hair clung to her face. She must be sweating. Her vivid magenta streaks glinted in the dappled sun coming through the branches.

"Z!"

He snapped back to attention. Jesus, he'd nearly driven off the edge into the culvert. He'd completely forgotten that he was even driving.

He maneuvered the van back into the proper direction and continued reversing down the driveway.

When they passed Gretel, she waved. He pretended that he'd just spotted her and waved back. Then he winced as she tripped on a spruce branch and tumbled into a snowbank.

As soon as they reached the road, Jason burst out laughing. "You like Gretel."

"What?"

"You were watching her. I saw you. You nearly crashed into a tree. That's how much you like her."

"I didn't nearly crash. And I like her okay." He reached the road and made a sharp swerve to head for home.

"I'm going to tell Eli."

"Tell what?"

"That you nearly crashed the van because you were looking at her like this." Jason widened his eyes as big as they could get and stuck out his tongue like a panting dog.

"The hell you are."

"Is there a rule against talking to Eli now?"

Of course there wasn't. Try as he might, Zander couldn't think of any of their rules that applied to this situation. "Insubordination and disrespecting your superior officer?"

"Nice try."

"Tell you what. I'll take care of dinner tonight. That's on your chart. You can go ski."

"Buying my silence?"

"Want it or not?"

"Yes," Jason said quickly.

A moment later they pulled up outside their house. Jason was already halfway out the door when Zander remembered the letter from the Office of Children's Services. Jason was old enough now for Zander to run stuff like this by him.

"Wait."

His younger brother sat back down and closed the door, but kept hold of the handle. "What now?"

"I got a letter about another home visit from a new caseworker. They usually only do that if there's a problem. Is there anything I should know about?"

Jason's eyebrows drew together. Just recently his voice had changed and his face had grown more bony. He too had their mother's hazel eyes and dark hair, just like Zander did.

Sometimes it hurt to see the resemblance.

"What do you mean?"

"Grades are good? No trips to the principal's office I didn't hear about?"

"No."

"Arrests? Drugs? Alcohol?" Zander was mostly joking about that, but it was worth throwing out there.

"Yuck, no. Dude, I'd never make the ski team if I did that shit. Can I go now?"

"So there's nothing?"

Something crossed Jason's face—maybe guilt? "Why don't you ask the caseworker why they're coming?"

Okay, well, that was a good suggestion. But he didn't want to look like he was *scared* of the caseworker.

Jason opened the door and made his escape, sending a swirl of cold air into the van.

Zander put the letter and the rest of the mail onto his box of groceries and hurried inside, Niko at his heels. Jason was already racing to his bedroom, stripping off his school clothes as he ran. Zander had gotten him a winter ski suit for Christmas. It was Jason's favorite possession in the world, second only to his skis.

"Can I borrow your ski poles?" he asked as he came racing back out.

"Yup. No pole-vaulting with them, though."

Jason came screeching to a halt. "How did you know?"

Zander burst out laughing. "Damn, I'm good, aren't I?"

"Did someone tell you?"

"No one told me. I'm just that good. Remember that the next time you think of some dumbass stunt like that."

Looking spooked, Jason loped out of the house. Zander chuckled to himself as he unpacked the box of groceries.

He'd broken two ski poles that same way when he was in high school. Why did kids always think they'd invented their stupid shit? Someone else had always done it first—and probably worse.

He stuck the letter from Children's Services on the pile of "important things he needed to deal with and better not forget about."

Before this new caseworker, Susan Baker, showed up, he had to find out what was going on. Because he knew his little brother well enough to know that he was hiding something.

CHAPTER FOUR

When Lloyd Morrison—mega-millionaire, father, and control freak—had cut Gretel off last fall, she'd panicked at first. She'd never had to completely rely on herself before, since she'd always had his credit cards as a safety net. She knew that he liked funding her life because that gave him a say in what she did. It worked out well for both of them.

But then two things had happened. One, he'd gotten mad at Bethany and wanted to punish her. Since Bethany didn't need his money, he'd gone after Gretel. That wasn't the real reason, though. Even Bethany didn't know the real reason. Gretel had done something he considered unforgivable—she'd played Robin Hood with his money. She'd donated funds to a group fighting to protect a butterfly sanctuary *from the Morrison Group*. Yup, her own father's investment firm was trying to develop that land, and she'd gone directly against him. To the tune of seventy-five thousand dollars.

Oops. Sorry not sorry.

"You can earn your own money and throw it away," he'd raged. "Let your sister take you in. I'm done."

She couldn't really complain because she'd brought it on herself. But yeah, she'd panicked.

Her mother, Aimee, had begged her to consider one of the wealthy older men who filled her contacts. Why get a job when she could simply marry a rich man?

But Gretel kept refusing her suggestions. It was time to grow up and fend for herself.

She'd accepted the position with the Noonans and taken an extra job at the Wicked Brew Coffee Shop, which had recently been purchased by a Hawaiian guy named Danny D. He'd changed the name from the Dark Brew to the Wicked Brew to give it some edginess.

"I'm here!" she announced as she twirled through the door.

"You always say that as if you deserve a medal." Danny D rolled his eyes as she waltzed toward the espresso counter.

The idea of showing up at the same time at the same place over and over again—that was new to her, she had to admit.

"Have you seen those roads? And have you seen my truck? It might honestly be faster to snowshoe into town."

She took off her parka—the hot-pink fur one she'd found at the thrift shop—and hung it on the coatrack in the back. She found an apron and tied it around her waist. For today's shift, she'd chosen a black lacy top layered over a form-fitting burgundy long-sleeve leotard. A striped spandex miniskirt over leggings and her zebra-print boots completed her outfit.

Joining Danny D behind the bar, she pulled herself an espresso shot. All the coffee she could drink—a reason to dress up —a chance to chat with the Lost Harborites—honestly, she loved this job.

"So you finally got out there with the snowshoes, huh?"

"Yup. And you know something? I am not a sporty person. I suck at skiing and tennis and swimming and jogging and skating and anything that has a ball—except for croquet, I'm pretty good at that—but I think I've found a sport I can get behind."

"Basically walking?"

"In my case, there's a lot of standing too. The occasional fall into the snow." She grinned at him and blew on her espresso. "But I love it because you're absolutely encased in fluff. Snowsuit, lots of fleecy gloves and so forth, fluffy snow. And it's literally impossible to go fast so there's no pressure. There's a reason why there's no Olympic event for snowshoeing. It would be like watching tortoises race."

He shook his head with a laugh and untied his apron. He wore a Kingdom of Hawaii bandanna to keep his dark hair off his face. He claimed to be a descendant of King Kamehameha and from his imperial manner, Gretel didn't doubt it. "You almost talked me into it."

"Into what? Don't let her talk you into anything, before you know it you'll be hot air ballooning over the South Pacific or something." Her sister Bethany strolled toward the bar, holding hands with her new sweetie, Nate.

"Now that doesn't sound so bad." Danny D balled up his apron and headed for the back room. "Don't burn the place down, Gretel. No freebies for anyone."

Gretel mouthed "ignore him," and poured mugs of coffee for Nate and Bethany. "Looks like we have cranberry muffins this morning, are you guys hungry?"

"No, we ate. Nate made pancakes." The adoring glance that Bethany gave Nate was sweeter than the triple dose of simple syrup Gretel added to her coffee.

Nate smiled down at her, just as blissful as Bethany. On the surface, the two of them seemed very different—Nate was lighthearted and fun, whereas Bethany was a doctor and more serious and reliable. On the other hand, they'd both dedicated their lives to helping others, so they weren't so different. And they'd fallen madly in love with each other after a few false starts. They were both wonderful people who deserved happiness. Gretel couldn't wait for their wedding next summer.

An actual wedding between two people who intended to stay together for life? Imagine that. Having witnessed Lloyd and Aimee's divorce, then two subsequent marriages apiece, honestly it was difficult.

"Do you both have the day off?" Gretel set to work preparing the behind-the-counter workspace the way she liked it.

"Yes, for once. Do you have any time off today? There's a new movie at the theater."

"I'm here until three, and then I need to drive Abby to a checkup."

Bethany frowned as she tucked a long strand of blond hair behind her ear. "You're working too much. I'm worried about you. When you're not helping Abby, you're working here, and you never have any free time. Why do you need this job, too? Isn't one enough?"

"It's fine. I'm making up for my lazy past when I didn't work at all." Gretel tossed back her espresso shot.

"You were not lazy. You were fun-loving," Bethany said sternly. "Don't you dare criticize my favorite person. Besides Nate, but he's in a different category," she added quickly.

Nate put a hand on his heart. "Ego check. Yup, still holding strong."

"I was a party girl." Gretel shrugged lightly. "No point in denying it, the evidence is all over social media. The internet is forever. Anyway, I like this job. I'm going to get a sound system in here and get some live music going. Danny has this dark moody vibe that he likes, but he couldn't say no to some local talent."

"That's a great idea. But you're trying to change the subject from your overbooked schedule. Can you cut back on your hours here, at least? Maybe Abby and Earl can make up the shortfall?"

Gretel had no ability to withstand her sister's concern. Her whole life, Bethany had been the one person she could rely on, the one person who loved her unconditionally.

"Our arrangement isn't about cash flow," she finally said. "They give me room and board and a truck and that's more than enough. They offered to pay me but I refused. Anyway, as soon as Abby's healed, she won't need me as much."

Bethany opened her mouth to respond, but Nate slung an arm around her shoulders. "It sounds like Gretel has it worked out the way she wants."

"Yes." She gave her future brother-in-law a tiny, grateful smile. "Even if they paid me, it wouldn't be much because they give me room and board. And I need quite a bit of money."

Bethany's eyebrows lifted. "For what?"

"I kind of...committed some money to some people."

"Oh my God. Are you in debt? Do you need a loan? Are there people after you?"

Crap, she'd phrased that wrong and now her sister was panicking.

"No, nothing like that. I don't owe the money. I donated it. Thinking that I had it, thanks to Daddy. But I didn't and now the group is in trouble thanks to me. So I need to work as much as I can to make up for it."

Bethany blinked at her in confusion. "What group?"

"It's a...butterfly sanctuary in Texas..."

Catching on, Bethany burst out laughing. "Oh boy. It's all making sense now. The one near Daddy's development?"

"That's the one."

"How much did you pledge?"

"A lot. But it's not your problem. It's mine."

Someone cleared their throat. "Uh, I got a problem. I need a quad shot cappuccino with two pulls of coconut syrup if you're done blabbing."

She turned to see Old Crow, one of the weather-beaten fishermen who mostly hung out in the harbor. "Well, look who the halibut dragged in. Shouldn't you be bugging the poor bartenders at the Olde Salt?"

"Toni told me to broaden my horizons," he grumbled as he leaned his elbows on the counter. "Besides, their coffeemaker broke."

"Oh really, is that the story you're going with?"

He scratched at the salt-and-pepper stubble on his chin. "Fine. You make a damn good cappuccino. When you stop gossiping."

She accepted the compliment with a gracious nod and slid over to the espresso machine. "No one in this town gossips more than the fishermen, so you can just eat those words for breakfast along with your quad shot."

"You know she's right." Nate laughed and tugged his hat back over his thatch of brown hair. "Didn't take her long to figure this place out. Though the firehouse could give the fishermen a run for first place."

"I've heard stitch-and-bitch is a good source too," added Bethany over the sound of the milk steamer.

"Ooh, I actually got invited to stitch-and-bitch!" Gretel finished the steaming process, added two pumps of coconut syrup to the cappuccino and carefully brought it to Old Crow. "They're going to teach me how to knit. I already know how to bitch pretty well."

"Speaking of gossip, did you hear about Ian Finnegan?" Bethany said. "He has a stalker. He warned all of us at the hospital so we can watch out for her."

"Yikes." Last fall, Gretel had spent a crazy night with Ian Finnegan, a neurosurgeon friend of Bethany's. Since there were champagne cocktails involved, she couldn't remember all the details, but it hadn't ended in bed. He had confessed that he had an enormous crush on her, but she'd let him down easy and their friendship vibe still felt pretty good. "I hope he's okay. I'll call him later."

Old Crow was staring down at his cappuccino. She'd mixed a bit of the foam with coffee and made a jaunty little crow on the foamy surface. "What the hell is that?"

"Coffee art. You know they have competitions for that."

He looked up at her, his weathered face set in forbidding lines. "But now I can't drink it. Don't want to mess it up."

She laughed and pulled out her phone to snap a photo of it. "There, now you can drink. Enjoy. Nothing lasts forever, you know."

Nate, still smiling, took Bethany's hand. "We'll get out of your way, Gretel. Good luck with all these degenerates."

"Oh, I can handle them just fine. They know who's boss around here." She winked at Old Crow, who was now sipping his drink with an expression somewhere between crusty and blissful.

The town had a saying—strange things happen around Lost Souls Wilderness. She would extend that to "strange people"— which were her favorite kind.

The rest of her shift flew by. During her downtimes, she scoured Craigslist for used sound systems. She sent off emails to a few potential sellers. Then she made the whole project even more real by posting in the town's Facebook group that an open mic night would be coming to the Wicked Brew soon. Within a few minutes, six people had responded with excited comments.

Let Danny D try to back out now.

Her mother called while she was filling a large order of coffees to-go for the real estate office on the next block. She tapped out a text telling Aimee she'd call her in a couple of days.

Her mother sent back a long text filled with uppercase words and exclamation points.

In other words, the usual.

After her shift ended, she raced to pick up Abby and Lulu for the baby's checkup. She actually dozed in the foyer, curled up in a hardback chair, during Lulu's appointment. Sometimes her small size came in handy.

She came awake with a start when Abby reappeared, covered in smiles. "She's doing great! She gained three ounces already."

"Woohoo!" Gretel clapped her hands and jumped to her feet. "That's great news! On a side note, the last time I celebrated someone gaining weight was with my anorexic bestie in Bali."

Abby shook her head in amusement. She was a tall, willowy woman who wore her hair in short curls that had never seen hair dye. She found all of Gretel's stories about her past life endlessly entertaining.

"Hey, I just got a message from Eli. He and the twins are playing over at Zander's house and we're invited to come for dinner. Zander picked up some pizzas from the Last Chance. Just so you know, no one in Lost Harbor ever says no to Last Chance pizza."

"Cool. Great. Pizza. I'm in." Did she sound funny? As if an unsettling thrill had shot through her at the mention of Zander?

Because it had.

"You sure? I can tell them to come on home. I know you and Zander are..." She trailed off delicately. Gretel had ranted about Zander once, early on, after he'd criticized the way she parked the truck.

"What? Me and Zander are what? I don't know what you mean. Go ahead and finish your thought."

"You're not his biggest fan, that's all. Though I really think if you got to know him more, you'd appreciate him. There is not a better, more honorable or responsible human being on this planet than Zander Ross."

Abby handed the baby to Gretel so she could get her coat on. The sleeping bundle settled sweetly into her arms.

"He's very responsible. He's also kind of...judgmental."

"Really, you think so?" Abby shrugged into her coat and pulled on her bright knitted hat. Earl had knitted it for her—how adorable was that?

"It's probably just me." Gretel handed the baby back and zipped up her own coat. "Since he has so much material to work with."

"Oh stop. If I catch him being anything but sweet to you, I'll hurl used baby wipes at him. You know I would, too."

Gretel giggled as they headed for the street, where they'd parked next to a snowbank.

Lost Harbor didn't have a single parking garage. Or a single parking meter. Or a single valet. It was weird.

But it did have Arctic sunsets the shade of peach bellinis and air like the purest champagne. She drank it in as she drove Abby and the baby up the ridge, each curve revealing a new vision to her dazzled eyes. It was almost enough to give her a buzz—without a drop of alcohol.

CHAPTER FIVE

Gretel had never been to Zander's house before. From the outside, it had the look of a gingerbread house with its steep roof and the smoke curling from the smokestack vent. On the front porch, a lamp hung from an ironwork bracket in the shape of a raven. That wasn't the only artistic touch; the whole house had a handcrafted feel to it. A jumble of skis was stored under the overhang, along with snowboards, snow shovels, snowshoes, skateboards, bicycles and even an old plastic tricycle.

Inside, it had the same unfinished feel as the Noonans', with pine board walls and open rafters, though it was much tidier. A wrought-iron spiral staircase led to an upper loft, which was closed off by a hatch. The kitchen and living room were all one big open space. A sturdy worktable occupied the center of the space. It held jars filled with crayons and pens, stacks of schoolbooks, and someone's science project, which appeared to be bug-related.

All the kids were sitting around the table playing a board game she didn't recognize. They were completely absorbed and barely noticed Abby and Gretel's arrival. Groovy joined Niko by the fire and they sniffed each other like old friends.

In the kitchen, they found Zander in the midst of taking pizza out of the oven. He wore jeans and a soft t-shirt, revealing mouth-wateringly defined arm muscles and a tattoo she couldn't make out.

Gretel's eyes widened as she scanned him, head to toe. She realized that she'd never seen Zander without his outdoor gear on. He was...ripped. Chiseled. Whatever the right word was for a perfectly honed masterpiece of masculinity.

"Smells good," said Abby, sniffing the steam coming from the pizza. It was lucky she spoke first, because Gretel was having trouble finding her voice. "But I hope you have more of those. My appetite is absurd these days."

"I got five." Zander greeted them with a nod. A very imper-sonal nod—maybe a judgmental one? "I learned my lesson the time I thought me and the boys could split two."

He gestured toward a stack of plates that sat on the stainless steel counter next to the sink. "Gretel, want to grab those and I'll bring the pizza? Abby, you just relax and don't try to carry anything. Earl told me he'd beat my ass if I didn't stop you from overdoing it."

Finally Gretel got her wits back. "What do you think my entire job is? The other day I had to tackle her to keep her from reaching for a jar on the top shelf."

"And then she had to stand on a chair to get it." Abby smiled at her affectionately. "It was pretty adorable, I'll be honest."

From his expression, Zander didn't do "adorable."

"Cover your ears, ladies." He put his fingers to his mouth and whistled. "Orders incoming."

At the table, Jason and Petey jumped to attention and swiveled to listen.

"Jason, put away the game in whatever manner you choose.

Petey, grab another chair from my bedroom. Eli, come get some forks and help Gretel with the plates. Littler kids, go wash your hands. Big kids too."

Incredibly, all the children launched into action and zoomed off to perform their assigned tasks.

Abby's face wore the same expression that Gretel's probably did—stunned and disbelieving. "How the heck? You should never have left the Marines, Zander. You should be a damn colonel or something."

"Discipline is important," he said seriously. He bent over to pull another pizza from the oven and Gretel tried to keep from staring at his ass. But not too hard—it was such a fine one. It deserved some appreciation. "We ran a drill before dinner to make sure they had it all down."

"You ran a *drill?*" Gretel slid a hot pad under the pizza as he set it on the counter. "They're little kids, not toy soldiers. Kids are supposed to have fun, especially when there's pizza—"

"I'm kidding." He grinned, which was such a rare thing for him that Gretel wished she could take a picture. It turned him from a serious grownup into a hottie about her own age. "I bribed them," he admitted. "I said if they made me look good we could talk about ice cream sundaes for dessert."

Gretel narrowed her eyes at him. "Bullshit. I've never seen you kid. You always say what you mean, which means you totally ran a drill."

He plopped down the pizza and planted his hands on his hips. "We practiced, but I wouldn't call it a drill. And I do kid sometimes. Like now."

Their gazes held in a standoff, which didn't end until Abby cleared her throat. "Well, whatever you did, bribery or drill or both, it worked like a charm. The dinner table is ready except for those plates. Can you guys relax so we can eat? Is there an order for that?"

"At ease," said Zander after a moment. "Or stand down."

"You can't aim your orders at me," Gretel told him. "I'm not really good about taking orders."

"Really? Shocker. Well, suit yourself. You can keep glaring at me if you want or you can come have some pizza."

"See, I'm so talented that I think I can probably do both."

He grunted, which she interpreted as a complete victory. Lifting her chin, she took hold of the stack of plates. As she carried them toward the worktable, she heard him say to Abby, "She likes the last word. I already learned that lesson."

"Don't make me throw a plate at you," Gretel warned him. "Because I'd probably miss and hit Abby and Earl would kill us both."

Zander's snort of laughter followed her to the table, warming her down to her soul.

ZANDER HAD NOTICED something interesting about Gretel. She had the ability to change the mood of a room—like, completely. Before she'd arrived, the kids had been focused on their game. Even the little ones were caught up in it—or maybe in the thrill of hanging out with the big ones. They'd interrupted the game only long enough to hurry up and complete whatever task he'd asked them to do.

After Gretel arrived, they were suddenly eager to talk. They even competed to share stories with her.

Jason wanted to talk about the practice session he'd attended with the ski team. "We went on an adventure ski out past Faraway Point and I kept up even with the seniors. They said I can definitely make the team."

Gretel reached across the table and high-fived him. "That's awesome, dude. I'm in awe of anyone who likes to go fast in the snow. I also think it's crazy, but hey. You love it, and I'm rooting for you. When can I watch you race?"

"Well, next year. If I make the team."

"It's a date. I'm going to mark it down in the giant empty space marked 'next year.'"

Yeah, Gretel didn't strike Zander as someone who planned ahead much.

"Gretel, can you dye my hair?" asked Petey.

Zander was still spluttering through a mouthful of 7Up when Gretel answered cheerfully, "Sure, what color? Or colors? If we do foils, I can do more than one."

"I want more than one," Petey declared. "At least five."

"Sounds complicated. Maybe we should start with two."

"Maybe you should start by asking permission," Zander told his little brother.

"It's my hair."

For a moment, Zander couldn't think of the right response to that. Petey made a good point; of course it was his hair. "But I'm responsible for you. And that includes your hair."

Petey aimed a death glare at him. "I can tell everyone that you aren't responsible."

"It doesn't work that way, kid."

Gretel chimed in—of course. Naturally she would think she had something to say in this situation. "Changing your hair color is a pretty harmless form of self-expression, if you ask me."

"No one did," Zander said gruffly.

"I do!" Petey raised his hand. "I ask her!"

Abby, who was a pro with his kids, butted in at that point. "One good reason not to use dye on your hair when you're young is that we're talking about chemicals that can be pretty toxic."

"So we'll use the nontoxic brands, or we can even use something like henna." Gretel's face lit up with that magnetic smile of hers. "Problem solved."

"Gretel, can I talk to you in private for a minute?" He shoved his chair back and stood up.

His brothers oohed as if they were the ones in trouble, but Gretel shrugged and followed him away from the table. The house was so small—almost more of a cabin—that the only place he could guarantee privacy was his bedroom. Even the bathroom wouldn't do because sound echoed off the tiles his mother had finished installing just before the crash.

He closed the door behind them, while Gretel surveyed his room curiously. The walls were made of rough white pine and a whimsical wrought-iron chandelier hung from the ceiling. Its best feature—aside from the king-size bed and the huge supply room that was now a walk-in closet—was a set of crank windows that opened onto the forest.

"You're the only boy I know with a chandelier in his bedroom," she said as she eyed it.

"This room used to be my mother's studio. She made that chandelier. The boys have my parents' old bedroom," he said curtly.

"Your mother *made* a chandelier?" Her eyes widened and she tilted her head back to stare up at it. The glow from the copper light shades turned her hair to fire.

"She was an artist. And a welder, among other things."

"Your mother was a *welder*?"

"Can we get back to the main topic?"

"Oh, sure. What was it again? I thought you just wanted to get me into your bedroom." She tossed a wink at him, as if throwing candy into a crowd.

"It's the only place they won't hear us."

"Yes, that's a good quality in a bedroom." Another wink, this one even more naughty and exaggerated.

"Stop that." He ground his teeth together. "I'm trying for a serious conversation here."

"All of your conversations seem pretty serious to me. Do you ever just sit around and shoot the shit?"

He dragged a hand through his hair. "Not very often, no. Back to my point." He paused, trying to bring his point back into focus. Hair. It had to do with hair. And hers was the color of fire-light in a glass of Cabernet right now.

"Hair dye," he ground out. "Don't encourage Petey to dye his hair. I won't allow it and you're just going to get him upset."

"Why won't you allow it? It's seriously so common these days. At my old school in Connecticut half the kids—"

"I don't care. We live here, and I'm responsible for Petey, and I say no to the hair dye." The truth was, he didn't know this new caseworker and he didn't want anything to look out of the ordi-nary when she showed up for the home visit. But he didn't know Gretel well enough to tell her that. He didn't trust her not to blab it all over town during a shift at the Wicked Brew.

"You're being very narrow-minded."

"Okay."

She drew in a long breath, as if trying to keep her cool. "Petey is very imaginative, he needs to express himself. I can relate to that. I was the same way when I was growing up. Obviously, I still am." She gestured at her outfit, which featured a blend of colors and layers that was uniquely Gretel. "I don't think it's fair that girls can have fun with their appearance but boys can't."

"Life isn't fair, is that big news?"

If life was fair, he would still be in the Marines. Or maybe he'd be doing something else. Sometimes he forgot the other dreams he'd had before enlisting.

"No. I know life isn't fair."

"Yeah? Did you figure that out when you were on a cruise or at a five-star restaurant?"

She drew in a sharp breath, and color flushed across her cheeks.

Fuck, he'd gone too far. He'd let his temper get away from him. He knew better than that. "Sorry," he muttered.

"No. Let it out. You think I'm just a spoiled rich girl who doesn't understand reality."

He didn't answer, since part of him *did* think that, but he didn't want to add fuel to the fire.

"Come on. *Express* yourself, Zander. I can take it."

She was goading him, he knew that. But Zander had all those years of military service under his belt, not to mention three years of playing single dad to his brothers. He wasn't about to let a barely five-foot tall Lower Forty-eight princess make him lose his cool.

"No hair dye," he said firmly, fixing her with a steady stare to emphasize his point.

Her nostrils flared, and he remembered what she'd said about taking orders—or not taking them. "If you're too strict with them they're going to rebel. That's like, a universal law of parenting."

"I'll take my chances."

"It's not just *your* chances," she cried. "What about your brothers? This is about Petey, not you."

She was persistent, he'd give her that.

"You're right. It's about Petey and the fact that you are not going to dye his hair."

"But...name one good reason—"

He interrupted. "Why are you so worried about his hair? Maybe this is about you, not Petey."

Her mouth dropped open, making him notice the pretty color of her lips. Not that he hadn't noticed before. He'd tried hard *not* to notice. But here in the close quarters of his bedroom, with his bed lurking right behind her, it was impossible to ignore their lovely curved shape and imagine their flower-petal taste.

She snapped her mouth shut; maybe she'd caught him looking at her lips. He dragged his gaze away and resorted to his best chain-of-command expression. "Since you aren't saying anything more, I'm going to assume we're done here."

She lifted her chin and stalked past him. "Oh, we're definitely done here."

And just like that, she took command of the moment. "And to think, there are so many other and better things you could have dragged me to your bedroom for. Oh well. I guess you'll never know."

He followed her out of the room. He might never know, but that didn't mean he couldn't use his imagination. He probably would. Later that night, right there in that bed.

CHAPTER SIX

When all the pizza had been gobbled up—and ice cream sundaes served—Gretel called on all her newly acquired maturity and offered to do the dishes.

She was still fuming over the way Zander had shut her out.

On the one hand, he was right that it was his call. She was just a random neighbor.

On the other hand, she hated to see young boys forced to fit into a box that might not suit them. Petey reminded her of one of her boyfriends in high school. A few years ago, he'd transitioned to a she, and their entire rocky relationship suddenly made sense.

But it wasn't her business. Point taken, Zander Ross. Ross the Boss.

"That's okay, we got it." Zander gave one of his piercing whistles. Jason, rolling his eyes, dragged himself over to the kitchen. Petey darted ahead of him and grabbed a dishtowel from a drawer.

As the rest of them watched, the three Rosses swung into the most amazing dishwashing drill Gretel had ever seen—or imagined. It was one step away from ballet, the way they operated in perfect coordination and timing. Zander scrubbed a dish, handed it to Jason, who rinsed it and handed it to Petey, who dried it and put it away. Partway through, Zander called, "Switch," and they all changed places so that Petey washed, Zander rinsed and Jason dried.

Abby laughed until tears came to her eyes. Gretel hoped she wasn't stretching her stitches, but maybe it was good for her to be so entertained.

When all the dishes were done, Zander had possession of the dishtowel. He tossed it long to Jason, who was jogging the length of the kitchen toward a laundry hamper against the wall. He caught it just in time for Petey to slide in and lift the top off. Jason slam-dunked the towel into the hamper and Petey plopped the top back on.

"Time?" Jason asked.

Zander was checking his phone. "Fifth best. Not bad. Good job. One hour before bedtime, Petey. Use it wisely."

With a grin, he ambled back to the table. Both of the toddlers, Iris and India, were sound asleep, curled-up with their heads on Gretel's lap. Eli was yawning from the aftermath of the sugar rush. Abby wiped tears of laughter off her cheeks.

"That was really something, Zander."

"It's one of our favorite drills. Breakfast is pretty good too."

"I'd love to see that sometime. We go for the barely controlled chaos technique. Gretel can tell you."

Gretel whispered so as not to wake up the little ones. "Sorry, did you say controlled? Did I hear that right?"

Abby and Zander both laughed.

"Need a hand getting all these kids into your rig?" he offered.

"That'd be great," Abby said, before Gretel could answer. She would have loved to tell Zander to back off, that she could handle it. But that would be ridiculous.

He leaned over and gently pried Iris' curled up hand off

Gretel's sweater. She inhaled the scent of dish soap and wood smoke as his head came close to hers. The skin of his neck looked almost vulnerable at that angle. There was a whorl of hair at the back of his neck; almost a cowlick. She wondered if he knew about it, or if he cared.

His big hands enveloped Iris and he lifted her away from Gretel. He draped her over his chest, her head snuggling into the crook of his neck.

Gretel's heart did the funniest little skip and jump at the sight of such a big guy cradling the tiny human that was Iris.

Abby handed him Iris' coat and Zander draped it over her. Groovy hauled herself to her feet and prepared to follow them out.

"Hand me the keys, I'll get the rig started," he told Gretel. *Ordered* her, practically.

Still, a warmed-up car was better than an icy one. She gave him the keys without comment and he disappeared with Iris. Abby roused Eli while Gretel managed to stand up without waking India. She settled her gently against her shoulder.

Gretel popped her head into the boys' room to say goodbye, and found them both reading on their stomachs on their twin beds. They weren't ordinary beds, she noticed. They looked handcrafted, and each of them had an animal carved into the headboard. Jason's was a wolf and Petey's was a raven.

"Goodnight, guys," she said softly. "It was fun hanging out with you."

"Night, Gretel." Petey lifted his head and gave her a wistful smile. "Maybe you can dye my hair when I'm sixteen."

"It's a date."

Still smiling, she carried her bundle of toddler through the steamy arctic entry and into the starlit night. The cold bit at her exposed cheeks. The snow crunched under her snow boots as she picked her way toward the Noonans' Tahoe. A rising spiral of exhaust rose from the tailpipe—lazily, as if fighting the weight of the cold air. She tilted her head to take in the brilliance of the stars against the profound darkness.

The night sky was like a never-ending show that didn't care whether or not anyone was paying attention. How many people were going about their business—eating out, sleeping, watching TV, partying, dancing—with no idea that such an incredible drama was playing out in the sky above their heads?

She'd never given the sky much thought before coming to Lost Harbor, except for a quick glance now and then. But then again, there were so many things she hadn't thought about. Like how the feel of a sleeping toddler in your arms could make your heart ache with happiness. Or the way a man's attention to things like buckling up a car seat could make him even more attractive.

"Thanks," she told Zander after he'd gotten both the toddlers buckled in.

"No problem. Happy to help."

He emphasized that last word, *help*.

Okay then. Game back on. "Funny thing. I was thinking about leaving Alaska until you got them into their carseats," she murmured, so only he could hear. "Better start writing your Bush Lines speech."

He gave a burst of laughter, causing Abby to poke her head from the passenger seat with an expression of surprise. "You sounded like a little kid for sec there, Zander."

"I guarantee I'm not a little kid," he murmured in Gretel's ear.

She couldn't think of a PG-rated response to that, so she let him have that one.

THE NEW CASEWORKER, Susan Baker, showed up a few

days later. She surprised Zander while he was in his workshop, which was never a good thing. He was in the middle of setting two freshly glued pieces of an old toboggan together. The glue was a fast-acting adhesive that left him only seconds to make sure everything was properly aligned.

Her knock at the door made him jump and smear glue across his work pants.

"Damn it," he exclaimed before he could even see who was there. "Hang on," he called to the visitor. Quickly he adjusted the two pieces into their proper position and set a clamp to hold them together.

He didn't worry about his work pants, since they were already covered with paint stains, pitch stains, plaster stains, and who knew what else.

He got to his feet and stretched his back, then opened the door to the stranger. She was a Native Alaskan woman, maybe around fifty, and she did not look pleased.

"I've been calling, didn't you get my messages?"

"No, sorry. Service is terrible out here. Who are you?"

"I'm Susan Baker from the Office of Children's Services. I assume you got the notification that I was coming?" She spoke in a blunt manner that reminded him of his platoon leader.

"Susan—Of course. Susan Baker. Nice to meet you." He rubbed his hands on his work pants and offered one. She declined.

"I have allergies," she told him. "Toxic substances, having my calls ignored, that sort of thing."

"I wasn't ignoring you. Did you try the landline?"

"I tried all the numbers in your file." She sniffed at the air. "What is that smell?"

"It's how I make money to support the family." He spoke more sharply than he'd intended, and she reacted immediately by narrowing her eyes.

"Tell me about that. Is it a struggle for you, being sole care-taker and sole money-earner?"

Oh no. If he had to have that conversation, he didn't want to be ambushed with it.

He gestured toward the door. "Why don't we go into the house and I'll get you some coffee?"

"I'm allergic to coffee."

"Maybe some tea?"

Did he even have any tea? Luckily, she shook her head. "I take care of my own beverages."

"That's smart." He ushered her out the door and they crossed the snowy yard to the side entrance of the house. Niko was out on a perimeter check, so at least he didn't have a dog to deal with.

"Why do you find that smart?"

Wow, this woman was sharp as a razor knife. She didn't miss a thing. By the time they reached the living room, he knew she'd catalogued every single dirty dish and balled up sock that had escaped the laundry hamper.

He hurried to put the sock back where it belonged. "It's usually much tidier than this, but Jason had an early ski practice and—"

She waved him off. "It's quite clean. I'm impressed."

The relief hit him like a blow to the chest. He felt his entire body relax. "We try," he managed. "The boys are a big help in that respect. I'm teaching them to hold up their end. Our parents always emphasized self-reliance."

She looked around one more time, then gestured to the work-table, which was still littered with the makings of a Lego fighter space station Petey had been working on.

"Can we sit?"

"Yeah, of course." He snagged the letter from the OCS and brought it with him. When he reached the table, she'd already opened up a binder and had a pen in hand.

Feeling outmatched in every way, he sat down across from her.

"So you've been taking care of Jason and Petey for three years now?"

"Yes. Since our parents passed."

"You were named as the guardian?"

His stomach tightened. "No, not technically. Their death was sudden and they hadn't named anyone specifically. I was the logical choice and I wanted to do it. I wanted them to be able to stay here in Alaska and stay together."

"And you left your military career to do it?"

"Yes. The Marines are all about duty. You don't get to choose what that duty is. Mine was clear."

She made a note on a page in her binder. He craned his neck to see what she was writing, but couldn't make out her hand-writing.

"So you saw it—see it—as your duty to come back to Lost Harbor."

Wait, that didn't sound right. "That doesn't mean I didn't want to. I love this place and I love my brothers."

"That's lovely. It's also not entirely the point. What is it that you feel you offer the boys?"

"Stability. Consistency. Family."

"And you're sure that's everything they need?"

Ice curdled in his veins. "What does that mean? Food, educa-tion, friends, of course they have what they need. Is something missing?"

She made another note.

"Is there a problem? If there is, I don't know about it and I deserve to. You can't just come in here and ask weird questions that sound like accusations."

"No accusations, Mr. Ross. You misunderstand. My job is to

make sure the best interests of the minor children are being served. That should be your job too."

"It is. Of course it is. What—"

"What about your personal life?"

"Excuse me?" He sat back in his chair and heard it squeak.

"You're a young, single man. I assume you have girlfriends. How do you handle that with your brothers?"

"Well, I...I..." *Think of something that makes me look good.* "I try to set a good example. Serious relationships only."

She raised an eyebrow, expressing all kinds of skepticism. "Are you in one now?"

Could a flirtation with the girl next door count? He swiped the back of his hand across his forehead, where a layer of sweat had gathered. "I suppose you could say that."

He braced himself for a request for more details, but she moved on.

"What if I were to tell you that another situation might be an option for Jason?"

"What situation?" He shifted position again. By now he was so agitated that one chair leg cracked under the pressure. Great, another chair to repair. "What are you talking about?"

"Calm down, Mr. Ross. Please. There's no need to overreact. You are the boys' guardian until further notice, and nothing will change without you being part of that discussion."

Zander felt as if his head was about to explode. "I don't understand any of this. It's coming out of nowhere. Jason and Petey belong here, with me. Together. All of us. You're talking about Jason going somewhere else? The hell—I mean, no way."

"You really shouldn't worry so much." She made another note in her goddamn binder, then snapped it closed. "Please answer your phone in the future."

"I—" Fighting to stop the panic, he scrubbed a hand across the back of his neck. "I'll do my best."

She rose to her feet and gave him a nod. "My assessment says that you're a caring surrogate father making the best of a difficult situation. Good for you."

He followed suit and came to his feet. "Thank you. Does that mean—"

She held up a hand. "Take the praise. Let's leave it at that."

Holy Jesus, this woman was unlike any caseworker he'd ever dealt with. "Yes, ma'am."

After she left, he returned to the chair and stared down at it. Then kicked it.

It shuddered and jumped across the floor. His toe throbbed. But damn, it felt good to release a little tension. And what the hell, it was already broken.

CHAPTER SEVEN

"Mom...mom...hang on. Stop talking for a second." Gretel adjusted her headset and smiled sweetly at the fire chief, Darius Boone. He was even larger than Zander, and more intimidating if only because he was in his thirties as opposed to his twenties. "What can I get you, Chief? And other chief?"

She added that bit just in time as Maya Badger stepped next to Darius. Just lately, Maya Badger had been named as Lost Harbor's newest police chief, after the townspeople got tired of her doing all the work while the old chief spent his time ice fishing.

"I'm buying," Darius told Maya. "My way of saying congratulations."

"Are you sure it's not your way of saying you need extra space now that we're down an officer?" Maya said dryly.

"You're so young to be so cynical. But now that you mention it..."

Maya rolled her eyes and turned to Gretel. "Macchiato, put it on my tab. And throw a muffin in there."

"A normal muffin, or a gluten-free sugar-free—"

"Make it a peanut butter cookie. And get one for the big guy too. I'm in a sweet mood."

Darius heaved a long sigh. "Okay, what do you need, Badger? I'll have a latte, Gretel. Large and hot."

"I like your style." She shooed them both away. "Now please go bicker—I mean discuss town business—at a table. I have a fight with my mother to get back to."

The two chiefs both looked at her in astonishment and then at each other. Maya laughed first, her smooth brown face breaking into a wide smile. "You are something else, Gretel Morrison. Glad you decided to stick around. I won't be at all surprised if you find yourself in trouble, though."

Gretel shot her a sassy smile and readjusted her headset. Since Maya was her future brother-in-law Nate's best friend, she wasn't too worried.

On the other hand, she had a reputation for being extra ethical, so—"On the house," she called after them.

She flicked the unmute button while she made their drinks. Her mother Aimee was still ranting, as if she hadn't even realized that Gretel had muted her.

Kind of the story of their relationship, come to think of it.

"Mom. *Mom.* I missed all of that. Can you boil it down to the essentials?"

"Oh darling, did you miss the bit about modeling the spring collection?"

"Uh, yes. I missed that. Congratulations, that's amazing." Aimee was a former world-class model, incredibly photogenic, and only in her mid-forties. She still got plenty of work, though she didn't need the money. Her three divorce settlements had left her in excellent financial shape.

"I don't mean me, darling. I mean *you.* They're looking for someone younger." Gretel winced at the hurt in Aimee's voice.

"Well then, they're fools. You're the best. And I'm not a model. You know that, Mom."

"You just need to work on your—"

"*No.* You know I suck at it. I'm too short and I can't control my facial expressions enough. No modeling."

"Okay. But there's something else to discuss. That honeymoon fund I set aside for you."

"No, Mom. I'm not marrying one of your douchebags. Moving on. What else is going on, Mom? Have you talked to Daddy?"

"He can't stop calling me. He's devastated. He wants you back in the family fold, honey. Would it kill you to just apologize and—"

Sweet Sofia Coppola, this conversation was a minefield. "He'll survive. Why isn't he happy that he has all his money to himself now?"

"*All* his money? What do you think I am, an amateur?"

"Of course not. Prenup, monthly allowance, blah blah blah. You know, you really ought to thank me for being born because that doubled your monthly check."

"You don't need to be so catty. Men don't like that, you know."

"Too bad for them." She removed two peanut butter cookies from the case and slid them each onto a plate.

"Baby, I'm worried about your attitude. When I was younger than you, I'd already married a millionaire and given birth to you! I was set for life at the age of twenty-three. And you're—where are you working again?"

"The Wicked Brew in Lost Harbor, Alaska, across from Lost Souls Wilderness."

"Which might as well be nowhere."

Not nowhere. Just very far from her parents. And yet, maybe not quite far enough.

"Bethany's here too. You should stop worrying."

"You shouldn't be so trusting with Bethany. Do I have to remind you that—"

"No! You don't have to. Please don't."

But this was Aimee's favorite story, so she couldn't be stopped. Gretel screwed her eyes shut and hoped she would tell the short version. "I was just the mistress, but I always knew the key was to be patient. Then after Bethany's mother died, God rest her soul, Lloyd turned to me, like I always knew he would. It was best for everyone that we got married, but poor little Bethany had a hard time. You can't trust—"

Gretel had heard enough. "Bethany loves me. She always has. You should just stop right there."

Aimee knew when she'd crossed the line. "Will you think about Fiji, darling? We had such fun there the last time."

Gretel pressed her lips together to keep the truth from spilling out—she'd spent most of that vacation completely buzzed.

"I have commitments here, Mom. I'm not leaving."

"Excuse you? I didn't catch that. You have what?"

Hmm...maybe Aimee wasn't actually familiar with the word 'commitment.' Come to think of it, Gretel had never heard her use it.

She put the cookies and drinks on a serving tray and stepped from behind the bar to bring them to Maya and Darius. The two of them were deep into an argument. All she overheard was "S.G.," who was a mysterious runaway who had turned up in Lost Harbor last fall.

"I can't leave," she said firmly. "I'm very busy here and there are people depending on me."

Her mother gave a trill of laughter. "Depending on *you?*"

Gretel bit her lip, wounded despite herself. As she unloaded the tray, Maya caught her expression. In a raised voice, the police chief said, "A lot of people depend on you, Gretel. We couldn't do without you."

Maya nudged Chief Boone, who spoke up in a deep rumble. "That's right. Lost Harbor needs you, Gretel. Please don't leave us."

A burst of sunshine warmed Gretel's heart. How sweet that two such professional and respected town officials would stand up for her. How unexpected.

"Who was that?" her mother was asking.

"That," Gretel answered proudly as she finished delivering their order, "was the police chief *and* the fire chief of Lost Harbor."

She mouthed 'thank you' to Darius and Maya and stepped back behind the counter, where Toni, the bartender from the Olde Salt Saloon, was waiting to place an order.

After a pause, Aimee laughed again. "I do hope they don't get too attached to you, baby. Have they seen your passport? When's the last time you stayed anywhere for more than two months?"

Gretel slammed the tray down harder than she meant to. "Goodbye, Mom. I can't spend all day getting insulted, I'm working."

"So I'll book the Fiji trip?"

She ended the call and rested both hands on the counter, heaving in deep breaths to get a grip on her emotions. Then she plastered on a smile and faced Toni. The slim, tattooed bartender looked like someone who never took shit from anyone, including her mother.

"Coffeemaker at the Olde Salt still broken?" Gretel asked her.

"Yep. Black coffee to go, hold the drama."

Still a little shaky from that conversation with her mother, Gretel filled a large to-go cup with coffee and snapped on the lid.

Toni handed her a five dollar bill, along with a sympathetic look. "If you need to let off some steam, come on out to the Olde Salt. I'm working all night. Haven't seen you out there lately."

"Yeah, I've been pretty busy. But thanks, a break might be nice." A champagne cocktail, maybe. She'd float on a cloud of bubbles into the sky, where nothing could wound her. Where her mother couldn't remind her that her primary reason for existing was to cement Aimee's relationship with a millionaire. Where she could chase away that sense of shame always lurking under the surface.

Not even playing Robin Hood had gotten rid of it. And now she couldn't even do that. Her wages and tips weren't doing much to fulfill the pledge she'd made.

CHAPTER EIGHT

After her shift ended, Gretel bundled up in her blue fake fur shortie coat and her Burberry beret. Even though most of the Olde Salt regulars were crusty fishermen and hardcore drinkers, they'd accepted her as one of them from the very beginning. She liked to amuse them with her outrageous outfits. She rarely paid for her own drinks there, but she'd never felt in any kind of danger.

To them, she was just another drinking buddy—with some extra flair.

She was still all jangled up from her conversation with her mother. She hated this feeling—it made her want to run, to flee, to escape, to get high, to blot out everything and find some fun.

As she scraped off the ice that had formed on the windshield of the old Nissan Frontier the Noonans had given her, she could already taste the prickle of champagne sliding down her throat. She'd been so busy lately that she hadn't had time for partying, or even a glass of wine.

When was the last time she'd had a drink? Jeez, she didn't even remember.

She snapped back the windshield wiper and chipped away at the ice under it.

When was the last time she couldn't remember the last time she'd had a drink?

Never, she realized with a shock. Because she didn't generally go long without one.

Was that a problem?

But she didn't have time to think about it because a small figure down the street caught her eye. She recognized that particular bright red parka.

Petey Ross was just emerging from Eller's Drugs. Eller's carried everything from fishing gear to housewares, birthday cards to crochet supplies. Before he'd taken more than two steps onto the sidewalk, a large man stepped from inside and grabbed him by the shoulder.

Petey tried to run, but the man tightened his grip. It looked as if he was furiously scolding Petey, who yelled right back at him. Gretel knew Petey well enough to predict what would come next —nothing good. Petey never shied away from a fight.

She tossed the ice scraper back into the truck and ran down the street.

"Hey! Hey you! Mister! What's going on here?"

The man wheeled on her as she skidded to a stop before him. Literally skidded—her zebra-striped boots had very little traction.

"This kid stole something. Are you his mother?"

She shot a quick glance at Petey, who was a red-faced ball of misery. But at least he wasn't throwing any punches.

"No, I'm not, but I was supposed to meet him here and do a little shopping with him. I was late, so that's on me." She dug in her coat pocket for her tips. "I'm happy to cover whatever he may or may not have taken, though it was probably by mistake and you should give him a chance to tell his side of the story. Petey, was there something you wanted to buy here?"

Petey nodded slowly and pulled an object from his coat pocket. It was a bottle of nail polish. He handed it to her and she turned it over. Kir Royale—a gorgeous shade of purple.

"Excellent choice," she told him. She turned back to the man. Without a coat, he was starting to shiver in his flannel shirt. "How much do we owe you?"

"Five dollars and seventy-nine cents, but that's not the point. Shoplifting is a crime and—"

"And he's a kid and that's a very important lesson to learn from his parent...al figures." She handed him six dollars and put the nail polish in her pocket. Petey would get it back once she'd sorted this out with him.

She put her hand around the boy. "You ready to go? I'm sorry I was late."

He nodded, then ducked under her arm and marched toward the truck. "We'll handle this," she told the man. She pulled a scrap of paper and a lipstick from her bag and wrote down her number. "Please call me if you have any more trouble."

"I should report this," he grumbled.

"Why? He's ten. Is this because it's nail polish? Because discrimination based on sexuality is illegal and—"

At the word 'sexuality,' the owner shuddered and backed toward the door. "Let's call it good. But straighten that kid out before he gets himself in trouble."

"*Straighten* him out?" But he'd already pushed open the door and disappeared inside.

In her truck, she found Petey with his arms folded defiantly across his chest. "You gonna tell Zander?"

"Well, I was thinking you should tell him. But if you don't want to, I will. One of us is going to have to. But it could be both of us. We can do it together." She turned the key in the ignition. "Wasn't Chloeann's dad doing the carpool today?"

"Yeah, but I had to work on a project with Trent. Zander's coming to get me."

That phrasing sounded extra morbid. "I'll text him and let him know you're with me."

"Okay." The relief in his voice told her that he wasn't quite ready to face his brother yet.

She could relate to that. She'd been in trouble almost constantly since about his age. But unlike him, she always got away with it. Probably because her mother knew how to sweet-talk authority figures.

After she'd alerted Zander, they drove through the town in comfortable silence. Petey ignored the picturesque storefronts with their profusion of twinkle lights that apparently stayed up all winter long.

She didn't try to quiz him about what he'd done. That wasn't her job, she figured. Her job was to keep him company while he worked it out in his own mind.

As they passed the turnoff that led to the harbor, where the Olde Salt perched like a drunken sailor at the end of the board-walk, she waved a wistful goodbye to her hypothetical champagne cocktail.

Sure, a drink would have been nice. But this was much more important.

"Ravens steal," Petey said abruptly. "They're really good scavengers."

"Oh yeah?"

"Sometimes they wait for other birds to bring down their prey, then steal it away from them. They're really smart birds. If they find a carcass, they'll call to the wolves or the coyotes to come in first so the meat will get exposed."

"Gruesome. You like ravens?"

"Ravens are awesome. They're my favorite bird."

"That's cool." Did the boy see himself as a raven, scavenging for nail polish? "I'm not sure that comparison is going to work with Zander."

"Zander's more like a bear," Petey said gloomily. "He's going to ground me to the den."

The boy knew what he was talking about. Zander was even more furious than Gretel could have predicted.

"You shoplifted from *Eller's*?" He laced his hands on top of his head and tilted it back with a groan. "Of all places. That man is a hard-ass."

"Exactly!" Gretel loosened her scarf so the melting ice crystals didn't drip down her shirt. "I paid him back and he still wanted to make a big deal out of it."

"Yeah, well...why shouldn't he? No one wants to be stolen from. Petey, you want me to go into your room and steal your stuff?"

"I was going to pay it back! I just didn't have my allowance with me."

"No excuses." Zander dropped his hands and planted his fists on his hips. "You're going to write a letter of apology to Eller's. You're going to do Jason's chores and your chores for the rest of the week. And I'm going to confiscate that nail polish. You shouldn't be able to keep something you stole."

Storm clouds had been building on Petey's face from "letter of apology" on. But that last part broke open the dam.

"*Zander! No fair!*"

"It's completely fair. Hand it over."

"*I don't even have it! Ask her!*" Petey ran to his room and slammed the door shut.

Jason snorted from his perch next to the woodstove, where he'd been waxing his skis. "Nice."

"Zander." Gretel drew in a long breath. "Can I speak to you in private?"

ONCE AGAIN, Zander found himself closed up in his bedroom with Gretel. This time, he wasn't the only furious one.

"You are being way too harsh on him!" she cried. "It's just a bottle of nail polish and I paid for it."

"That's not the point. He shoplifted. That's not okay." His jaw tightened and his gut roiled. This was exactly the kind of thing that could be a red flag for the caseworker.

"Then we'll say it's my nail polish and I'll just give it to him."

"The hell you will. He needs to get this. Don't get in the middle of it, Gretel."

Her eyebrows drew together in an offended frown. Turquoise daggers flashed from her eyes. "You should be grateful I *did* get in the middle of it. That idiot would have hauled him off to the police."

What a disaster that would have been. "Thank you," he managed stiffly. Truly, he did appreciate it, but his worry about Susan Baker blotted out everything else.

"Very gracious of you." Sarcasm radiated through her voice. "I'm overwhelmed."

"I'll pay you back the money for the nail polish. I'll buy it from you."

"And do what with it?"

"What does that matter?"

She took a step toward him and tapped him on the chest. Her touch reverberated through him. "Because it does. Because Petey wanted it enough to break the rules, and he knows how you are about rules. So he must have wanted it *really badly*."

Flabbergasted, he stared at her while his thoughts churned. He hadn't thought about it like that. He was entirely focused on the potential threat to their family.

"So he wanted it enough to steal. How does that let him off the hook?"

"My point is, I think you're being extra hard on him because it's nail polish."

Out of nowhere, the thought came—he wanted her to touch him again. He shoved it aside. "What are you getting at?"

"You're freaking out because he's a boy and he took nail polish. Just like you wouldn't let me dye his hair."

Finally Zander put it all together. He gave a short bark of laughter. Ironically, it eased the tension inside him.

And there it came—another touch from Gretel. This time, she swatted him lightly on the arm. "Why is that funny?"

He caught her hand and held it against his chest. Not for any reason other than he wanted to feel it there. "The first time Petey watched a YouTube makeup tutorial, I asked him why he was so interested in it. He said he was curious, and I should butt out. So I did."

She curled her hand against his chest, but didn't pull away. "And?"

"Petey's kind of...an explorer. And he's a kid. He's going to be who he's going to be. Gay, straight, something else, whatever. That's not my job."

Finally she tugged her hand away from his chest. He still felt an electric tingle where it had rested. "What is, then?"

"My job is to make sure he's safe and doesn't break any laws while he's figuring shit out."

She ran the tip of her tongue across her lips. He couldn't help tracking that pink bit of flesh. What did the rest of her body look like under all those layers of winter clothing?

"What about the man at Eller's? I saw his face when he saw the nail polish."

"That guy's a dick. Always has been."

"I basically accused him of being homophobic."

He grinned. "You're not wrong. Better you said it than me."

One corner of her mouth lifted, then the other. It was a glorious process, watching those fresh-petal lips curve into a mischievous, dazzling smile.

And maybe he should stop staring at her mouth right about now.

"I think you might be telling the truth," she murmured.

He raised an eyebrow at her. "Why wouldn't I be? I don't lie."

"Okay, then why won't you let him dye his hair? That didn't involve any kind of law-breaking. If he's trying to figure out—"

He cut her off with a gesture. "No hair dye. No nail polish."

"And no explanation?"

"No explanation." The finality in his voice made her beautiful smile vanish.

Seeing it go created an empty ache in his heart, but what could he do? He couldn't tell her about the caseworker's veiled threat. He didn't even know the full situation yet.

Maybe you can trust Gretel. The thought came out of the blue.

He considered it. She'd come to Petey's rescue. She'd handled the situation at Eller's pretty damn well. She obviously cared about Petey.

He wanted to trust her. He wanted to talk to her. He liked talking to her—even though he wasn't generally a big talker. With Gretel it was different. Why not just take the leap and explain about Susan Baker?

Unless...what if this was his dick talking? Gretel was outrageously attractive to him. When she was around, he always knew exactly where she was—as if he could sixth-sense her location. His ears picked up her voice quicker than any other sound, as if he was tuned to her specific vocal frequency. It was weird.

How was he supposed to make good decisions about someone

who scrambled his brain as much as Gretel did? He wanted her, bad. His cock was already partially hard just from this conversation—and it wasn't even a sexy one.

If he trusted her enough to tell her about the caseworker, things would change between them. They'd probably get closer.

But he couldn't sell out his family's secrets just to get a smile from Gretel.

He had responsibilities and they came first.

"Okay then." She whirled around, her blue fur coat swinging behind her. His gaze dropped to her ass, which was encased in a clinging skirt that barely came to her thighs. Under that she wore thick wool leggings and zebra-print boots and damn, the sexy sight could bring a guy to tears. "I guess I'll go now. Good luck and all."

"Gretel," he called after her, making her pause in mid-flight. "Thank you. Really. I owe you one."

She shot him a quick, unreadable glance, and disappeared out the door.

He let out a long rush of breath and adjusted his jeans. Damn. He needed to get a grip on this attraction before it got him into trouble.

But still—he did owe Gretel. And he knew just how to thank her.

CHAPTER NINE

A few days after the shoplifting incident, Gretel padded out in her panda slippers from the guest room she inhabited at the Noonans'. They'd gone to great lengths to make it as comfy as possible for her—they'd acquired a queen-size bed, bought her an electric heater, and even added an extra router so she could get Wi-Fi in her room.

Earl was back from the North Slope, which meant that she didn't have to get up early and help Eli get off to school. When Earl was here, she was able to work more shifts at the Wicked Brew and do things like practice her snowshoeing.

She could drink coffee made by someone else for once. Which she enjoyed to the max, especially when Earl splurged on the high-end coffee beans he loved.

After pouring herself a mug, she petted Groovy for a while, then wandered into the playroom, where the toddlers were knocking over a set of blocks and laughing hysterically. They really knew how to keep each other entertained. Abby sat in a rocking chair, nursing the baby and keeping an eye on the toddlers.

"Is Earl on car-pool duty?"

"Morning shift only. He'll be home soon."

Gretel shivered and wrapped her long angora sweater around her. It had a unicorn on the back and she loved its silky warmth. It was so comfy that it worked as a kind of shield against hurtful things like Zander shutting her out.

"Are you chilly?" Abby asked right away. "I haven't checked the fire in a while, would you mind? After that you should help yourself to the coffee cake Earl made. He's having fun playing homemaker, the big beast."

The affection on her voice took any hint of sting out of her words. No one who knew Abby and Earl had any doubt about their love for each other, but they did have a rough-edged way of showing it sometimes.

Gretel shuffled into the living room and added a log to the fire. The last log.

Darn it. She'd have to go out into the deep freeze to collect some more. Wasn't Earl supposed to do that sort of thing when he was here?

She spotted the coffee cake, still in its pan on the kitchen counter. He'd used some of the currants that the family had gathered in the fall. The cake's warm aroma made her mouth water and her grumbling disappear.

"All is forgiven, Earl," she murmured under her breath. She cut a small square and popped it into her mouth, then wandered into the arctic entry. After kicking off her slippers, she stuck her feet into her boots and sorted through the coats looking for one of hers.

Finally she located her blue faux fur and pulled it on over her fuzzy pajamas. Yawning, she pushed open the door that led outside and right away realized her mistake. Cold air blasted right into her mouth. She slammed the door and snapped her mouth shut.

"Everything okay?" Abby called.

"Peachy!" she croaked.

She was definitely awake now. Every nerve tingled from the shock of that elemental collision between her and the outside air.

It must have dropped below zero.

She grabbed a scarf—Eli's, she believed—and tried again. This time she angled her body sideways so that she wasn't getting the full blast head on.

"Wooooh," she called into the bitter wind as soon as she'd made it outside. "Let's do this! Bring it, baby. Bring it!"

The wind answered with a howl. It tugged at the scarf, bit at her cheeks—but not in an attacking way. It felt more like an exuberant dog—Groovy. Like a wild, barely trained force of nature begging her to play with it.

"Okay, I'm here, aren't I? Gotta make this quick, though. Unless you want to blow a few sticks of wood out of that shed for me." She murmured the words into Eli's scarf to avoid another episode of wind-down-her-windpipe.

Leaning into the full force of the wind, she trudged down the path to the woodshed. *Please cooperate*, she silently begged the sled. *Just this once. I'll be extra nice to you. I'll take you down a real hill for fun instead of making you work all the time.*

God, she was so silly, talking to a sled. Smiling at her own absurdity, she took the last step into the woodshed and stopped short. The wind whistled through the planks of the shed as she blinked whirling snow out of her eyes.

The orange plastic sled was gone. Nowhere to be seen.

A sleek new sled had taken its place. It had actual metal runners, polished wooden boards, and vintage writing on the side. "Flame Runner," was its name.

"Well, look at you, handsome stranger," she murmured. Here in the shed, she couldn't feel the buffeting of the wind, and didn't mind speaking out loud again. "Where did you come from? Did Earl find you?"

Then she spotted an envelope wedged between two of the sled's slats. She tugged it out and saw that it was addressed to her.

"This doesn't count as 'help' because I owe you. Found this at the dump and restored it. It's a classic. Enjoy, it's yours."

It was signed with a big Z.

Wow. This was Zander's handiwork? She ran a hand over the smooth fine-grained wood with its perfect sheen of varnish. She knew about his woodworking projects—but she hadn't realized that he had this kind of skill. The sled was a work of art. Having grown up with expensive things, she knew how to recognize quality. This was top-of-the-line meticulous craftsmanship, on the part of both the original creator and the loving restorer.

It was almost too beautiful to pile full of wood. But the cold was creeping in around the edges of her coat, so she set aside that worry and set the sled—more of a toboggan, really—onto the snowpack.

It stayed right where it was supposed to, sturdy and solid, its own weight keeping it from squirreling all over the place the way the plastic sled used to. Quickly she loaded it with several armloads of firewood, until it was filled to the top of its side rails.

Now the big test. She gripped its leash and walked toward the house. With a quiet *swish,* it followed behind her as sweet as a lamb. Not once did it threaten to tumble over or lunge down the snow bank. On the entire path to the house, not a single stick of wood went overboard.

"Flame Runner, I think I love you," she sang to it. "I wanna know for sure—"

Up ahead, she spotted Zander emerging from the ski trail that connected the two properties. "Hey, you," she called.

He changed direction and skied across the yard toward her.

"How's it working?" With his eyes gleaming green against his wind-chapped face, he made her mouth water.

"Like a dream." She dropped the tether and stepped toward him. She probably looked like a homeless woman in her pajamas and winter gear, but she didn't care. He was still skiing toward her when she stepped directly into his path. He dropped his ski poles and grabbed her in his arms. His momentum kept them sliding a few more feet.

"Watch where you're go—" he began, but she cut him off by planting a kiss right on his lips. It was a quick kiss—touch and withdraw—but it felt like a thunderclap. The detonation echoed through her.

They came to a stop but he didn't release her. He stared down at her with a look of shock. "Was that a thank you or—"

"Of course," she said lightly, even though her heart was fluttering like a trapped moth. "This sled is my new best friend. It's beautiful, Zander. Really wonderful. I had no idea you were so talented."

He lifted one eyebrow, but still didn't release her. "Do you thank everyone with a kiss on the lips?"

"Maybe I was aiming for that spot right *next* to your lips. That little scar." She touched the mark with her mitten. His eyes darkened.

"You still didn't answer the question."

"Is this an interrogation? I can take the kiss back if you want."

His lips quirked. "Then I'd have to take back the sled."

"I guess you're stuck with that kiss then."

"I guess I am." He tilted his head, considering. "I have more sleds where that came from."

Oh no. This was trouble. Her insides were starting to melt in a liquid pool of heat. Her nipples were hardening against his chest, though luckily several layers of winter gear separated her from Zander. "Are you ever going to let me go?"

"I'm thinking about that."

He was so warm, and it felt so good to be held against him while the cold wind whipped around them. Frosty crystals had formed on the hair that curled under the edge of his hat. His head lowered, his lips came closer, she could feel his warm breath on her face. Anticipation flooded her veins in a hot rush.

Then the door of the house opened and Groovy galloped into the yard. She spotted Gretel and Zander and hurtled toward them with her tongue lolling.

Gretel found herself in a controlled slide toward the ground. Zander held her steady as her boots touched the snow. Good thing, because as soon as Groovy reached them, she began running tight little circles around the two of them.

"No, Groovy! You'd better not knock over my new sled!" Gretel cried and rushed to secure her load.

Too late. Curious about the new object, Groovy bumped against the Flame Runner, sniffing and pushing, and somehow got it sliding toward the snowbank.

And once again, there went half her firewood.

First she groaned, but then she had to laugh. Zander was laughing too, as he skied toward the fallen sled.

"You grab Groovy while I get the wood," he called.

"Groovy! Come here, you wild thing." When she finally got a hand on her collar, she saw that Zander was already herring-boning up the bank, sled in tow.

That took strength. So did holding her in his arms, entirely off the ground, for the eternity it had taken for them to almost kiss.

That almost-kiss was going to haunt her, she could tell already.

"I have bad sled karma, that's all there is to it," she said cheerfully as he skied to her side. She took the tether from him and headed for the house.

"I was actually going to see if you wanted to try the sled out on Wolf Pack Hill."

"Wolf Pack...is that safe?"

He smiled. "It's the best sledding hill around. It's supposed to warm up a bit, should be perfect sledding weather."

She hesitated. Was this a ... date? How would she feel about it if it was a date? "It sounds fun, but I have to check my schedule at the Wicked Brew."

His face shuttered a bit. "Okay. Let us know. Petey in particular is hoping you'll come."

Ah. So it wasn't a date. It was a Ross family outing.

"Tell Eli too. I don't know if the twins are ready for Wolf Pack Hill, but everyone's invited."

And not just a Ross family outing, but the Noonans too. It was for the best. Safer that way.

A gust of wind whirled past her and she shivered. "Let's plan on it. I'll bring the hot cocoa. Employee perk from the Wicked Brew. Thanks again for this miraculous magic carpet, Zander!"

She hurried back to the house, the sled in tow, Groovy capering at her heels, a tingling sensation still coursing through her. She assumed it was from the cold, but even later, after she'd warmed up by the fire, it hadn't left her. Those tingles were entirely Zander Ross-inspired. Damn it.

CHAPTER TEN

Zander loved all winter sports, from hockey to skiing—he even played with the Lost Harbor Puffins when he had time. He didn't really consider sledding to be a sport. It was a little-kid thing, a way to have fun in the snow, like building a snowman or making snow angels.

But sledding with Gretel Morrison was a completely different kind of experience. She had a way of making everything more fun. With her bright smile and playful lighthearted spirit, she had all the kids laughing and vying for the right to climb into her sled on the first run.

Wolf Pack Hill was perfect for sledding not only because it was long, with the optimal degree of steepness. But also because it was safe; it had been cleared for pastureland at some point, and no trees had ever grown back. There was no possible way for anyone to get hurt sledding Wolf Pack.

At the top of the hill, someone had installed a platform made from four by fours, with a burn barrel mounted on it. On good sledding days, when it wasn't too cold and there was a good layer of snow, people often gathered here with firewood and thermoses.

Someone would start a fire in the burn barrel and the adults would gather around catching up on the news while the kids hurtled down the hill, then slogged back up towing their sleds.

But today, they had the hill to themselves, except for a couple in ski gear enjoying the view. Earl got a fire going in the barrel while Abby nursed the baby in the warm car. Zander unloaded all the sleds he'd brought along; they had a huge collection that they'd gathered over the years, from circular pieces of foam to kick sleds that you could ride upright.

Jason went right for the fastest one and raced to his favorite launch spot on the steeper side of the hill. He went airborne, on his belly, howling like a wolf.

Gretel gasped as she watched him fly through the air. "He knows what he's doing, right?"

"If there's snow involved, he knows what he's doing," Zander told her. Ever since she'd gotten out of the Noonans' Tahoe, in her fluffy pink hat and silver insulated jacket, his heart had been doing odd things. Sudden lurches of joy alternating with quiet moments of trying-to-be-reasonable.

"Someone's waving at you," Gretel told him, gesturing toward the couple in ski gear.

Recognizing them, he waved back. "That's Doug and Sandy Stern, the ski coaches at the high school."

"Married ski coaches?"

"Yup. Stern and Sterner, that's what the players call them. He was an alternate at the Olympics once. She was a champion biathlete. They're the reason why Lost Harbor High has such a great ski team."

"So they might be Jason's coaches? Maybe I should butter them up with some hot chocolate." She held up the giant thermos she'd brought.

"They're *going* to be his coaches. I got an email from them basically guaranteeing Jason a spot. They said he's 'surpassed all their expectations' and they invited him to practice with the team for the rest of the school year."

"Wow. Jason must be so psyched about that."

"He's already planning his cross training regime for the summer. They actually want him to work out with the team before school, but—"

He broke off, because something had just occurred to him. When he'd emailed back, he'd explained that Jason would only be available for afterschool sessions. Early mornings were out of the question because of the drive and the carpool schedule.

The Sterns had pushed back on that, suggesting various options for transportation, even offering gas money. Although he'd been pretty offended by that, he'd kept it simple and answered, "When he's on the team we can discuss it again. For now, that's the most he can do."

They'd dropped it with a gracious, "We understand."

But it had been weird.

He looked over at the coaches again and saw that Jason was jogging over the snow toward them, looking eager and excited. The way he only looked while skiing.

He sorted through everything he knew about the Sterns, which wasn't much. They were a dynamic couple with a big fancy house close to town where they threw fundraising parties for the ski team. They were a hundred percent focused on skiing. They had plenty of money, lots of connections in Lost Harbor and beyond. They had no children of their own, but they often took in ski students and foreign exchange students.

Was the "other option" Susan Baker had referred to ... them? Or was he just being paranoid?

"Zander!" Gretel nudged him with her elbow. "You look like you just saw a ghost. Is everything okay?"

"I—" he shook it off. "Yeah, fine."

The ski coaches couldn't just take Jason away, could they? They were a family. They needed to stay together.

"I need to make a quick phone call," he told Gretel. He had to get to the bottom of this or he wouldn't have any fun sledding. He stepped away from Gretel just as another car pulled over at the top of the hill. He waved at Lucas Holt and his fiancée, Megan Miller, along with her eight-year-old, Ruby. Ruby went racing ahead while Lucas and Megan unloaded their sleds. A perfect nuclear family with a twist—Ruby's father lived in California and sometimes Ruby flew down there for advanced math tutoring.

No one would try to take Ruby away from Megan and Lucas. Zander knew that Megan and Dev, Ruby's father, had run into some custody issues—how much time Ruby would spend with each parent, and where. But they'd worked it out and now Megan, Lucas and Ruby had a beautiful little family.

He dialed the number Susan Baker had left with him. All he got was a voicemail.

"Hi, this is Zander Ross and I'm calling with an urgent question. Please call me back. If someone is trying to—if there's a threat to—sorry, I just need to know what's going on. Please call me back. I have a right to know."

When he ended the call, he swung around and surveyed the scene of happy kids gliding down the snow, shouting and laughing. Stern and Sterner were gone.

Where was Jason? He panicked when he couldn't locate him. Then his brother's curly brown head popped up from the bottom of the hill, way past the point at which they usually stopped. He was making his way up the long hill with his sled held over his head. It was probably an extra workout he'd devised—climb the hill without using his hands.

The kid was crazy.

The panic faded and the world tilted back to normal. Jason

wasn't going anywhere. Their family needed to stay exactly the way it was. Losing one brother was not an option.

Gretel and Petey were flying down the hill in the sled he'd restored for her. Gretel sat in back, with Petey between her legs, which meant that she had the controls.

They spotted Jason and aimed toward him, shouting something he couldn't make out. It looked as if Petey was leaning to the right to make the turn happen. As they passed Jason, he jettisoned his own sled and jumped on behind Gretel.

Everyone shrieked and the toboggan tilted on one runner and they all went tumbling into the snow in a laughing pile.

Not proper sledding protocol.

But what the hell, everyone was fine and Zander was tired of being the prison warden.

He grabbed a round foam sled—those things could really move—and jumped onto it in a kneeling position. Using a paddling motion of his hands to gain speed, he raced down the hill in their direction. The three of them were trying to untangle themselves, but every time one of them got free, someone else would tug them back down into the snow.

Petey was gathering up snowballs and winging them every which way—at Gretel, at Earl zooming past with the toddlers, at the sky. Jason was still trying to get the snow out of his face but he was laughing too hard to manage it. Gretel spotted Zander first.

"Watch out, boys, here comes trouble!" she shouted. "Get those snowballs ready."

"He's probably gonna be mad," Zander heard Jason say as he careened toward them on his spinning perch.

"Watch out!" Zander shouted as he shifted his weight on the sled. Timing it perfectly, he made a rooster tail of snow spurt from under the sled—right onto Gretel and his brothers. They all tumbled back into the snow, bright splashes of winter coats against the white.

"It's on!" Jason howled.

Exhilarated, Zander kept going. He let fly a long whoop of pure joy at the speed and the wind against his face and the snow whirling around him.

When he finally spun to a stop, he glanced up the hill and saw Gretel standing up, legs braced apart, brandishing a fist at him.

"You're going down, Zander Ross!"

After that came chaos. They turned the sled on its side and used it as a shield while they pelted him with snowballs every time he tried to come up the hill. But then Ruby felt sorry for him and joined his cause, using herself as a human shield while he crawled behind her.

"Double fudge sundae, what do you say, Ruby?"

"You don't have to pay me in dessert. I fight injustice wherever I see it." Her dark eyes shone down at him over her widespread arms.

"Lucky for me."

But even Ruby could only do so much, and when they reached the sled his brothers gave a war cry and attacked with armfuls of snowballs, while Gretel whirled Ruby out of the way.

Then Gretel raced back to her battle station and the snowballs rained down and it was all a blur up until the point when he and Gretel found themselves behind the sled, with his brothers and Ruby on the other side.

Completely sheltered by the sled and the snow fortifications the boys had built around it, the two of them paused to catch their breath. Gretel's flushed face was the deep rose of a peony, smudged with snow. And it was only a few inches away.

The last time, outside the Noonans' house, she'd kissed him and he'd been stopped by the dog before he could kiss her back.

He hadn't been able to stop thinking about it since. All of that desire came rushing back tenfold. It would have taken an avalanche to stop him from hovering his face over hers, scanning for sign of an objection.

Her lips parted and she tilted her face toward his. "Quick," she whispered.

He dipped down and brushed his lips against her mouth. Her lips were soft and chilled, with the flavor of snowflakes and chocolate, but they quickly warmed under his kiss. Even more quickly, he lost control of his common sense, and what was supposed to be a quick peck went much deeper. His tongue swept against hers, seeking her sweetness, the hot tender velvet.

She responded by eagerly opening her mouth under his. Every movement of his tongue met a willing sparring partner. The kiss became a waltz, a tease, a dance, as if they were spinning down the hill together on the smoothest, silkiest ride of all.

The sound of his brothers shouting about snowballs faded away, along with any thought of other sledders. Right here, right now, in this little patch of sheltered snow, they were alone and the world was theirs. He could hear the beating of her heart, the flutter of her breath.

Gretel, he thought, then wasn't sure if he'd said it out loud or if her name had simply taken over his brain. *Gretel*.

Then a snowball landed on the back of his head and smashed into a million bits of snow, half of which went down the back of his neck.

He pulled away with a gasp of shock. Just in time, too—Petey peered over the edge of the sled.

"Gretel, get up! I have a plan! You can be on my side."

Petey disappeared and a second later he plopped next to them in the snow. Gretel's face flushed even deeper red as Zander helped her up and brushed the snow off her suit.

"Smart kid," he murmured. Then, his voice rising so that Petey could hear him too, "But you're still going to lose."

Yup, it was the most fun he'd had in the snow in—forever.

CHAPTER ELEVEN

After that day on Wolf Pack Hill, Gretel gave herself a stern lecture about keeping her distance from Zander. He was a serious person with real responsibilities and...well, she wasn't. It couldn't possibly work between them, no matter how wildly attractive she found him.

Even if she made it through the winter—which she totally would, just to hear him grovel on the Bush Lines—she had no idea what was next for her. Would she stay in Lost Harbor while Bethany and Nate started a family? Would Auntie Gretel be a thing? Or would she get itchy feet and start dreaming about Argentina or New Zealand? Or would she finally go to college—assuming she could find a way to pay for it? Or would she cave into her mother and accept one of her weekly offers of a plane ticket somewhere? Or—

The point being, she had no idea what her future held. How could she inflict that kind of uncertainty on Zander? It wouldn't be fair.

Besides, this winter was about focusing on herself and trying to make good on her donation pledge. It was about standing on her own two feet and relying on herself. Not other people, not clubs, not champagne cocktails.

Lost Harbor had a very active AA meeting, she discovered. Drinking problems were pretty common in a town like this. The group met in a back room of the Unitarian church every Tuesday and Thursday evenings. The first time she went, she tiptoed in and grabbed a chair at the very back of the room. By the time the facilitator noticed her, she'd already listened to several people's stories and had to wipe tears off her face. One older woman had blacked out while babysitting her grandkids and hadn't been allowed to see them since. A younger guy had lost his license after injuring his best friend. The guilt was eating him up.

When it was her turn, she'd introduced herself and said, "I'm trying to be a better person, and I don't think I can be if I drink to escape. Does that make sense?"

The silent sympathy and lack of judgment meant so much to her.

She'd been back three times since then, and always left feeling moved and...*real*. Grounded. As if the people at the meetings saw past her frivolous exterior and knew that it was just one part of her, and there was so much more.

Sometimes she forgot about that.

She needed to focus on herself, not get distracted by her hunk of a neighbor. She came up with a strategy—every time she started craving Zander, she strapped on her snowshoes and worked off her lust with exercise instead.

She got quite good at snowshoeing. The woods around the Noonans' became almost a second home.

That was where she was one afternoon when she heard a strange sound coming from the direction of the road. She was fairly deep into the forest, picking her way up the side of a valley dotted with alders buried under several feet of snow. The only way she knew there were alders under her feet was that Earl had mentioned it. He'd also told her that there was a stream wandering through the valley, though it was probably frozen solid by now.

The sound was a loud crashing thump, followed by silence. She was in the midst of taking a photo of a baby spruce so covered by snow that she couldn't see a single branch or spruce needle.

"Hello?" she called up the slope. No answer.

She replayed the sound in her memory and realized that there had been another sound before that—an engine. She couldn't hear anything like that now.

Had a vehicle crashed into the forest?

Changing direction, she headed straight up the ridge, toward the approximate location of the sound.

"Hello," she shouted again. But the shape of the slope made the sound of her voice bounce back at her instead of carrying uphill.

After that, she saved her energy for the climb. It was a good thing she'd been doing so much snowshoeing and built up her fitness. Even so, her thigh muscles were burning and she was heaving in deep breaths of chilly air by the time she crested the ridge.

Up ahead she spotted a vehicle, its nose snug against the base of a tree. From this angle, she couldn't identify it, but she could see someone small emerging from one of the doors.

She recognized that bright red coat. "Petey?" she shouted.

Finally, someone heard her. "Gretel!" She heard the fear and tears in his voice. "Something's wrong with Chloeann's dad!"

Even though it wasn't really possible to run in snowshoes, she launched into a kind of lope that took her across the snow as fast as humanly possible. By the time she reached the car, Eli had also left the vehicle. Both of the boys looked completely freaked out.

"What happened?" she cried as she stumbled to their sides.

The two boys started talking at once. "We dropped off Chloeann because she had so much homework and he was taking us home when he just--"

"He made a weird choking sound and then he jerked back, like this—"

"And we started driving into the woods." Eli finished the sentence. "We hit the tree and then he kind of fell forward on the wheel and we didn't know what to do. Is he okay?"

Gretel snowshoed to the driver's-side door and wrenched it open. Jeff Durst was slumped over the wheel, his body tilted to the side. She reached past the layers of winter gear—jacket, scarf —and finally touched his neck. At first she couldn't tell if the frantic pulse she felt belonged to her or to him. She took a breath to calm her racing heart, and decided it was his pulse, not her own heartbeat in her fingers.

"He's alive," she called to the kids. "We need to call for help." She dug in her coat pocket for her phone. She always kept it zipped in an inner pocket so the cold wouldn't kill the battery. After pulling it out, she saw that she had no service—of course. When were they going to put up that damn cell tower?

"There's never any service here," said Petey, not very help-fully. "What are we going to do?"

Eli and Petey were looking up at her like two scared bunny rabbits. She noticed that Petey had a bruise on his forehead. What if he'd gotten a concussion from his head bumping the window? What if they were both traumatized from witnessing a seizure—or whatever had happened?

They were counting on her to handle this situation.

What would Bethany do?

That was no help at all. Bethany was a doctor and by now she'd be administering first aid to poor Jeff Durst, saving his life and completely taking command of the situation.

"Okay, here's what we're going to do," she told the boys. "You two stay in the car and try to keep Mr. Durst warm. I'm going to loosen up his scarf so he can breathe easy. Then I'll hike up to the road and wave someone down. I should be within earshot so if anything happens or you need me, just yell loudly. Okay?"

The boys looked at each other, uneasy. "What if the car explodes or something?" Eli asked.

Gretel had no idea if that was a possibility or not, but maybe it was better not to take a chance. "Then we should get him out of there." How could she do that by herself? She didn't want the kids anywhere near a potentially exploding car. God, this was terrifying.

Petey dropped to his knees in the snow and peered under the car. "Nothing's leaking. I don't smell gas. Zander taught me how to tell. The car's not going to explode."

He might be only ten, but the kid was smart and taught by a former Marine. Gretel believed him. "Then we'll leave him there and get help. Come on, kids."

Petey got back to his feet. "I'm gonna stay with him in case he wakes up. He might be scared. Eli, you can go with Gretel."

What a brave kid.

But Eli—at all times—preferred to do whatever Petey was doing. "I can stay too," he said in a small voice.

Gretel knew he was still scared, but she'd rather the two boys stayed together then separate. And time was passing quickly. "Hopefully this won't take long. Remember, yell if you need me."

She gave Eli a quick hug and a whispered, "you're doing great," to keep his spirits up. Following the tire tracks the SUV had left in the snow, she headed up the hill. Even with a trail, it seemed to take forever to make it to the road. The last few feet were torture for her already sore legs.

Once she reached the pavement, she bent over and rested her

hands on her knees while she heaved in a few breaths. Then she yelled into the woods, "Can you guys hear me?"

The answering yell from Petey sounded closer than she'd expected. They must only be twenty yards or so down the slope. Maybe her nerves had made it seem farther. Jeff's life might depend on her getting help, after all.

She took a position facing toward town, where no one could zip past without seeing her. This road didn't get a lot of traffic. Only a few families lived past here—the Noonans, the Rosses, and the residents of an Old Believers Russian village located ten miles or so farther into the hills.

Zander was probably still in town, waiting to pick up Jason from his ski practice. Maybe Earl hadn't come home yet. But with a sinking heart, she remembered that he intended to replace the heat tape that kept the water flowing into the kitchen. He and Abby were both already home.

If no one drove past, she'd have to race on her snowshoes all the way to the Noonans, and that would take precious minutes that Jeff might not have.

As the seconds ticked past, she came up with more backup plans. Maybe she could try to drive the van, if it still ran. Could she somehow move Jeff without hurting him, then back the van up the hill to the road?

Ridiculous ideas.

What else? Signal flares? Maybe Jeff had something like that in the van? Should she have checked that first? Were her poor decisions about to cost a man his life?

She was on the verge of tears when finally—finally!—a car rounded the curve from town. It was a tidy blue Toyota that looked oddly out of place in the Lost Harbor universe of work trucks and Subarus. A city car, with a woman at the wheel.

Gretel waved madly to get the driver's attention, even jumping up and down in her snowshoes. The driver turned on her hazards and pulled over next to Gretel. She rolled down the passenger-side window.

"Do you need some help?"

"Yes! I need a cell signal, can you drive me up the road a bit until I get a bar?"

The woman frowned and cupped a hand around her ear. Gretel saw that she was Native Alaskan, with gray threaded through her dark hair. "You want to go to a bar?"

"No! God no. I need cell service." She came closer so the driver could hear over the sound of her engine. "A vehicle went off the road down there. The driver had some kind of medical crisis. We need to call 911 and I can't get a signal."

Finally the woman seemed to understand. "Get in." She gestured for Gretel to hop in. Something in her blunt manner made Gretel hurry to obey, but first she yelled down to the boys. "I'll be right back! Hang tight!"

"Is someone with the car?" the woman asked as Gretel snapped off her snowshoes. She planted them in the ridge of snow left by the plow truck. They'd be easy to spot, she figured.

"Yes," she said, then stopped before giving any more details. She didn't know this woman, after all. Crime in Lost Harbor tended to be drug or alcohol-related, and domestic in nature. She probably wasn't at risk from an unfamiliar woman, but she might as well be extra cautious.

As they got underway, she stared at her phone, waiting for the infuriating "no service" to disappear and a bar to show up.

"How long had you been waiting for someone to drive by?" the woman asked.

"It seemed like forever! But I honestly have no idea. I was so happy when I saw your car. So few people live out this way. I was starting to worry that it could be hours before anyone came." Ugh, she was babbling, something she did when she got nervous. *Change the subject.* "Do you know someone out this way?"

"I'm headed for the Rosses. Do you know them?"

"Of course I know them. Very well, actually." Curiously, she dragged her gaze from her phone and glanced at the driver. What connection could she have with Zander and the kids? "Are you a friend of the family?"

But she missed the woman's response because just then her phone pinged. A bar appeared, then disappeared too quickly for her to place a call.

She groaned in disappointment. "Actually, Petey Ross is back there with the vehicle. It's his carpool. But he's okay," she said quickly. "Neither of the kids was hurt."

"Jason's there too?" She knew their names; she must be a friend.

"No, Jason's at ski practice. Zander's going to bring him home. He's going to freak out when he hears about this, but he can't be in two places at once, poor guy."

"Poor Zander has a lot to juggle, doesn't he?"

"Oh my gosh, he sure does. I honestly don't know how he manages." She was about to go on about Zander's situation—and maybe ask a few questions of her own—but the phone dinged again. Two bars this time.

"Pull over!" she cried. "Right here." She was already dialing 911 as the Toyota veered to the side of the road.

"Nine-one—"

Gretel cut off the dispatcher in mid-911."Car off the road! We need paramedics! The driver is Jeff Durst and he had a heart attack or a seizure or something. He needs medical help."

"Slow down," said the dispatcher. "Where is the vehicle located?"

"Wolf Ridge Road."

"Where on the road?"

"Past the Durst place, do you know where that is?"

"Do you know the mile marker?"

"How would I know the mile marker? What *is* a mile marker? I mean, I know it marks the miles, but is it on your phone or something? How can I figure it out?"

Sounding maybe a little amused, the dispatcher said, "It's okay, we'll use your cell signal to find you."

"No, I'm not with the vehicle. There's no cell service there. But I put my snowshoes there as a marker. And I'm going right back there now."

"Good thinking," the dispatcher assured her. Great, apparently she'd done something right, despite her ignorance when it came to 'mile markers.' "Someone's on the way. Is there anything more you can tell me about the victim?"

"No, except I checked his pulse and it was very fast. Two boys are with him and they're going to keep him warm and be there in case he wakes up."

"Do you want to stay on the line until the EMTs arrive?"

"No! I need to get back, as long as this amazing angel of a good Samaritan doesn't mind driving me." She gave her rescuer the most grateful smile in her extensive repertoire of smiles.

After she hung up with the dispatcher, she made one more call—to Abby Noonan. "Abby, it's Gretel. I don't have the Dursts' number, but Jeff was in an accident. The kids are all okay," she said quickly before Abby panicked. "EMTs are on the way, but I was thinking you should call May Durst and let her know what happened. He had some kind of attack while he was driving and went off the road."

"Oh my god. I'll call her right away, absolutely."

"Also, Petey and Eli need a pickup. I wouldn't mind one too, since I don't think I can snowshoe another inch."

"Of course. Earl will come right away."

"Perfect. Zander won't be back until later, so—"

"Petey will stay with us until then. I'll call Zander right after I call May."

"You're a doll." Gretel hung up and sat back on her seat, utterly spent now that the adrenaline was wearing off.

Her rescuer turned the Toyota around and headed back down the hill.

"I seriously can't even begin to tell you how grateful I am," she told the woman.

The good Samaritan gave her a creaky smile, as if she didn't do much of that in general. "I'm glad I was at the right place at the right time." She sounded less brusque than she had at first.

"No kidding." Gretel scanned the side of the road for her snowshoes, or for a paramedic van, or anything breaking up the monotony of trees and snow. "I think it was destiny, or at least serendipity. It's such a funny coincidence that you know the Ross family. I can't wait to tell Zander."

"Are you going to see him today?"

"Of course. I see him all the time."

Just then Gretel spotted the glow of blue and red flashers past the downward curve of the road. The paramedic van was almost here, and with any luck, Nate would be in it. At that point she could completely relax. Or almost completely, because she'd still be worried about Jeff, and she still wanted to make sure Petey and Eli got home safely. "I'm Gretel, by the way."

"Susan Baker. I'm sure we'll be seeing more of each other."

Gretel realized Susan Baker must think she was closer to the Ross family than she actually was. She opened her mouth to correct her, but she was already bringing the car to a stop on the downhill side of the road, poised to head back to town.

"You're not going to the Rosses, after all?" Gretel asked in surprise.

"No, I'll come some other time. This doesn't seem like the best time for a visit."

"Are you sure? Do you want me to give Zander a message?"

Gretel got out of the car, anxious to get to the boys and make sure they were still okay.

"No need. I'll call soon. You can tell him that."

Was it Gretel's imagination, or did that sound almost ominous?

CHAPTER TWELVE

Zander screeched his work van to a stop outside the Noonans' house and tore inside. As soon as he spotted Petey, he swept him into a bear hug that had the boy squirming in protest.

"You're okay? What's that bruise on your forehead?"

"It's fine. The paramedics put ice on it, but it doesn't even hurt. Jeez. Mr. Durst had a stroke! Can you believe it? In the middle of driving!"

Zander shuddered at the very thought of it. As soon as Abby had called him, he'd charged into Jason's practice—luckily it was an indoor workout day—and they'd headed for home. The details kept ringing through his brain like an echo.

Stroke at the wheel. Car into a tree. No cell service. Gretel to the rescue.

Where was Gretel? He located her in the play corner with the toddlers, sitting cross-legged while they all built a pyramid of blocks.

She glanced up and met his eyes—pure sympathy shining from those turquoise depths—and he felt a rush of gratitude.

She'd been there for Petey—for the second time—and he'd never forget that.

But there was a whole roomful of people and he couldn't properly express his feelings in that situation. So he just mouthed, "thank you," to her and put a hand over his heart.

The smile that lit her face was something to see—not just radiant, but filled with pride too, as if he'd offered her something priceless with his simple 'thank you.'

A chaos of conversation followed, with Petey determined to recount every single thing that had happened. And maybe a few things that hadn't happened.

"I'm pretty sure Eli and I heard a bear while Gretel was gone."

"That's very unlikely, kid. All the bears are hibernating right now. And they don't hibernate this close to people. You know that."

"Well, maybe we woke this one up when we crashed. It was such a loud sound, like *bam*."

Zander caught a flinch from Gretel. She probably didn't want to relive all this, even if Petey did, in excruciating detail.

"Come on, guys, let's get home and get some dinner."

"Can Gretel come? I want Gretel to come. She saved us!"

He focused on Gretel again, even though he hadn't actually fully looked away from her yet. "Sure. But it's up to Gretel. She might be too tired."

"Why don't you guys stay here?" Abby spoke up from the kitchen, where she was stirring some kind of delicious-smelling sauce. "There's plenty, despite Earl's immense and endless appetite. Moose-meat spaghetti sauce."

Petey made a face and angled a pleading glance at Zander. Lately he'd been refusing to eat meat, which made cooking a lot more complicated.

"We should probably get back. Jason has a lot of homework tonight."

Jason loitered by the door, the hood of his sweatshirt drawn up over his head. Until Zander had explained the situation, Jason had been furious about leaving practice early.

This ski obsession was getting out of control, in Zander's opinion.

He met Gretel's gaze again, and lifted his eyebrows in invitation. "I'll drive you there and back. No snowshoeing required."

"Please, Gretel," begged Petey. He hurtled across the room at Gretel and flung his arms around her. "It'll be so much fun. *Please.*"

Sometimes little brothers really came in handy. Who could resist that? Gretel rolled her eyes. "How about a little more drama, kid? Think you can manage it?"

"*Pleeeeeease!!!*"

Gretel climbed to her feet, which were encased in knee-high fleece slippers. With an impish smile, she crossed her arms over her chest. "Someone's going to have to carry me, though. My feet are too sore to put boots on."

"I will!" And Petey actually did. He wrapped his arms around her legs and lifted her off the ground. He made it a few steps until he staggered to a stop. "Zander! Help!"

Zander flexed his muscles, playing the strongman, and strode across the room. He plucked Gretel away from Petey and whisked her to the door, where she slid to the floor, laughing.

And he tried desperately to hide the effects of that brief contact.

MOST OF DINNER consisted of Petey recounting his adventure over and over. They got word, halfway through, that Jeff Durst was conscious and alert. He'd experienced some damage to his right side, but with therapy, it would be manageable.

The relief brought by that news put everyone in a happy mood.

It wasn't until after dinner—a Petey-friendly vegetable stir fry with a slab of venison for Jason— that disaster struck.

Zander asked, casually, who had picked Gretel up by the roadside. She slapped her hand against her forehead. "I can't believe I forgot to tell you! It was a friend of yours. Oh my God, I can't remember her name—" She snapped her fingers to summon the memory. "She told me, right at the end, but everything was so crazy at that point—Susan something?"

He frowned as he racked his brain for a Susan. "I don't have any friends named Susan."

"She said she would call you and arrange another time to visit."

Visit. That word rang a bell.

"What did she look like?"

"Native Alaskan, maybe around fifty. Dark hair with a little gray. She could easily get rid of it, I thought about offering as a thank you for—what's wrong?"

Oh shit. Dread settled into his gut, sinking through him like a deadweight. He leaned back in his chair and rubbed his forehead to chase away the sudden tension.

"What did you tell her?"

"Tell her? Nothing. I didn't mention her hair at all, I just thanked her for—"

"*About us?* What did you tell her *about us*? Our family?" His sudden intensity made her jump.

"I don't know. Nothing. I asked if she wanted to send you a message and she did, and I already gave it to you. She said she'd call you soon to come out and visit. Why?"

"Jeez, Z, what's wrong with you?" Jason frowned at him. Petey was staring at him as if he'd lost his mind. Maybe he had, a little.

But Gretel was a loose cannon. She loved to chat and get into long conversations with people. He needed to know exactly what she'd told Susan Baker.

"Gretel, can I speak to you in private?"

Her pretty eyes widened. "*Again?* Are you kidding?"

"No. Please."

She must have picked up on his worry because she snapped her mouth shut and followed him into his bedroom.

"I've missed this place," she joked as they stepped inside. "It's been too long." Then she turned serious as she faced him. "What's going on?"

"Can you tell me, word for word, everything you said and everything Susan Baker said?"

Gretel cocked her head, one of her earrings catching the light. She wore an unusually subdued bulky sweater in basic black. But nothing ever looked basic on Gretel. It clung to her body like fur on a kitten.

"Why?" she demanded.

"Because...it's important."

"Why is it important?"

"Why can't you just tell me? Trust me, it's important."

"*Trust* you? That's ironic, when you don't even trust me enough to explain why it's so important! Who is Susan Baker? Why are you so worried about her?"

He swung away from her, scrubbing a hand through his hair.

"God, Zander, don't you ever get tired of keeping everything to yourself?"

Yes, he did get tired of it. Sometimes it made him feel like the weight of the entire world was on his shoulders. *Just tell her, jackass.*

"Can you commit to not telling anyone else? Not the Noonans, not your sister, not the dude at the Wicked Brew, not fucking anyone."

She crossed her arms over her chest and he realized that he'd offended her. Too bad. He needed her to know how important this was.

"I've always been good at keeping secrets," she told him stiffly. "I never spill. There's a certain movie-star divorce that I knew about way before it happened. TMZ actually offered me a hundred thousand dollars to talk. If I didn't then, why would I now?"

He squinted at her, not sure if she was joking, and wondered how they'd gotten so far off the topic.

"Okay. I'm sorry. I know how much you like talking to people, that's all."

Her expression softened just a smidge. "Talking to people is different from spilling their secrets."

"Yeah." So maybe he'd underestimated her. Wouldn't be the first time.

"So now that you know I'm as good as a bank vault, tell me what's going on," she said. "Who is Susan Baker and why do you care what I told her?"

He drew in a deep breath. He still didn't know if he could fully trust her, but she'd just come through in a crisis—in a big way. Maybe he should give her the benefit of the goddamn doubt.

"Okay, I'm going to tell you, but you can't say anything to Jason or Petey. I haven't talked to them about it yet."

"I promise. I won't."

"She's a caseworker for the Alaska Child Services Department."

Gretel's fine eyebrows drew together in confusion. "Okay...so?"

"So I'm still kind of a probationary guardian of my brothers. My parents didn't leave a will. Caseworkers from the department check in now and then. I'm happy they do, because I know they're just looking out for the boys. I don't mind it. But Susan Baker is new. And I think she has something up her sleeve. I think someone wants to take Jason."

"*What?*" Her reaction was exactly what he would have hoped for—appalled and outraged. "Can they do that?"

"I don't know. Maybe. If the state determined that I'm not a fit guardian, she probably could. Or if she decided that Jason would be better off somewhere else." He swallowed back the lump in his throat that developed every time he thought about this.

It must have shown on his face, because she stepped toward him and wrapped her arms around his waist. It was a comfort hug, not a sensual one, but that didn't take away from how good it felt.

"So that's why you freaked out about Petey and the nail polish?"

"I don't care about the nail polish. I care about Petey breaking laws. If she thinks he's turning into a delinquent, forget about it."

"And dying his hair?"

"People have funny ideas about that kind of thing. She could read it as a rebellion. Decide he's unhappy and needs a more conventional family. A big brother only goes so far." His hand hovered over her back. He wanted to run his palm down her spine and watch her arch and purr.

She pulled away while he was still wrestling with that temptation. "So basically, that's why you're such a hardass all the time. Because you're worried about this caseworker."

"Not *all* the time," he corrected her. "Give me a break."

"Okay, not while sledding. Or while—kissing."

His cock twitched just from hearing the word. But he hadn't dragged her in here to flirt. This was a serious situation. He had to make her understand just how serious.

"After my parents died, before I got back, Children's Services was talking about separating the boys. They were both freaking out. I told them I'd never let that happen, that we were all going to stay together no matter what. I knew I had to prove to the state that I could do this. That I could provide a good environment for them." He snorted. "I even speak their language now."

Her sympathetic gaze drew him in, made him want to lose himself in her beauty. But he couldn't lose focus here.

"That's why I need to know what you told Susan Baker. Can you remember if you said anything that would make me look bad? Like I'm not a fit guardian, or that things aren't going well?"

She tilted her head to one side as she considered. "Okay, starting at the beginning."

Good, she was taking this seriously.

"I asked who she knew out this direction, and she said she was visiting you. So I assumed she knew you. I told her Petey was back with the car, and you were staying in—Oh!" Her hand flew to cover her mouth. "Shit. I think I said you were going to freak out when you heard about the accident, but that you couldn't be in two places at once. She said something about how you have to juggle a lot of responsibilities."

"And then what?" Zander braced himself for disaster.

"I said I had no idea how you manage everything." She winced and screwed up her face. "That sounds bad. But maybe it's good. It shows that I respect you and how hard you work and..." She trailed off, biting her bottom lip. "Did I mess things up? I'm so sorry if I did. I had no idea about any of this."

Zander turned away and interlaced his hands on top of his head. He knew in his gut that Susan Baker was looking for any excuse to push her agenda, whatever it was. She would pounce on this. The car crash, the fact that he'd been in town when it happened, Gretel's words.

It wasn't Gretel's fault, of course.

It was *his* fault.

"This isn't on you. How were you supposed to know, unless I told you?" he said in a grim voice. "I was afraid to tell anyone. Now she's going to jump all over this."

He felt her step closer to him, then a light touch skimmed his back. "You don't know that. Maybe it's not as bad as you're thinking," she said softly. "It's not like I told her how you run the house like a boot camp or anything."

He gave a hollow laugh. "That ought to be a compliment but it seems like you didn't mean it that way."

"Well, what do I know? I had zero consistency growing up. My father's on his fourth wife. My mother's had three divorces. I might have enjoyed a boot camp experience for a change. Maybe," she added quickly. "I have to admit it's hard to picture. I did have a supercute pink camouflage bomber jacket in middle school though."

He pictured her in a pink camo jacket, with maybe nothing much on underneath, and that image cheered him right up.

What the hell. The damage was done. The caseworker would do whatever she decided, but he wouldn't take it lying down. He'd fight back, like a good Marine should.

He turned and cupped his hands around Gretel's face. She looked so worried, not a trace of a smile on her beautiful lips.

"It'll be okay," he assured her. "Don't worry about it." He skimmed both of his thumbs across her cheekbones. Her eyes fluttered shut and he felt the brush of her eyelashes against his fingers.

Then her eyes opened and he fell head over heels into the dazzle of her eyes.

"There's more," she said. "I think she thought we were a thing."

"A thing?"

"I didn't tell her that," she said quickly. "But she said something like, 'I'm sure I'll see more of you,' and I didn't really answer. Is that a problem?"

He shrugged uneasily. "I don't know. I kind of implied that I had a serious girlfriend. She might think it's you."

She let out a brief peal of laughter, which he tried not to take personally. "Well, if it helps at all, I think she liked me. I can be very charming, you know."

"I've noticed."

That comment brought a slight flush to her cheeks. "I'll find an excuse to run into her again and I'll rant and rave about how wonderful you are."

He lifted one eyebrow sardonically. "Really, you'd lie for me?"

"It's not a lie." She curled one hand around his wrist. The lightness of her touch made his breath catch. "You're not as grumpy and annoying as I previously believed."

"Thanks." More wryness.

Her lashes fluttered again. "You're...not like anyone I've ever known, put it that way."

There was so much he didn't know about her life, but yeah—she probably hadn't run into very many ex-Marines raising their younger brothers. "I'm just an ordinary guy trying to keep things together."

"You are not ordinary, Zander Ross. Not one little bit. You have—" She twisted her face adorably. "What's the word?"

She seemed to be searching her memory, so he came up with a few options for her. "Good looks? Charm? A hot bod?"

"No. Character." Finally, her lips curved, and she swept a

sexy glance up and down his body. "Okay, now that you mention it, a hot bod too."

He crowded her backwards toward the raw pine boards of his bedroom wall. "Now that I mention it? All those boot camp workouts and you never even noticed?"

She giggled and held onto his forearms as her back touched the wall. "It's hard under all that winter gear, you know. If I'd met you on a beach, it'd be different."

"Oh yeah? What would you be wearing on this beach?"

She pursed her lips, sending a shock of heat to his groin. "Not much. Definitely lots of sunscreen. Maybe a tiny bit of bikini."

"How tiny?" His voice was nothing but a growl. Tension throbbed between them, hot and urgent. Damn, this attraction had been simmering for a while. Any second now it would boil over.

Her pupils widened until the turquoise nearly disappeared. Her lips parted and her tongue darted across her lower lip. "Sorry, what was the question?" she asked.

The fuck if he knew. He couldn't even remember what they'd been talking about. All he knew was that she was a magnet and he was a helpless hunk of metal being drawn in, closer and closer, until her light fragrance surrounded him—blossoms caught in a summer breeze.

"I have no idea," he admitted. His head lowered to hers and their lips joined as if they were puzzle pieces locking together. She arched her body against his, her breath coming fast. Even though there was a pretty big size discrepancy between them, the crucial pieces fit—he felt her nipples like diamonds against his chest, the mound between her legs pushing against his upper thigh.

She tilted her hips, going for another angle, and he helped by sliding his hands under her ass. God, she was so delicate and fine-boned—except she wasn't, not really, because she ground against his thigh with a fierceness that told him she was a woman who owned her desires—without apology.

Now *that* was a turn-on.

Just ask his cock, which had swelled into a raging beast trapped behind his fleece sweats.

She noticed—God, how could she not? Her hand loosened from his forearm and slid down to his groin. When she touched his erection through the fleece, he gave a choked groan. *Keep your cool.*

Their lips still clung together, as if neither of them wanted to lose the connection. Lust and need roared in his blood, and he could taste the same on her lips. He closed a hand around one of her breasts—so perfectly formed, with a tender peak of flesh.

He would sacrifice a kidney to see her naked right now.

His bed was right over there, just feet away. He could snatch her up and toss her onto it. Strip off her cozy black sweater and her peacock-feather-patterned leggings and expose the sweet skin just waiting for his tongue. He could spread her open and lick his way down her stomach, from nipples to clit—

Someone pounded on the door.

"Zander! Someone's on the phone for you!" It was Jason, his just-hit-puberty voice veering between deep and boyish. "What's taking you so long?"

He wrenched himself away from Gretel.

Looking dazed, she blinked at him while her hands flew this way and that, touching her hair, her neckline, her mouth, as if checking to make sure everything was still attached to her.

"Gotta go," he croaked. "Sorry."

She nodded, and he stepped back. He had to call on all of his self-discipline to do it. It was so hard to separate from her.

"Coming!" he called to Jason. He shot Gretel one more look, pouring every ounce of his blazing desire into it, then charged out the door, nearly knocking Jason over in the process.

Jason tried to peer past him, but Zander blocked his line of sight. "Gretel's coming. She...uh...had a thing."

Apparently his brain had been fried by that kiss, because he couldn't think of a single actual explanation to give his brother.

Then again, from the look on Jason's face, he didn't need to explain. The kid got it.

CHAPTER THIRTEEN

Even though Zander didn't blame her for anything involving Susan Baker, Gretel still felt terrible about it. If she was the cause of the Ross family breaking apart, she'd never forgive herself.

So what if Zander kissed her as if she were the pot of gold at the end of a rainbow. No matter how much he wanted her—how much they wanted each other!—his responsibilities to his family came first.

That was just the way he was, and to be honest, that was one of the things she liked best about him.

The way he kissed wasn't too shabby either. Or the way he touched her body and ground his thigh between her legs and generally drove her into a state of rip-her-own-clothes-off madness.

Over the next few days, she did her best to keep some distance between her and the incredibly tempting man next door. She'd already screwed things up for him with Susan Baker; she didn't want to make things worse somehow.

She worked extra shifts at the Wicked Brew, and attended her first stitch-and-bitch gathering at Nicola Bellini's house.

Mrs. Bellini had recently suffered a stroke, so she herself wasn't yet able to knit or crochet. But the group had decided to meet at her house anyway in order to offer her some companionship.

To Gretel's surprise, not all the stitch-and-bitchers were women. Two men were also part of the group, both of them with the weathered look of fishermen or other outdoor laborers.

Zoe Bellini, Nicola's daughter, caught her look of surprise.

"We get a few men in the winter. Those guys will be busy fishing in the summer, but they like to catch up on their knitting in the winter." Her wild dark curly hair was held back by a bandanna printed with sunflowers and her smile lit up the living room.

Zoe, along with the rest of the Bellini family, ran the Last Chance Pizza shop. She'd recently gotten together with the world-famous singer Padric Jeffers—or rather, gotten back together with him, since they'd grown up together in Lost Harbor. Gretel wondered if she'd get to meet the superstar, who was overseeing the construction of a new recording studio in Lost Harbor. If there was an opportunity to invite him to perform at the Wicked Brew, she was going to jump on it.

"I hope I'm not a total embarrassment," Gretel told the group cheerfully. "I've never knit a stitch in my life." She held up the bag of supplies she'd purchased at Eller's. "I got a little bit of everything, just in case. Where should I start?"

As Zoe Bellini set out plates of jam cookies and a pot of tea, several kindly crafters offered Gretel their assistance. The one who ended up next to her was a grizzled black man who introduced himself as Harris Badger.

"Oh, are you related to Maya Badger, the police chief?"

"My daughter. She's my claim to fame now." He smiled cheerfully. "I used to stand on my own laurels. Now she's outshone me and I don't mind a bit."

"Harris used to run the Coast Guard station in Far Point," Zoe explained. "We liked him so much we refused to let him leave even after he retired."

Harris chuckled as he showed Gretel how to hold the knitting needles. "That's how I took up knitting. It was lonely out there in the winter. So first thing you do, is you gotta cast on."

Gretel focused on Harris' instructions while the conversation flowed around them. At first it was hard to remember which piece of yarn was supposed to go where, and how to keep the needles from simply slipping out of their loops. But Harris was a patient teacher, as if he had all the time in the world to spare from his own project.

"What are you making?" she asked him, after she'd painstakingly completed one entire row of her practice square.

"Sweater for Maya. We got a competition going. She made me the most beautiful blanket you ever saw for Christmas. I'll need something extra special to top that."

"Maya knits?" This day was full of surprises.

"Not on the job. She's very picky about workplace rules. She doesn't relax until she's off the clock. But yeah, she knits. She does a lot of things that aren't police-type stuff. Oops, you dropped a stitch. See that hole there, looks like it's unravelling? You can't let that little bugger get away. Let me show you how to fix it."

He helped her retrieve the runaway stitch while she tried to keep track of every movement of his gnarled hands. She wondered if knitting kept them nimble.

"Whew." She let out a breath of relief when he returned the needles to her. "That was stressful."

"Ain't nothing in knitting that can't be fixed," said an older woman with a long gray braid draped over her shoulder. She'd been introduced as Mrs. Holt. Lucas Holt's mother, Gretel figured. "That's the beauty of it. Say, you're the girl living with the Noonans, is that right?"

"Yes, that's me!" Gretel turned her needles this way and that, trying to remember how they were supposed to fit into her hand. Deftly, Harris got them reoriented for her. She gave him a grateful smile.

"How're those Ross kids doing?"

Since she seemed genuinely concerned, instead of looking for gossip, Gretel answered, "Quite well."

"You see a lot of them, being neighbors?"

"I do." Remembering Zander's paranoia about Susan Baker, she didn't want to say too much, so she turned the question around on Mrs. Holt. "Do you know them well?"

"I knew their parents very well. Brenda Ross was quite a craftswoman. She made an iron gate for my cow pasture. Just beautiful. My yak loves it."

"Did you say *yak*?"

"I have a yak, yes. Tibetan yak, ornery fella. I light a candle for Brenda every month. I know she'd be proud of Zander. After the accident, it was touch and go what would happen to the kids. All their family was in the Lower Forty-eight, and no one was jumping up and down to have them. It would have broken Brenda's heart to send them away from here. She wanted to raise her boys here on the edge of the wilderness. She was quite the woman."

The rest of the group murmured their agreement.

"Todd Ross w-worshipped her," added Nicola Bellini. "Living here was her idea. Left his Delta Airlines career behind and never l-looked back."

"They were good people," Mrs. Holt said somberly. "When Zander decided to step up and come home, I bet Brenda breathed a big sigh of relief."

Harris chuckled. "If anyone heard it, that would be you. She thinks her husband came back as a yak," he explained to Gretel.

Mrs. Holt shrugged off that comment. "I told Zander the next time I saw him, I said, 'your mother would be crying tears of joy knowing that her little ones are taken care of.' I said, 'you keep those boys together, come what may. They're going to need you more than you can even imagine.' He listened, too, which is a lot more than my own kids do."

A murmur of laughter rippled through the group.

"You know Lucas always went his own way. Brenda and I used to complain about how our sons just up and left soon as they got old enough. Now they're both back, Lucas and Zander, and I just wish Brenda was still here to see it."

The needles slipped in Gretel's hands and one of them stabbed her in the wrist. "Ow," she said loudly.

Harris peered at her hands and whistled. "Looks like we have our first knitting injury. Is that blood?"

Several of the ladies jumped to their feet, but Gretel waved her arm in the air. "No no, it's a bit of jelly from those amazing jam cookies. I'm okay. No blood has been shed in the making of this row of misshapen stitches. Although considering my track record when it comes to sports, I wouldn't be at all surprised to be Lost Harbor's first knitting victim."

Pretty soon she had them all laughing, and by the time conversation resumed, the topic had changed to the mystery of S.G.—the runaway girl who had hidden out in the firehouse.

The stitch-and-bitchers threw out all kinds of theories. Was she the lone survivor of a twin-engine plane crash in Lost Souls Wilderness? Had she been kidnapped from an off-the-grid homesteading family? Smuggling came up, as did the Russian border, which was hundreds of miles away, but then again, S.G. did look Russian.

Gretel didn't contribute to the discussion, even though she

knew more about S.G. than most, since Nate had first discovered her in the firehouse and Bethany had treated her sprained ankle.

No, her thoughts were entirely focused on what Mrs. Holt had said about Brenda Ross. That she'd be crushed if her family was broken apart. That Zander was fulfilling his mother's wishes by raising the boys here in Lost Harbor, on the family homestead.

Some stranger shouldn't interfere with that dream. And Gretel couldn't allow her own careless words to wreck it either. Surely there had to be something she could do to help. She just had to get creative.

CHAPTER FOURTEEN

Susan Baker called Zander a few days after the car-pool accident.

"How is everyone? Any injuries?"

"Just the one—the driver's stroke. My brothers are both fine."

"Jason wasn't even there," she pointed out.

"Right. He was in town with me. I brought him home. But he's fine too. We're all fine." Hm, awkward babble. Great. Always impressive to a caseworker.

"Very fortunate. Not so fortunate is the fact that I had to leave Lost Harbor before I got a chance to visit. I'm in Kodiak now. I will have to reschedule."

"Great." What a relief that she wasn't right outside his door with an order to remove Jason. "Whenever you're available, we'll be here. If you give me a heads-up—"

"What would be the point of that? No one gets a heads-up. That's not how it works. But I will tell you that it probably won't be for at least a week."

"Great," he said again, then corrected himself quickly, "I mean, whenever. We will welcome you with—"

"Rotten tomatoes," she said dryly.

Wow, a sense of humor. Very well-hidden up until now.

Should he take advantage of her slightly more friendly tone? "I have a guess about what this other living situation is that you mentioned. Would you be able to confirm or deny?"

"Nope. No point in speculating until it's a real offer."

"An *offer*?"

But she'd already hung up the phone. Susan Baker definitely had her own way of going about things. He heaved out a long breath and went to the big chore board. In the special notes area, he scrawled "Family Meeting tonight."

Then he went out to his workshop and vented his frustrations with a belt sander on a table that needed to be stripped of several decades worth of varnish.

Between the custody question and his combustible attraction to Gretel, there was plenty of frustration to be vented.

The family meeting got him nowhere. He told his brothers that there was a new caseworker on the scene, and that she was keeping a close eye on them. Petey promised to be on his best behavior. Jason didn't say much, but then again, he was busy wolfing down practically an entire salmon.

After dinner, Zander asked Jason to help him in the work-shop for a minute. When Susan Baker came, she'd want to talk to the boys individually. If anything was on Jason's mind, he wanted to know now so it didn't bite him in the ass later.

"How's school going, Jason?" he asked as the two of them unpacked a case of polyurethane.

"Good."

"Skiing?"

"Good."

So far, so monosyllabic.

"You excited about the high school team?"

Jason shot him a scornful "dumb question" look, as if that one didn't even deserve a monosyllable.

"How about home? Anything you want to complain about?"

"What do you mean?"

"I know I can be strict, but I'm just trying to keep things on track. Do you think I need to lighten up?"

Jason brushed aside a shank of hair that kept falling in his face. "I don't know."

Not much of an answer. Jason didn't like to talk, not the way Petey did. Not that Zander was much better.

"So you're happy? Everything's good?"

"I miss Mom," Jason said abruptly. "And Dad. I wish they knew I made the ski team."

"Mom probably would have welded you a trophy by now. Or a ski rack."

A smile split Jason's face. Zander noticed pimples on his chin. Poor kid.

"Yeah, probably." Jason pulled his ski hat out of his pocket and put it on. "Are we good? I want to do a quick run through the woods before bed."

"Homework done?"

"Yeah." Jason aimed his long body toward the door of the workshop. The kid was almost as tall as Zander, though still not as muscular. Give him time.

"If something's bothering you, will you tell me?" Zander called after him.

"Yeah, Z. Something's bothering me. Begins with the letter Z."

"Oh, real funny. Nice one."

With a smirk, Jason vanished out the door. Zander quickly put away the remaining cans of poly.

He still got the feeling that Jason wasn't telling him everything. But he was thirteen, after all. What thirteen-year-old boy wanted to talk about his problems? Look how long it had taken

Zander to tell Gretel about this situation—and he was twenty-seven.

All he could hope was that Jason knew he could talk to him if something really bad came up.

In the meantime, he needed to know if his wild theory about Stern and Sterner was correct.

The next day after school, while Jason was stretching out with the others on the snowy field behind the high school, Zander approached Doug Stern. He was in his forties, extremely fit, with a clean-shaven face and the look of a Viking invader.

Or maybe that was just Zander's paranoia talking. He was perfectly courteous as he greeted Zander.

"So, uh..." Now that he had the man's attention, he wasn't exactly sure how to put this. *Are you planning to steal my brother?* "How's Jason doing with the practice sessions?"

"Good, good. I knew he would. He's a real talent. Eager to learn, too."

Really? Zander almost said. Stubborn, know-it-all Jason? Eager to learn? Maybe from his ski coaches, but not from his big brother.

He kept all that to himself. "Good to hear."

"I have high hopes for him next year. This team could really dominate. I wish we had him this year, but—" The coach shrugged. "Rules and regs."

"Right. So when you say that you wish you had him..."

"Nothing against the current crew, but there's no one else with Jason's potential. An athlete like him can be a kind of tent-pole. Everyone else tries to keep up and so they level up their own game. It's a coach's dream."

"He's that good, huh?"

"He is."

So far, Zander wasn't hearing anything about Jason going to live with the coach. He drew in a breath for courage.

"I've heard that you foster students sometimes."

He was quite proud of that one. Direct and yet indirect.

The coach gave him a cryptic look, then turned to answer a shouted question from one of the students. "Sometimes," he told Zander when he was done. "We have a lot to offer, my wife and I. A stable family environment, extra training if the student wants it. It's worked out well for us in the past. We may well do it again. Why, do you have someone to suggest?"

Was Stern angling for information now? "Not really. Seems like it would be a tough thing for a kid to leave home. I know it happens, but there's got to be a really good reason."

"Oh sure. A student has to be very serious about skiing for us to take him or her on. We're very choosy. But if someone has real talent and we think we can help, we consider it."

Zander studied the coach's expression, trying to read between the lines. Was he saying that he wanted to foster Jason or didn't want to? If they wanted to, why didn't they come out and say so directly, to Zander?

Maybe his theory was completely off-base. He didn't know what to think anymore.

Coach Sandy Stern blew the whistle and the students jogged across the snow to huddle together.

"Gotta get to it," said the coach. "Good to talk to you, Zander. Keep up the good work with Jason."

"Thanks," Zander said to his back, as he hurried toward the group. The coach skied over to his wife, who smiled at him without interrupting the flow of her instructions to the kids. The two coaches looked so comfortable together, so *solid*, so respectable and trustworthy in their high-performance ski jackets and ultra-pricey skis. The perfect couple. The perfect ski coaches. The perfect parents. The perfect family.

CHAPTER FIFTEEN

The next time Aimee called, Gretel was somewhere she'd never imagined she'd be. An outhouse.

"Hello, darling, how does a cabana on the beach at Baja sound?"

Pretty fricking great, she had to admit. But not out loud. "Been there, got the sand rash."

"Oh come on, sweetie. How cold is it there?"

"The thermometer outside the outhouse says five-point-two degrees."

"In Baja it's seventy, so—wait, what did you say?"

Gretel laughed quietly to herself. "Outhouse. It's like an outdoor shed plopped over a hole in the ground. But don't worry, there's a kind of toilet you can sit on and plenty of toilet paper."

Nothing but shocked silence on the other end of the phone.

"Mom?"

"Are you *in* one right now?"

"Yes! Ironically, it's one of the few places with decent cell service. Wanna FaceTime?"

"No!" Aimee shrieked. "I will not FaceTime with an outhouse. Is there 911 there? Should I call for help?"

"Mom, calm down." Oddly enough, her mother's over-the-top reaction made Gretel decide she didn't mind the outhouse. "We had a plumbing issue in the bathroom, so we have to use the outhouse until Earl fixes it. It won't be long."

"Honey, every word you utter is like a stake through my heart. You're supposed to be an ornament to society, not some kind of pioneer mother's helper. All you have to do is find the right man with the right bank account."

Gretel put down the phone and let her mother vent while she finished her business.

When she picked the phone up again, her mother was saying, "This Alaska whim isn't funny anymore. Have I taught you nothing?"

Gretel squirted hand sanitizer on her hands. "The bit about always carrying sanitizer has come in handy. The part about men, I'm trying to block out."

"Gretel, darling, I'm begging you. Just come with me to Baja for one week. There's a lovely man I want you meet. He's a little less wealthy but also a little younger and you could always use your honeymoon fund to make up the difference."

"How much is in that fund by now, anyway?" Her mother had started it years ago as a kind of incentive for Gretel to get married. She'd forgotten about it until now.

"Oh lord, I don't know. It must be almost a hundred. If I check, will you come? A little sunshine will open your eyes. You're on some strange trip right now...oh! Is that it? Have you been drinking?"

"Well, they say strange things happen around Lost Souls Wilderness. But as a matter of fact, I haven't had a drink for weeks now."

"Weed? Molly? Ecstasy?"

"Oh my God, Mom. I'm not doing drugs. I'm doing my job. And it feels good."

Sure, using an outhouse at five-point-three degrees didn't necessarily feel *good*. Or maybe it did, in a "I survived so I must be a capable human being" kind of way.

"Job." Her mother said the words with disgust. "Jobs are for people who don't have your advantages. Why did I work so hard to make sure you had everything for you to just throw it away?"

"By 'work so hard,' do you mean marry rich and get good prenups?"

"Yes," Aimee said simply.

"Kinda sounds like getting married was your job, if it was so much work."

"But that's my whole point, it's *better* than a job."

Gretel tugged on her gloves and pushed open the door of the outhouse. It had an open window shaped like a crescent moon, meant for venting. Apparently it was a common design for Alaska. But it meant that inside the outhouse was only a few degrees warmer than outside the outhouse.

"Did you know there's such a thing as outhouse races? You put the outhouse on wheels and race while you're—"

"Goodbye, cruel child. Call me when you've come to your senses."

"Love you, Mom. Oh, quick point of clarification. Does 'come to your senses' mean 'get married' in Aimee Morrison Brandt Tartikoff language?"

Her mother clicked off the call.

Just in time, because Gretel was chilling down and needed to get back inside the toasty-warm house. She snapped a photo of the outhouse with its cute little window and sent it to her mother, then tucked her phone in her pocket.

Not that she didn't love her mother—she did. But Aimee had always seen Gretel as a miniature version of herself. When

Gretel was little, Aimee would dress her in matching mother-daughter outfits. The two of them had competed in mother-daughter beauty pageants until Gretel had rebelled. It had taken literal years for Gretel to realize that she wasn't a carbon copy of her jet-setting, glamorous, light-as-air mother.

Sometimes she still wasn't sure about that either. She loved to travel, after all. She and her mother had that in common. Gretel loved seeing new places and meeting the people who lived there. She loved chatting and making new friends.

The difference was that Aimee's idea of traveling was finding the best restaurant in each new city and ordering the most expensive bottle of champagne. Also, she was hyperaware of everyone's social status, and factored it into every relationship.

Gretel puffed out a breath, creating a cloud in the cold air. She'd been working on making a ring, like a smoke ring. As soon as she mastered it, she'd show it off to the kids. Her father, who loved his cigars, had taught her how to make smoke rings.

Weird thing to teach a kid.

Here, children learned more basic survival skills—how to chop wood, how to start a fire, how to keep a fire going, how to change tires, how to fish, how to do basic carpentry, how to drive on icy roads.

She'd learned her own survival skills—how to shift between two completely different households, how to be adorable and make people smile, how to flirt, how to tell if someone had money, how to dress to showcase her looks, how to be the life of the party, how to get invited to the right parties.

What wasn't on that list: how to rely on herself, how to manage her money, how to *earn* money that wasn't given to her by her father, how to pay her debts, how to feel confident in her own abilities, her own self.

That part was a work in progress.

Aimee's words came back to her. *It must be almost a hundred.*

It wouldn't be much of a honeymoon if it was a hundred dollars. Did that mean that it was more like a hundred thousand? That seemed like an outrageously expensive honeymoon, but probably not to her mother.

She shoved open the door to the arctic entry and Groovy came tumbling out, as if she'd been penned up just inside. She leaped out the door and darted straight for the nearest tree, sniffing wildly.

"I guess we all have our survival strategies," she told Groovy. "Marriage or sniffing trees, whatever works, am I right?"

And just like that, the idea came to her. A survival strategy that might work for everyone.

CHAPTER SIXTEEN

As car-pool driver of the day, Zander's purpose for stopping at the Noonans' was only to drop off Eli. He wasn't supposed to be scanning every inch of the property looking for Gretel. But he couldn't quite stop himself.

Eli dashed inside, his backpack bumping up and down, and a second later, Gretel emerged. Instead of actually putting on a coat, she'd wrapped her blue fake fur around her shoulders. She must be in a hurry, because she hadn't bothered to fasten her snow boots either.

She hopped across the yard toward his Suburban, so adorable it set his teeth on edge.

"Hi Zander, hi Petey. Zander, can I speak to you in private? Do you have a few minutes? Actually, it might take more than a few minutes."

His eyebrows climbed. Was this some sort of come-on? "Um...now?"

"Doesn't have to be in a bedroom," she said quickly. "It doesn't even have to be today. I'm working at the Wicked Brew tomorrow, maybe you could swing by."

"Okay, that should work. I need to get Petey home, he's got a science project."

"And it *sucks!*" called Petey from the backseat.

"Also, we have to discuss his vocabulary," Zander said dryly. "I'll see you tomorrow."

She nodded and waved them off, smiling as he performed a turnaround.

Wild with curiosity, he swung through the usual evening routine of dinner and homework and chores. Jason got dropped off late by a friend from the ski team and dove right into his homework, with barely a grunt of greeting.

What would it take to get Jason to actually communicate?

Then again, who was he to complain? It had taken him so long to tell someone about the new caseworker.

Don't be like me, kid, he wanted to tell Jason. *You might miss your shot.*

The next day, he volunteered for car-pool duty. Gretel's Nissan truck was already gone when he stopped at the Noonans. Great, they could have that private conversation as soon as he dropped everyone off at their respective schools. Never had he been so efficient with the drop-offs. He was dying to know what Gretel wanted to talk to him about.

The Wicked Brew Coffee Shop sat smack in the middle of town. Its sign featured a black cauldron, with coffee steam rising from it. The steam formed shapes—a raven, a bear, a wolf, a whale. Danny D had put up the sign when he bought the place and changed its name, and it screamed rush job. It actually drove Zander nuts that it was so badly carved.

The Wicked Brew was an especially popular hangout for teenagers, who appreciated the free Wi-Fi. Even in the summer, the clientele was mostly locals instead of tourists. It was...funky. That was the best word for the place.

He spotted Gretel right away, as soon as he stepped through

the door, which was painted a deep royal purple. She was chatting to Danny D behind the counter. Her hair was drawn to the top of her head like a pile of fireweed fluff, with two chopsticks holding it in place. She wore a tight black top that exposed her collarbones and the tops of her shoulders. A locket dangling from a choker nestled into the divot at the base of her throat.

All these details registered before she even looked his way.

When their gazes locked, she gave him a little wave, then said something to Danny. He nodded and assumed her position behind the espresso machine. She came around the counter and headed his way. He noticed that she seemed...uncomfortable. Awkward, even. That was unusual for her.

"Hi Zander. Come on back. Danny said I could have the supply room for the next half an hour."

"Supply room," he murmured. "That's a change from my bedroom."

"Right, and here's another change. I'm not going to yell at you. I want to help you." She spoke over her shoulder as she led the way down a short, very dark and cramped hallway to a storeroom at the end. The aroma of roasted coffee beans filled his nostrils as they stepped inside.

He inhaled long and deep. He'd only had one cup so far this morning, and he usually drank at least three.

"Oops, I forgot to ask if you want some coffee. I'll be right back."

She darted out the door, while he shoved his hands in his pockets and tried to shut out the memory of her ass in those crimson velvet leggings.

Something about her always managed to push that lust button.

In a minute, she was back with a large mug of steaming black coffee. "Costa Rican Dark Roast, direct from the cloud forests," she said nervously. "You know what would be fun to do? Go on a world coffee tour. Coffee beans are grown in some of the most beautiful places in the—"

"Gretel." He put a hand on her shoulder, trying to ground her. "What's this all about? I know you didn't invite me here to talk about coffee. I love it too, but we don't have to have that convo in a supply room."

"Right. Right. So here's the thing. I've been thinking about your situation with Susan Baker, and I want to help. I don't want to see the Ross brothers get split apart. I know how that feels and it sucks. I grew up between two homes, or really more like multiple homes because my mother kept remarrying, and my father kept buying more houses. I would hate for the boys to have that kind of stress if there's no need for it."

"Gretel."

She paused in her headlong rush of words. "Yes?"

"What's your idea? I'm open to anything. You don't have to be nervous."

A nervous laugh was her response to that. When she rubbed her palms on her leggings, he tugged one of her hands free and turned it over. "You're sweating?"

"Happens when I get nervous. You should have seen me when I jumped off a waterfall in Hawaii. I was sweating so much—"

"Gretel."

"*What?*"

"Just spit it out. Imagine you're jumping off a cliff. Just make up your mind and—"

"Let's get married," she blurted out.

"*What?*" He must have roared the word, because she took a quick step backwards, as if the force of his voice was a fire hose. "Sorry." He tried again. "*What?*"

Okay, that one was at least a few decibels lower.

"What are you talking about?"

She lifted her chin and he realized that she might be wounded by his spontaneously stunned reaction.

"Little confused here, that's all."

"Right. I should have led up to it more, but I got nervous and —" She tugged her hand away. He'd forgotten he was holding it. "I went into some online forums and learned a few things about what child services departments pay attention to. Basically they look for red flags, right? Falling grades, acting out, signs of abuse, that sort of thing. But there's also a preference for two-parent households. It makes sense because raising kids is hard. Two people have more to offer than one. So a one-parent household, like you, is going to be under more scrutiny. Following me so far?"

"Yes, but—"

She held up a hand. "Let me finish, or you're going to make me too nervous. If you're married, that's one less thing they can use against you, in case they're looking for things to use against you."

"But who's going to believe that I suddenly got married?"

"Susan Baker already thinks we're in a serious relationship. It's the logical next step."

Logical? None of this was logical. The whole concept was ridiculous. And yet, the idea of informing Susan Baker that he wasn't just a single dude raising his brothers on his own...was kind of tempting.

Slowly, almost to himself instead of to her, he said, "I could always tell her that we were already engaged when she stopped by, but we were keeping it secret until we told the boys."

Gretel clapped her hands as her face lit up. "That's brilliant! A secret engagement! How romantic."

"No no no, that just slipped out, I'm not onboard with this yet." Was he actually considering this? It was such a bad idea. Or was it? God, he didn't know.

This time, Gretel didn't look offended by his resistance. "I know, it's unfair because I've been thinking about it for a few days now, so I have a head start. Here's the thing. I know that Susan Baker liked me. That's understandable, because I'm such a delight and all-around charmer."

When he didn't laugh, she got serious again.

"But I never told her specifically what our relationship is. Neither of us did. So we can say that it's anything we want. Why couldn't we have been secretly engaged? It would explain why I knew where you were the day of the car-pool crash. It would explain why I was so upset."

He rubbed at his temples, where a persistent hammer-tacker throb had set in. "But...marriage...or a fake marriage...I don't know..."

"No. It couldn't be fake. It has to be real. Like, registered with the State of Alaska real. You know she'd check. I only met her briefly and I know she'd check."

"Oh, she'd definitely check." He picked up the mug of coffee from the shelf where Gretel had set it down. But he was afraid to take a sip in case she said something else outrageous and he spewed it everywhere. "So it would be in name only. Just a formality."

She twisted her face to the side. "I don't think that would work either. Everyone has to believe we're really married. The Noonans, your brothers, Bethany, my family. Everyone in Lost Harbor. Otherwise, she'll know. And that would be worse than not doing it at all. We can't look like cheats."

His head was literally spinning. Or maybe the room was doing the spinning. Or maybe the entire world.

"You want to marry me?" he asked flatly. "Why? None of this is your problem."

"Well, guess what? It's not just for you. I have my own reasons."

"Then I need to know those reasons, like now. We need

complete and total honesty here. This is my brothers we're talking about. My family." He drilled her with a stare borrowed directly from his unit commander. No one could withstand that.

"Fine. I have a couple reasons. One, to get my parents off my back and show them I'm serious about that. Two—okay, this is the main one. Once I get married, I'll have instant access to a fund my mom set up for my honeymoon. She says it has almost a hundred thousand dollars in it. I would offer to split it with you but I need it to pay a debt."

"What sort of debt? This sounds sketchy. If there's anything sketchy, I don't want to be involved because of my brothers."

"Are butterflies sketchy?"

"What?" Why did every word out of her mouth confuse him even more?

"Back when I had bank accounts and credit cards from my father, I pledged a pretty substantial donation to a butterfly sanctuary. I wanted them to be able to stand up to my father's company."

He blinked at her. This was definitely a side of Gretel he hadn't known about.

"Instead I got cut off and I couldn't give them anything. Last I heard, they were considering taking the purchase offer but I think there might still be time. It's funny because I hadn't even thought about that fund because I had no intention of getting married, but now..." She shrugged. "There's an actual reason to."

"Kind of a weird reason. Two weird reasons, if you count Susan Baker."

Gretel rolled her pretty eyes. "My mother's been married three times. My father is on his fourth wife. I haven't exactly had good role models when it comes to marriage. I'm not even sure I believe in it. But if I can help someone by getting married, then maybe it does have a purpose."

"You don't believe in marriage?" He had to ask. If they were going to do this, he needed to know what it meant to her. He hadn't given a ton of thought to marriage himself—too busy, really. But he'd always assumed that someday he'd fall in love the way his parents had, and then he'd get married.

"I said I'm not sure. I didn't, before. I was pretty cynical about it because I witnessed so many marriages firsthand that were basically business arrangements. I mean, I've personally seen four prenups with my own eyes. How many unmarried twenty-five-year-olds who aren't lawyers can say that?"

He wasn't sure what to say to that. He'd never seen a prenup except on TV. "My parents were married for thirty-five years, never had a prenup, died still happy with each other, far as I know. They had their rough times, but they liked being married."

"Well, in my experience, that doesn't happen very often. The point is, marriage is kind of a...partnership. Both people have a goal, and the other person helps them reach the goal."

"That's beautiful," he said dryly.

"That's practical."

He snorted. "You don't have a practical bone in your body."

She planted her hands on her hips. "You don't know everything about my bones."

He couldn't stop his gaze from dropping down her body, doing a complete sweep of her petite build and delicate curves. True, he didn't. But he wanted to.

And how would this "marriage" fit in with that?

Complete honesty, he reminded himself. "What about sex?"

"What do you mean?"

She hadn't even *thought* about that part of it? "Would this be the kind of marriage where you have sex, or the kind that's just on paper?"

"I already said it can't be just on paper."

His eyebrows climbed up his forehead. If he was understanding this right, they might be headed for the bedroom. And to

the actual bed, for once. This just got more and more surreal—
and also more appealing.

"I mean, I'm pretty sure we'd both enjoy that part," Gretel
said, sounding totally reasonable. "Just based on, you know, all
the kissing."

"All the kissing," he repeated. His cock twitched. He'd been
hoping "all the kissing" would lead to something more, but he
hadn't imagined it happening this way. "What if we don't?"
When she looked confused, he added, "Enjoy it?"

"Oh. I hadn't thought about that," she confessed.

"If we don't enjoy it, and we're married and stuck with each
other, what then?"

"Look, one thing I learned from my father, and it's not necessarily a good thing, but it comes in handy sometimes. Everything
is negotiable. All we have to do is put it all out there on the table
and hammer out an agreement. Off the top of my head, if we get
married and then discover that we can't stand each other and
don't want to have sex—then we don't. I'll stay for enough time to
make it look legit, then I'll leave town. No one would be the least
bit surprised. It's kind of what I do."

He was already shaking his head. "No, that would make it
look like I was being too reckless with my brothers' well-being."

"We'll make sure it doesn't look like that. If anything, we can
make it look like you're protecting your brothers by dumping
me."

He squinted at her, trying on for size the idea of dumping
her. It didn't really compute. "Did this whole idea come from
Bethany? Didn't she and Nate pretend to be together before they
actually got together?"

"Wow, you heard about that?"

"Abby told me."

She shrugged. "That was totally different. It was fake. This
won't be fake. If you want, we can put our own private asterisk

next to it. Marriage with an asterisk. Or 'marriage' in quotes." She demonstrated the quote marks with her fingers. "We'll be committed to each other, for better or worse, but we can say it's for a limited amount of time. I was thinking three years because Jason will be sixteen by then."

Oh my God. She'd lost her damn mind. "An expiration date. Good to know."

"It's negotiable."

He let out a long laugh. "Negotiable" and "marriage" were two concepts he'd never put together like this before.

An impatient frown creased her forehead and she bit her lower lip. "Look, it's just a thought. You can say no right now. I won't be offended. I was thinking that it's a way we can both get something we want. That's all. But if the idea is really that repulsive to you—"

"Repulsive?" He came toward her and caught her hands in his. "It's not repulsive, for fuck's sake. Nothing about you is repulsive, not even close. I'm honestly...touched that you thought of this. I'm honored. So don't go getting it all twisted, okay?"

She gave a little sniff and a nod. Had he really hurt her feelings with his wary reaction? He cupped her chin in his hand and lifted it so their eyes met. "Do you believe me?"

Her lips quirked—or one corner, anyway. "I'm trying to decide."

"It's just...I'm trying to think about this rationally. Pros and cons. Logistics. Details. But it's kind of hard when you're two inches away from me and looking so fine and smelling so sweet."

Now the other corner lifted as well. There was that dazzling Gretel smile.

"So here's what I'm thinking." His voice dropped to a growl because she just turned him on, every bit of her. "We have a little time before Susan Baker gets back from Kodiak. Let's make the most of it."

"How?" Her turquoise eyes skimmed back and forth, scanning his face.

"Let's do some speed dating. Like a courtship on speed. We'll get to know each other—a lot better than we already do. We'll kiss. If that goes well, we'll make out. If that goes well, we'll have sex. If that goes well, then—and only then—will we talk about this again."

Her tongue did that thing where it ran between the seam of her lips and drove him crazy.

"And then?" she croaked.

"Then we'll decide."

"What if we run out of time? What if she comes back?"

"If she does, we'll wing it. But I'm not worried. It's winter, and the flights to Kodiak get canceled all the time. With the forecast over the next couple weeks, she's probably stuck there for a while."

Her skin was so soft against his hand, and he could feel the rapid beating of her pulse under his fingers. Was she scared? Nervous again? Happy?

"I'm not used to thinking about marriage as a business deal," he said softly. "I don't think it will be, for me. It has to be...something. Do you understand?"

Slowly, she nodded. "You want to see if we would actually get along together."

"Yes. It's for your sake, too. I don't want you to get stuck in a situation that isn't good for you. I'm not always the easiest guy to live with. Just ask my little brothers."

"Oh, I've already heard. And seen it, with my own eyes."

He laughed.

A question struck him. "Would you move into our house? What about the Noonans?"

"Abby's a lot better. She doesn't need me as much anymore. She can actually lift her arms over her head and drive. And they're right next door, so I can still help out when they need it. I already thought about all this and we can't let Susan Baker surprise us. I'd have to move in—or at least make it look like I've moved in. I don't know. It's—"

"Negotiable," he finished along with her.

They smiled at each other. Perfectly in tune. Weird.

CHAPTER SEVENTEEN

And that, Gretel realized as she got back to work, was the most honest conversation she'd ever had with a man about a relationship. She was great at breakups—those were easy compared to this. She always poured on the sweetness and light, soothing the guy's wounded ego until he felt proud about how great he was handling the end.

Working out the nitty-gritty of an actual relationship? Totally new experience.

Yet another one brought to her by Lost Harbor, Alaska.

Danny D was in a lousy mood, muttering about the oncoming series of storms predicted for Misty Bay and the entire Aurora Peninsula.

"Surf's up in Molokai," he kept saying. "Winter storms, they're the best for the waves. Not here, man. Here they mean get your shovel, baby."

"I love the winter storms!" His scathing glance made her dial back the perkiness. "If you need a couple days off, I can fill in. You can hang out in your summer fantasyland."

In the winter, Danny liked to crank his heat up to eighty and walk around his house in his board shorts and sunglasses. He filled a kiddie pool with water so things didn't get too dry, then set up a chaise lounge and pretended he was still a lifeguard at the resort where he used to work.

"Might take you up on that." He slung a towel over his shoulder and went to unload the dishwasher.

Poor Danny. The long dark nights must be getting to him, as she'd been warned they would. When it didn't get fully light until ten in the morning, then right away started getting dark again by four-thirty, people could get depressed. Light lamps and tropical vacations were basic survival strategies.

So far, the short days and long nights hadn't bothered her.

She looked for something wood to rap her knuckles on, but could find only a wooden spoon. Close enough. Knock on wood, she wouldn't suffer from seasonal affective disorder as so many others did. Was it some kind of natural immunity, or the fact that this was all new and exciting to her, or was it—Zander Ross?

Just thinking about Zander gave her a warm sensation deep in the core of her being. The look in his eyes during their discussion of "marriage"—she couldn't help mentally putting quote marks around the word—still thrilled her. Intimate and intense. Real. As if he was looking deep into her heart and appreciating what he saw.

And his suggestion that they should conduct some kind of "courtship"—on speed? She found that so adorable. That was something people used to do back in the fifties, or pioneer days, or Renaissance Faire times. Courtship was a quaint, old-school concept that had long since been replaced with "hanging out" or "hooking up."

It sounded boring, to be honest.

Unless it was with Zander. That didn't sound boring at all.

She was still working when she got a text from him.

Up for an adventure?

Always. What do you have in mind?

It's a surprise. No guesses.

Behind the bar, she gave a little hop of joy. She loved surprises. And adventures. *Sure.*

Meet me at my house tomorrow after all the kids leave for school. Dress warmly. Unless you have to work?

She was a little disappointed that this surprise wouldn't be taking place indoors. Say, in his bedroom. But that was what courtships were all about, she supposed.

Nope. See you there.

That night, she was so excited she could barely sleep. Every time she dozed off, images of Zander filled her head. His bare chest, skin gleaming with sweat, muscles bunching as he braced his naked body over her. His black-green eyes hot with desire, eating her up. His face set in stern lines—not grouchy, as she'd first thought. But intense. Focused. Passionate.

She tossed from one side to the other, trying to chase the images away so she could sleep. But even in the dreams that followed, Zander appeared. He cupped her face in his calloused hand and whispered that he couldn't stop thinking about her. That he dreamed about her every night, and that he wanted her every minute. Then they were sledding down the main street of Lost Harbor, but standing up, as if they were surfing. She was holding onto his waist, exhilarated, shouting that they were going to crash.

She woke with a start and sat up in bed. It was just growing light outside—pearly blue dawn tapping at the window. It must be late. The kids were probably already gone off to school.

A note sat on the kitchen counter; Earl was taking Abby in for a checkup.

A completely free day lay before her. A free day *with Zander*.

She sent him a quick text—*I'll be there in half an hour*—then grabbed a bowl of cereal and poured herself a cup of barely warm coffee left from the morning chaos routine. A check out the window told her it was snowing, but only lightly. The sky was a flat misty gray that promised more snow to come.

Dress warmly. Hopefully that didn't mean "dress ugly," because she had no intention of compromising her style just so she could fend off frostbite. She dragged on a base layer of silk long underwear, then a thick pair of snowflake-patterned fleece leggings, along with her favorite new sweater, found at the thrift store, silver angora with a howling wolf stitched on the front, along with the words "Born to howl."

Parka, scarf, gloves, and a fake fur pillbox hat that looked almost Jackie O-ish except with ear flaps—and she jumped into her Nissan Frontier and headed for Zander's.

Even though Zander had told her not to guess, of course she had. Snowshoeing? More sledding? Snowball fight? Snowman construction project? But none of her guesses even came close.

A sled for two sat in Zander's expansive snow-covered yard—with six dogs harnessed to it, in three pairs. Eager, excited dogs who nipped at the snowflakes falling from above—and at each other.

Zander knelt by the dog in the front left position. He rubbed her head and whispered in her ear.

Gretel wasn't sure why she thought that dog was a "she." But somehow she was sure of it.

Zander rose to his feet, grinning. He wore a full snowsuit and fresh snowflakes dotted his dark hair. "My buddy's a dog musher, and I'm his backup when he's out of town. He wants me to take these guys for a run. He says they're getting antsy and need a real workout."

"Wow." Her mouth fell open as she stepped closer. One of the dogs cocked his head at her; his eyes were yellow, like a wolf's. "Do they like this? Pulling a sled?"

"Hell yes. They love it. Fiona's the lead dog." He gestured to the dog he'd been whispering to. "She's unbelievably fast. She was the lead of a team that came in second in the Iditarod. Now she's retired from racing but she still loves to run. She keeps the other dogs in line."

"What are their names?"

He ran down the line, naming each dog and bestowing rubs and pats to each. Most were some kind of husky mix, with thick fur and sturdy bodies and enough energy to power a train.

"In the old days, before we had so many roads, dog sleds were common around here. Some homesteads can only be reached by sled. The dog sleds can go across ice, frozen rivers...even the bay, when it used to freeze over. It doesn't do that anymore."

She crouched down and offered her hand to the closest dog so he could sniff it. "You sure they don't mind being harnessed like this?"

"Dogs are pack animals. They do well in teams, like this, as long as they're treated well. And these pups are treated like the champion athletes they are." One more scratch behind Fiona's ears, and he stepped over to the sled. He offered his hand to Gretel.

Gretel glanced again at the dog team. Fiona was looking curiously behind her, as if wondering who this unfamiliar human was. She caught the dog's eye and got a whoosh of intuition—Fiona was wondering what the holdup was. She wanted speed and snow and woods.

Holding Zander's hand, Gretel settled herself into the sled. Zander tucked a blanket around her. The proximity of his head, bedazzled with snowflakes, made her breath catch.

It stopped entirely when he paused, so close she could see his pupils darken, then slowly dropped a kiss onto her lips. She stayed still, letting him take the lead, giving herself over to the sensation of his firm mouth savoring hers. The contrast between his warmth and the cold air just outside their little bubble sharpened the sensation.

She sighed, her warm breath mingling like mist with his. His dark gaze held her for a moment, the strong lines of his face softening. "Hi there," he said softly.

"Hi."

They smiled at each other, as if it was Christmas and they were just about to open the present they were most excited about.

He stepped behind the sled. "I have to push off, they can't go from a dead stop. Be right there."

He took hold of the back of the sled and yelled, "Hike!" to the dogs. As he pushed, the dogs lurched forward in a chaotic tumble. Gretel grabbed onto the side, ready for the sled to dump her into the snow—as usual. But it steadied as the dogs got themselves straightened out. Zander jogged behind, pushing until the sled was well underway. Finally he hopped into the sled and snuggled next to her.

He worked with the reins, calling out directions, as Fiona yelped at her team. The exuberant dogs settled into a coordinated pace and the sled glided forward from the snowy yard into the forest. The runners of the sled made a crunchy sound, as if they were carving through an ice field. The dogs yipped and bumped against each other.

In the woods, the dogs really got into their groove. They loped at an easy pace, smoothly synchronized with each other and with Zander. He chose a course over new snow, winding through the deep forest toward the valley below.

She scrunched down in the sled to avoid the lower branches

of the spruce trees, but even so, her head brushed against one of them and a cold spritz of snow scattered across her face.

She didn't mind; it felt like a "hi there" from the forest—a greeting in the language of ice. It made her laugh out loud. In fact, she'd been smiling ever since the sled had gotten underway. What a joy to be here with these trees, this snow, these dogs...this man. It took her breath away. It was magical.

CHAPTER EIGHTEEN

When they reached the stream bed at the bottom of the valley, the mature spruce gave way to baby trees barely poking their tops above the snowpack. No trails had been broken down here. No human had ventured this far, at least recently. Virgin snow glistened on the branches of the spruce. A raven croaked overhead, its glossy black wings startling against the snow-heavy sky.

Zander called out, "Whoa," and they came to a stop and the dogs sat down in the snow, panting and bright-eyed. Gretel gazed around at the low slopes rising on each side of the valley, everything coated with a meringue of snow.

"Ready to go fast?" Zander grinned down at her. Frost clung to the scruff covering his jaw. His hood kept falling back, but he didn't seem to mind. His eyes shone bright, wild with exhilaration. Reddened cheeks, windblown hair—she'd never seen this side of him, as if all his cares and duties had been blown away by the rush of their ride.

"They can go faster?"

"Oh yeah. I was holding back because of all the branches, but down here they can go and go. They love it. They're just waiting for us to say the word."

"What's the word? What are those words you say to them?"

"Hike to run, whoa to stop. Gee to turn right. Haw to turn left. Want to try?" He handed her the reins.

"Really?" Her jaw dropped. "You...trust me that much? You've seen how many times I get dumped into the snow."

Another grin split his face. "I'll be right here. Nothing will go wrong. I got you."

And that felt like such a true statement. That was how Zander made her feel, in general. That with him around, things would be okay.

She took the reins and nestled in close to his side. "Hike," she called to the dogs—but mostly to Fiona. Fiona was in charge here. The dogs knew it and the humans knew it.

"You're a bad bitch, girl," she called to her. "Show your stuff."

This time, the sled didn't lurch at all. It zoomed across the snow as if gravity had loosened and they were all skimming a few inches above the snow. Joyful laughter spun from her lips, snatched by the wind. She was floating, no, she was flying. The cold air rushed past her face, and sang in her ears. It was a wild cry, the voice of the wilderness calling her like a siren.

Zander kept her anchored with his strong arms and steady presence. With the reassurance of his nearness, she let the dogs go at the speed they were craving. She felt their joy course through the reins and into her own bloodstream. *This is life. This is it. Right here.*

Eventually, Zander nudged her to bring them into a slowdown. They came to a stop in a clearing dotted with moose tracks. Some of the dogs pranced in place, some plopped their butts down in the snow. Spruce trees weighted with snow seemed to nod at them from both sides. Other than the panting of the dogs, the hush was absolute.

"I love it down here," Zander said softly, gazing at the clearing and the forest beyond. "My mother used to say that she felt connected to the trees around here. She believed that trees are wiser than people. I think about that every time I'm in the woods."

Gretel smiled with delight. "I totally agree with her. But what does responsible, practical Zander think?"

With a cryptic look, he said, "That you don't know everything about my bones, either. I'm not always practical."

Electricity throbbed between them.

He had a good point; if he was always practical, he probably wouldn't be considering her crazy marriage-with-an-asterisk scheme.

But then Zander did turn practical. "We should give them a short rest, then turn back. Want to hand out some treats? I have to check something."

He dug in one of his coat pockets for a Ziploc bag of dog treats, handed it to her, then stepped out of the sled. He opened a water bottle and gave each dog a drink and a compliment and a rub.

"Wait. Zander. Before you go. That was amazing. Thank you so much."

With a smile, he lifted one eyebrow. "Pretty good first date, right?"

"The greatest," she said sincerely. There was some stiff competition for that title—but all of those other first dates seemed to fade away in comparison.

She busied herself feeding treats to the dogs while Zander followed the moose tracks into the woods. They all wore little booties on each paw. She wondered if someone had crocheted them.

When Zander came back, he carried a set of antlers, awkward as a coat rack.

"The male moose shed their antlers this time of year," he explained. "I've been noticing this guy roaming around these woods. I knew he'd drop them soon."

"What do you want them for? They're so huge."

"I can use them in my woodworking. Clean them up, polish them, work them into some kind of art installation."

While he lashed the antlers to the back of the sled, she rubbed her forehead against Fiona's. "Such a good girl," she murmured to the lead dog. "Thank you for not toppling me into the snow."

Zander was watching her with amusement when she finally left the dogs and climbed back onto the sled. "You like to talk, don't you? To dogs, to sleds, to people?"

"Well, people are my favorite, but yes. I don't like to leave anyone out."

"Lost Harbor doesn't have a lot of people. Seems like an odd place for you." She understood the real question he was asking.

"You're wondering why I'm here. In Alaska. At the Noonans'."

"Basically, yeah."

She tugged her lip between her teeth and tried to figure out how to explain it.

"Remember that big blizzard last fall, when Abby was still pregnant? Bethany was her doctor, and she asked me to help her out, play with the kids and so forth, especially when Earl was gone. I was with them when the blizzard hit and all the power went out. We had to light candles and keep the woodstove going or we might literally freeze to death. It was...survival, you know? And then Abby had a seizure."

It had been the most terrifying moment of her life. Abby, eight months pregnant, suddenly gripped by convulsions. Gretel had rushed to catch her before she hit her head on the table. She'd managed to maneuver her onto her back and get all the furniture out of the way. She'd yelled at Eli to take the twins into the bedroom and keep them there—she hadn't wanted them to get hurt somehow.

With no cell service, she'd used the landline to call 911, and then Bethany because the dispatcher said it would take at least half an hour for the ambulance to get there. Bethany and Nate had rushed to the Noonans; Gretel had never been so relieved in her life. They'd taken care of Abby while Gretel had comforted the kids.

"I heard the story from Abby. She says you came through like a champ."

Gretel smiled at the compliment. "Thank you. The thing is, it was literally the first time anyone was depending on me. And I handled it. I wasn't just flirty-funny Gretel the partier. It's like—I used to think of myself as like the powdered sugar on top of a cake. This time, I was..." She trailed off, searching for the right image.

"The cake?" Zander frowned in puzzlement.

"No, more like..."

"The main dish?" he suggested. "Something not so sweet?"

"Okay, so it's not the perfect metaphor." Gretel cupped her hand to watch the snowflakes gather on her mitten. "The point is, I handled the situation. *I* was the grownup. Me, Gretel Zsa Zsa Whitney Morrison."

Zander looked slightly stunned—probably by that recitation of all her middle names.

"My mother likes celebrities," she explained.

"Fair enough. I'll memorize your middle names later. Go on."

" So then, when my father cut me off *for real*, I wasn't as panicked as I could have been. Because of that incident at the Noonans'. They need me, and no one *ever* needs me. People might like me, or enjoy having me around, or like the way I look lounging in a bikini on their yacht—but they don't *need* me."

He gave her another of those cryptic looks. "Are you so sure about that?"

She sighed. "You don't understand because people *do* need you. Look at your brothers. Look at your friend the dog musher. These dogs. They need you."

As if she knew they were talking about her, Fiona gave an impatient *yip* and pawed at the snow.

Gretel and Zander looked at each other and laughed. "I think she's saying she *needs* you to get off your ass and start the sled," Gretel told him.

"Yup. She was born to run. We think she's part wolf. See those long legs?"

"Part wolf!" That made her give the lead dog another look. Fiona pranced in place, nipped at her neighbor, who was trying to lie down. "No wonder I like her." She unzipped her parka to show off her sweater, with the howling wolf and the lettering "Born to Howl."

He laughed and tipped his head back to let out a long howl of his own.

Zander the lead wolf, taking care of his pack of brothers.

She could totally see it.

His howl set off a chain reaction of barking and yodeling from the dog team. When they got that out of their system, Zander turned the team around and they headed back down the stream bed, toward the set of tracks they'd left up the slope and into the forest. For the uphill portion, they both got out and walked next to the tiring dogs.

By the time they'd returned the team and the sled to their home, Zander didn't have much time before he had to leave for car-pool duty. Not nearly enough time for kissing—although they made the most of it while Zander boiled water for hot cocoa.

Standing behind him at the stove, she ran her hands under his sweater, then under the other layers until she hit damp, warm skin. She felt him shiver at her touch.

"Playing with fire," he warned. "If I'm late picking up the kids, I'll be in big trouble. I might even have to get married to make up for it."

"That sounds terrible," she murmured. "What kind of crazy girl would you get to do that?"

"That's the thing. I have the highest possible standards. It would have to be someone I can't get out of my head. Someone incredible. Someone with the most amazing smile I've ever seen. The kind of girl you dream about. You know, those naked dreams that you don't want to wake up from."

Startled, she stilled her hands on their journey across the ridges of his abdomen. He turned, questioning, and shifted them so they weren't standing so close to the stove. "Did I say something wrong?"

"No, it's not that. It's—you were in my dream last night."

"That's funny. You were in mine. Were we doing something fun in your dream?"

"Sledding. Standing up, like on a surfboard. What were we doing in yours?"

His eyes darkened. "I'd rather show you." He set his hands on her hips and tugged her against his groin. The hard curve of his erection pressed against her, just above her sex. She wanted it *on* her sex. She wanted *him*, damn it.

No one but him.

It had to be *his* hands gliding under her sweater, his strong body pressed against hers. She wanted his mouth coming down on her like an oncoming storm. His lips setting fire to her blood. His groans reverberating through her body.

He slid his hands between her legs and cupped her sex. Her entire body gave a jolt of reaction—all her nerve endings firing at once.

"Zander," she whispered into his shoulder.

"Hm?" He found her most sensitive spot with one of his long fingers. She squeezed her eyes shut as pleasure welled under his touch.

"How long does 'courtship on speed' usually last?"

"You think I'm an expert? I've never courted anyone before."

He rubbed her gently, increasing his pace bit by bit until she thought she might burst into flames faster than the burner under the hot cocoa.

"Then we can make up our own rules?"

She tugged him closer so she could slide a hand down his pants. The hot skin of his lower belly twitched and his erection rose up to meet her. The first touch of that hard shaft sent a sharp bolt of lust through her.

He gave a strained laugh; she felt its vibration in her bones. "Don't you do that anyway?"

"Mostly," she admitted. "Since the ones I got taught made no sense to me."

"You're wicked. You're the queen of chaos, that's what you are." Whatever he was doing with his hand, it was making her body arch shamelessly. Desire poured through her like rich thick coffee syrup, undiluted and dark as pitch. Then it slid into something else—a pulse of release, a rush of pleasure that was more like a tease than an orgasm. A promise of climaxes to come.

"And you're, what? The law of the land? Mr. Ross the Boss?" She nipped at his chin. "Are you going to boss me around and tell me what to do?"

"Count on it." With a deep growl, he gripped her hips. She caught her breath, anticipating his next move, his next caress. Instead, he set her away from him. Tension sang in every line of his body. He practically snarled with regret. "But only when I'm not on car-pool duty."

Now that was discipline. Wow. "You're sure?"

"No. I'm already late. Do you want Petey hanging out with those idiots who keep daring him to throw snowballs at the principal?" He tucked his shirt back into his pants. He looked wild with lust.

"No, of course not. Ugh. Those troublemakers." She drew in a long shaky breath. "This is my fault. I never should have touched you."

"Hey." He tugged her back to his side. "Never apologize for that. Believe me, every time you touch me, it's better than all the times that you don't touch me. No matter how it ends up. You get me?"

She must have looked confused, because he gave a wry laugh and ran a hand through his hair. He pocketed his truck keys.

"Never mind. You've scrambled my vocabulary. You coming?"

"To pick up the kids?"

"Yeah, if you have time. You can recite your middle names again. I want to get this courtship thing done as quickly as we can. Otherwise I might implode."

"Let's do it."

CHAPTER NINETEEN

Zander hadn't done much "dating" in his life. He'd lost his virginity to his high school girlfriend, who had since moved away from Alaska. In the Marines, he'd hooked up with his share of women, but he wouldn't call that "dating." Definitely not "courtship." Since moving back to Lost Harbor, he'd kept things very simple with the women he met. No strings, no attachments, no expectations.

This thing with Gretel—courtship, negotiation, whatever it was—fell into its own unique category.

Lust. Friendship. Fun. All of that, plus a weird layer of surreal seriousness. He remembered a documentary he'd seen about arranged marriages, in which the couples were brought together by their families, but were given time to get to know each other before committing to the marriage.

It almost felt like that, except their families didn't even know they had a role in this. The boys noticed that Zander and Gretel were spending a lot of time together. So did Bethany. Gretel told him that her sister had quizzed her relentlessly when she dropped in for her morning coffee at the Wicked Brew.

Other people noticed too, which they decided was a good thing. It would add authenticity to the story they were weaving for Susan Baker. The more time they spent together, the more real it looked. The more time they spent together, the more Lost Harbor got used to the idea of Zander and Gretel.

But mostly, the more time they spent together, the more time he *wanted* to spend together.

It almost didn't matter what they did. Cuddling up watching DVDs on the couch during a storm was great. Ice skating on the pond that the town hot-mopped was wonderful. He loved snowshoeing through the woods with her, because she brought such a sense of wonder to every adventure, and she was so curious about everything.

He showed her bunny tracks in the snow—and the mark made by the owl that had swooped in and claimed the rabbit. He taught her how to warm her hands in her armpits, and how to recognize a spot where a moose had bedded down for the night—and might be back.

He asked her about her globetrotting days, and she told him about backpacking through Thailand and sailing in the Mediterranean. He enjoyed her stories, but they also drove home the reality that Lost Harbor, Alaska would never be enough for her. No matter what they decided about "marriage," she would still want to see the world.

But he'd show her whatever he could of *his* world, while she was here.

On the night of the new moon, in the clear aftermath of another storm, he tapped on her bedroom window and lured her into the darkness. She came out, still yawning, but always up for an adventure. He kneeled at her feet to help her get her snowshoes on because she was still half asleep. He fitted a headlamp over her hat as she blinked at him sleepily.

It was adorable.

He snowshoed ahead of her, breaking the trail, his headlamp casting a narrow cone of light across the snow, which lit up with sparkles as he moved. It took only a short time to reach the lookout, and once they did, Gretel finally woke up.

"Oh my God." She grabbed his hand. "That's...wow. That's incredible." Ethereal veils of lights shimmered across the sky in luminous white, tender spring green and faded blood red.

"Aurora borealis. The northern lights. Solar flares hitting our atmosphere. We don't always see so many colors here. Usually they're just white."

The lights danced in a fluid flow across the entire horizon. They fluctuated in intensity, with one area of the sky fading while another dominated. The shapes were always changing, too, as if they were following an invisible symphony conductor who dazzled with light and harmony.

"Are they singing?" she asked in a whisper.

"No, they don't make any sound."

"Are you sure? I think I can hear them. It's like a hum, but harmonized." She cocked her head, trying to home in on something. "Maybe it's something else."

"I don't know. My mother used to say they sang. But science says they don't." He wondered if she realized she was still holding his hand.

"Pfff. Science, schmience," she scoffed. "I agree with your mother."

She adjusted her neck, which must be starting to cramp from looking up at the sky. Now that was a job he could handle. He pulled off his glove and replaced her hand with his. Gently, he rubbed out the knot until he felt her muscles relax.

She made a sound of appreciation, low in her throat.

"Now I hear a hum," he joked. He adjusted her position so that she could lean back on him without bending her neck so much. "Is that better?"

"Yes. You're like a big warm wall."

He chuckled and looped his arms around her. She nestled closer against him. The cold clear night kept sending tendrils of icy air at the edges of their clothing and their exposed faces. "I'll take that as a compliment. At least the big and warm part."

They stayed like that for as long as they could stand it, taking in the drama of light and color playing out in the heavens. The cold tried hard to chase them away, but Gretel was so riveted by the lights that he didn't have the heart to call an end. Instead he checked the skin of her cheek to make sure she wasn't chilling down too much, the way he used to do with Petey, and his father had done with him.

"Did you know that the Japanese believe it's good luck to see the Auroras on your honeymoon?" he murmured to her.

"Too bad we're not on our honeymoon yet. You should have jumped on my proposal," she joked.

"I did jump on it. This is just...you know, foreplay." He rested his chin on the top of her head.

"So you think we'd get along with each other?"

"I think we'd have a lot of fun trying to find out."

She turned and looked up at him. "Wait, are you saying we should do it?"

With her face lit only by the Northern Lights, she was even more luminous than usual.

"Do you still want to?"

He hadn't intended to have this conversation right now. But here they were, and time was running short. Susan Baker could be back at any moment.

She twisted her face, as if trying to decide, and in that moment he realized that he'd feel empty and disappointed if they didn't go forward with this. He'd gotten used to spending time with her. More than "used" to it. Time with Gretel was always the best part of his day.

And that, he realized, was the biggest risk of all. He could fall so thoroughly in love with her that if—no, probably when—she left, he'd be crushed. Deeply so.

But if it helped keep the Ross family together, he could take the hit. That was what Marines did.

"Yes," she finally said, a smile breaking over her face. "It's both unselfish and a little bit selfish of me, but yes. It helps you, and I can help the butterflies and...I like you."

I like you.

Huh.

Obviously, he was the only one who'd be getting his heart crushed. Suck it up, Zander.

"A lot," she added softly, probably noticing his expression.

Too late. He got the message, and honestly, it was a good wakeup call. Despite their "courtship" and the fun they had together, this wasn't a romance. It was a mutually beneficial agreement.

"The thing is, it's a real sacrifice for me," he told her gravely.

"Excuse me?" She frowned and tried to draw away from him, but he held her close.

"It means you'll be staying, and I'll have to go on the Bush Lines and make an ass of myself."

Glee lit up her face. "I hadn't even thought about that part. I guess my evil plan is working." She rubbed her hands together.

"Unless my evil plan is to draw you into my web and then drive you so crazy with my bossy ways that you get the first airlift out of here."

She laughed, then looked at him from under her eyelashes, a scorching, smoldering look that sent him into immediate lust mode. "What if I like your bossy ways?"

"Then...move it, woman. We need to get out of this cold and into a bed. Immediately."

With that reminder of the cold, she gave a full-body shudder. "Not gonna argue with that."

He rubbed his hands up and down her arms. "We've been standing still too long. You'll warm up when we get moving."

As he massaged heat into her, her eyes got that hazy, happy look that always reminded him of a cat curled by a fireplace. "I like it when *you* warm me up."

"Then you ain't seen nothin' yet. There's a lot more heat where this came from. Come on."

He struck off across the snow, while she took one more look at the glory of the Aurora, then followed him into the woods. He wasn't cold at all. His entire body was on fire for her.

And his entire brain was busy trying to figure out how they could make this happen. Her bed, in the midst of all those Noonans? Hell no.

His bed, with his brothers right across the hall? Another hell no.

Could he arrange for the boys to have an overnight somewhere? Could they book a room at the Eagle's Nest, the nicest hotel in town?

AND THEN MAGICALLY, about a month into their "courtship on speed," everything fell into place. Jason was invited to travel with the ski team to a weekend meet. And Petey asked if he could have an overnight at the Noonans' so he and Eli could work on an extensive, multi-pronged snow-and-ice fort they were perfecting. It had tunnels and arched doorways and enough space to sleep in. They were lobbying hard to be able to camp out in it overnight.

He gave Petey permission for whatever Abby and Earl felt comfortable with. Petey could barely hide his surprise, but he didn't question his good fortune. He just packed his backpack and hopped in the truck, ready for his ride.

Zander sent Gretel a text to invite her over that night.

Slumber party? She asked.

Don't count on any slumber.

She sent back some winky faces. *I'll tell the Noonans I'm going to stay at my sister's.*

When he dropped Petey off at the Noonans' that afternoon, he did his best to speak normally to Gretel, instead of revealing the excitement raging through him.

Of course Gretel had to make it even harder by playing innocent. "So, you have a free night, Zander Ross. Are you going out on the town? Should I tell the female population of Lost Harbor to watch out?"

"Hopefully they're already lining up for a chance at this." He flexed his muscles, making a joke of it.

But he caught the way her gaze lingered on his chest. He definitely wasn't the only one nearly jumping out of his skin with anticipation.

"Gretel, you should go over there and keep Zander company." Abby spoke from the rocking chair, where she was nursing the baby.

"Oh, I totally would, but I promised my sister I'd spend some time with her. We've both been so busy, what with her saving lives with medicine and me saving lives with coffee. Sorry, Zander, you'll just have to get through the night on your own. I hope it's not too hard."

Subtle emphasis on the word *hard*.

The wicked girl.

He drove back home and raced through the house for a whirlwind cleanup. It shouldn't matter—in fact it would be better for Gretel to see the full reality of the household she might be joining —but somehow, he wanted to impress her. He found some local shrimp in the freezer and made a quick stir fry in case she was hungry.

He'd once heard her mention to Abby that she could never get enough shrimp.

What about dessert? Ice cream supply, check. Including the pistachio he'd made sure to buy. Fudge sauce, yes. Whipped cream in a can, yes. All he needed was Gretel's naked breasts so he could lick that cream off her nipples.

He lost himself in that fantasy for a moment, only to be interrupted by a knock on the door.

Going for a cheesy playboy pose, he opened the door with a leer and one hand braced on the doorframe.

But it wasn't Gretel. It was Susan Baker.

He dropped the leer in a flash, but she'd already seen it. "Expecting someone else?"

"Uh, yes."

"Your girlfriend, I presume. My timing is always off." She didn't seem to regret that fact at all. In fact, she wore a smug smile.

"You're back from Kodiak."

"So it seems. May I come in?" She peered past him. "Are your brothers here?"

"No, they're both gone for the night."

"Ah. So you're taking advantage of the situation."

He winced at the way she made that sound. "It's not—I mean —look, do you ever just call ahead?"

"I happened to be in the neighborhood."

A truck roared into his yard. Susan wheeled around just as Gretel's Nissan Frontier veered past her Toyota. The caseworker gave a little gasp at the close shave.

The door opened and Gretel jumped out of the truck, landing with one foot in a snowbank.

Honestly, they were like a magnet for her, those snowbanks.

She yanked her leg out of the snow and shook it off, then ran full-tilt across the yard.

On the way, she met his gaze and gave him a wink—as if to say, *I see what's going on, I got this*—and everything in him relaxed.

He stepped toward her just as she flew into his arms. They embraced for a hot, passionate moment, then Gretel, flushed and laughing, slid down to the porch and turned to Susan Baker.

"I'm sorry to be so rude, I just get carried away every time I see my fiancé. I remember you. You're the good Samaritan who gave me a ride!"

"Susan Baker, yes."

"Ah, the caseworker from the state. Yes, Zander mentioned you. I'm happy to meet you."

The caseworker frowned between the two of them. "Did you say 'fiancé'?"

"I did! We've been engaged for a while, but we've kept it low-key. That's why I didn't say anything when you helped me out."

The woman's dark eyes filled with suspicion. "I haven't gotten any updates to the file."

Gretel held onto Zander's hand and gazed up at him with an adoring, besotted expression that totally worked for him.

"Well, we haven't officially done the deed yet, that's why. But we're about to. It's really just a formality at this point. I can't wait to be part of the Ross family. I think an angel brought me to them."

Zander dug his elbow into her side, afraid she was overdoing it.

But Susan Baker seemed to have a romantic streak under her blunt exterior. "It's nice to see two young people so much in love, and so willing to make a commitment. I don't see that enough."

"Oh yes, we're all about commitment," Gretel said earnestly. "Especially considering the boys, you know."

The caseworker tapped a finger against her briefcase. "I admit, I've been worried about the boys."

Zander could think of a million things to say to that, but decided to leave the talking to Gretel.

"That's one of the reasons we kept it quiet, so the boys could get used to us being together. Change can be so disruptive. But the boys come first. Susan, would you like to come in?"

The caseworker waved her off. "I'll let you two enjoy your evening. Zander, call me when get a chance. We need to set up a time when I can speak with your brothers."

"I'll do that." He settled his arm snugly over Gretel's shoulders and kept it there until Susan Baker's car had reached the road.

Then Gretel drew away, gasping. "We have to hurry."

"Yes. Bedroom, now." His heart hammered crazily.

"Not the bedroom, silly. We have to fill out the paperwork."

"But—we don't—I don't even—" This was moving so fast. Was it really happening?

"She's expecting us to get married. Didn't you catch that bit about commitment?"

"Yes, of course, but—"

"I already looked it up. We need a minister licensed with the State of Alaska and two witnesses."

"Gretel." He squeezed her upper arms, trying to ground her.

But she kept rattling on. "Who do you know that's a licensed minister but who's not actually a church minister, because that doesn't feel right, you know?"

"*Gretel.*"

Finally she focused on him. "What?"

"None of that is going to happen today. It's four-thirty in the afternoon. We have all night to figure it out."

She blinked at him. Her nose was pink from the cold and he noticed a stray snowflake on the tip of her eyelash. "All night?"

"All night. But I already have plans for this night, and they don't involve paperwork."

Her lips parted. "But what about—"

"Don't worry about Susan Baker. You have her wrapped around your little finger. We finally got some time alone. In a house. With a bed. How about we make the most of it?"

A slow smile curled up the corners of her lips. He'd never get tired of watching her lips do that.

He bent down and scooped her up, her knees hooked over one arm, her back resting on the other, a perfect warm bundle against his chest.

"I know we're doing everything out of order, but I figure this part should go in there somewhere."

He nudged open the door with his foot and stepped across the threshold.

CHAPTER TWENTY

How was it that Zander made everything so romantic without even trying? It was the way he looked at her as he carried her across the threshold—as if she was a dream literally coming true in his arms. As if she was the most magical being he'd ever laid eyes on.

She felt the flex of his muscles as he kicked the door shut behind him, then strode across the living room. "I really hope you're not hungry or thirsty or have anything else on your mind other than getting into bed," he growled. "I'm done waiting. I'm not leaving this fucking house until I've made you come at least twenty times."

"What if the Northern Lights come back?" she teased. Her heart raced in response to his hot words.

"I don't care if there's a meteor about to hit this house. If it does, I want to be fucking you when it happens."

Wow, the F-word from Zander. He usually avoided that in front of the boys. He must be really letting loose.

She was all for it, one hundred percent.

At the same time, this suddenly seemed like a big step.

They'd been dancing around this for quite some time. What if it was an anticlimax? Not what you wanted in a climax.

When they reached his bedroom door, he couldn't quite manage the doorknob, so he had to angle her into the right position to open it. It took her a few tries.

"Sweaty palms," she murmured.

"Nerves?"

"A little. What if we don't have any chemistry? What if we don't...fit?"

"Fit? Of course we fit. Everyone fits. Besides, penetration is only one part of sex, and—"

"I don't mean like that!" she cried. She'd read a few sex scenes in old romance novels in which the virgin heroine was afraid the hero's enormous penis wouldn't fit inside her petite body. She'd always found that ridiculous. "I mean sexually. What if we don't vibe with each other?"

"Then we get a vibrator," he said seriously, before a grin split his face. "I'm not opposed to sex toys."

"Oh really? This is so fascinating. What's your favorite sex toy?"

Nerves forgotten, she finally managed to turn the knob and he carried her into the room. He set her down on the bed, more gently than she would have expected.

"My favorite sex toy is anything that makes you feel good," he murmured as he unzipped her parka. She'd almost forgotten that she still wore all her snow gear. He unwound the scarf from around her neck. "This scarf, for instance, could be my favorite if I used it to tie you to my bed while I lick your entire body."

She squirmed as a tendril of heat curled through her body.

"I wouldn't use that scarf," she warned. "It's my first knitting project and it might unravel at any moment."

Laughing, he folded it carefully and set it on top of her parka. "Hands off the scarf. Got it."

He came back to the edge of the bed and she decided it was her turn to make a move. She took hold of the waistband of his jeans and tugged him closer. The outline of his erection was already clear. Through the denim, she traced it with her finger, making a complete tour of that ever-growing bulge.

He stared down at her, eyes dark with desire. A muscle ticked in his jaw and the tendons along his neck went tight. He looked as if he wanted to pounce on her.

She rose up on her knees at the same moment that he reached for her. It could have been a disaster, but it worked out perfectly, putting her at the exact height for him to tug her sweater over her head. She was wearing another of her favorites, extravagant peonies mingled with stripes. Underneath—well, underneath she wore a simple thermally beneficial long-sleeved shirt. And underneath that, a t-shirt. But underneath *that*—she'd put on her very sexiest corset bra, with laces up the front.

He laughed as he peeled each layer off her—until he got to the final one. Then he gave a wolf whistle. "Wow."

Worth every penny she'd charged on the credit card she no longer had.

He traced the edge of it, where brocade met bare skin. Shivers traveled from the pad of his finger across her nerve endings, all the way down to the liquid core of her belly.

Slowly, his heated gaze warming her skin, he untied the bow at the top of the bra. The two edges separated and she hauled in a suddenly free breath. He kept going down the row, loosening each lace, until the bra opened enough to expose her nipples.

He let out a sound that was either appreciation or agony—or some combination. "God, you're gorgeous." She looked down, all her focus on his large, warm hands as they delicately explored her breasts. How could he manage to touch her with so much sensitivity, when he normally used those hands for power tools and axes and snow shovels?

But then she remembered that he was basically an artist who happened to work with wood. Of course he was sensitive. He worked magic with antique toboggans and moose antlers. Why should nipples be any more challenging?

If they were, he was definitely up for that challenge. She sighed and shifted back and forth as his teasing caresses stoked the fire that he'd already sparked inside her. When the bra was completely loosened, it fell to her waist. Now she was entirely exposed to his touch and his gaze and never before had she felt quite so desirable.

He cupped her breasts in both of his calloused hands and lowered his mouth to one nipple—the right one. Which was significant because her right nipple was her favorite. When he engulfed it in his hot, wet mouth, she gave a gasp of sheer pleasure.

"You picked the best one," she murmured.

"What?" He lifted away from her nipple for a moment. She glared at him for halting the delicious sensations. With a chuckle, he put his mouth back where it had been.

"My right nipple's just better. It's more sensitive," she explained.

He tongued it harder, making her moan.

"It looks better, too." Her voice grew ragged under his intense suckling. "The other one has a pucker in the areola. I don't know why they're different, but they aa-ahhh—are." A spasm of heat twanged through her body. "See?" she gasped. "The other one wouldn't do that."

"Okay, you got me curious." He shifted over to the left nipple. She closed her eyes, letting him do his thing—but just as she'd warned him, the sensation was weaker than in the other nipple. He noticed the difference, too. "Okay, good to know." He went back to her right nipple and immediately the wild pleasure flooded through her again.

She noticed that he didn't see it as some kind of challenge and waste a bunch of time and energy working on her left nipple. The first time she'd told a guy about that quirk, he'd treated it as a kind of Mount Everest, determined to be the first to make her left nipple respond like the right.

Zander just made a mental note of it, as if he was mapping the terrain of her body, and that was just another feature to remember.

For all of his honed physique and military studliness, he was surprisingly not arrogant and full of himself.

Speaking of honed physique...she dragged herself out of the stupor of pleasure he was creating with his mouth on her nipples and reached for his hoodie.

Zip. Down came the zipper. Out came the rippling muscles under his gray USMCA t-shirt. She pushed it up, over his abdomen, feasting her eyes on each new ridge as it was revealed. He helped her by ditching the hoodie and reaching over his head to tug off the t-shirt. Finally, she saw the full picture of Zander Ross' chiseled torso. Each muscle was taut and toned, his skin marred by a scar here and there, dark curls gathering between his pectorals and swirling all the way down below his opened waistband.

Breathless, she spread her hand across the middle of his chest, feeling firm muscle everywhere her fingers reached. "Boot camp?"

He shrugged. "Boot camp helped. I got a head start growing up here. I was always a physical kid. Also, we have a weight room. Jason and I work out there. Petey comes and goes. He likes pushups but can't stand pull-ups."

She touched a curl—soft and springy—and followed it down his body to the edge of his pants.

"No surprise what you're going to find there," he laughed, his voice sounding strained. He caught her wrists before she could go any further. "Not yet," he managed. "You're going to come first."

"Oh really?"

"Really. My bed, my rules." He firmly lowered her down onto her back.

She couldn't come up with an argument against that. Especially because he was now sliding her leggings off her body. And then her long underwear.

He stopped there and slowed waaaay down. He ran his fingertips down her thighs, then back up the insides of her legs, to the vee in between. Flutters followed everywhere he touched.

She'd also worn one of her sexiest pair of panties—basically a thong with a butterfly discreetly covering her mound. It was definitely doing its job on Zander. His breath was coming fast and that telltale muscle in his jaw was jumping. He traced the shape of the butterfly with his index finger, which was absolutely maddening because he touched everywhere except the kernel of nerves that craved it the most.

But the more she wriggled and pushed at his hand, the slower he went. He left caresses like flickers of firelight along her inner thighs. Sent warm breath wafting across her sex. She might as well be naked, the way he scorched her with his gaze. The delicate fabric provided no shield against it, or the relentless approach of those skilled fingers.

She flung her arms wide and grabbed onto the red comforter covering his bed. Who had a red comforter? The random thought flitted through her mind. She would have pegged him for black or blue or brown. Simple, non-flashy colors. Stoic. Reserved.

But Zander had another side—a very different side, all fire and spice. He had a red comforter side and right now, she was at the mercy of that part of Zander. Sensations flowed through her body at a speed and intensity that almost scared her. *Hang on,* she told herself with the bits of sense that remained. *Hang on and enjoy every second.*

She dug her fingers deep into the comforter and closed her eyes. The sight of Zander's iron-tense muscles was too much sensory overload. His touch was all she could handle—barely. Especially when he returned to her nipples—well, the right one—and set about teasing and licking and suckling until she cried out in strangled desire.

"God, Zander! Please!"

He released her nipple with a wet pop and slid down her body to her sex. Frantic, she pushed against him, seeking friction and contact and heat and hardness.

And he gave it to her. As she wanted it.

Oh, *the bliss* of that first touch. Just right, with his thumb directly on the spot that trembled and throbbed. Pleasure speared through her and brought a cry that came all the way from her heart. Just a sound, no words, because there was no way she could come up with actual coherent thought. Not when he was stroking her swollen clit with a mixture of ruthlessness and sensitivity that ripped her apart.

In a good way.

It turned her into a wild thing thrashing back and forth on his bed. It was a miracle that he managed to keep his thumb right where she needed it—but he did. With the other hand, he kept her anchored to the bed so she didn't go flying off. *Strong hands.* They sure came in handy.

For an eternity—or a flash—she hung suspended and trembling over a high cliff of bliss. Then he lowered his mouth back to her right nipple and tugged at it with firm lips...and that did it. She erupted into an ecstatic chaos of convulsions that rampaged through her entire body. The orgasm kept going and going, stoked by his fingers and his tongue. He'd taken absolute control of her body and all she could do was surrender.

She came down slowly, like a wave receding on the beach. Stranded like a mermaid in love with a prince.

Silly thought; she waved it away. "Holy wow," she murmured instead. "I'm out of words, and that doesn't happen very often."

"Words, who needs 'em," he joked. Even though he was obviously aiming for lightness, his rapid breathing and pitch-dark eyes gave the game away. The same fire that had just virtually consumed her was still alive in him.

She grabbed the waistband of his still-opened jeans and finished unzipping them. "We need these pants out of our life," she told him. "They can go wait in the corner until they're needed."

With a snort, he stood up and peeled them off his body. She watched avidly as his powerful thighs emerged, then the rest of his muscular form.

"Could you just...turn around?" she asked innocently.

"Why?" He looked over his shoulder, toward the window.

She wanted to laugh; didn't he know how impressive his body was? Didn't he want to show it off from every angle? Most of the men she knew—

What was the point of thinking about most men? Zander wasn't like the men she'd known in the past. Nothing like them.

"I think I saw a moose at the window," she told him. He turned all the way around to check it out, while she checked out his ass in his black boxer briefs. Firm, defined, muscular. She wanted to bite those fleshy cheeks.

When he turned back around, she saw from his expression that he was onto her. "That was petty."

"Petty? No way. I've been wondering what you looked like in your underwear for too long to be denied. In the classic words of Elvis Presley, 'a little less conversation, a little more action please.'" She sang that last bit, since it was one of her favorite songs.

"This kind of action?" He did an Elvis move with his hips, showing off his bulge, now the size of a small boulder.

"How'd you guess?"

He lowered his briefs, allowing his erection to jump free. Long and thick, determined, it pointed directly at Gretel. She reached for it, greedy and impatient. It settled into her hand, hot and eager, raring to go.

"Hello, you," she said directly to it. "Aren't you a handsome one?"

"It's not a dog," grumbled Zander. The catch in his voice made her sympathize with his situation. She knew exactly how he felt; aroused to the point of being ready to burn everything down if he didn't come soon.

"Any chance you and that big human up there have a condom lying around? We can improvise if you don't." To prove it, she swirled her tongue across the swollen skin of the head. His shaft gave a sharp jump in response, and her pussy throbbed. As if they were having a conversation between just the two of them.

He groaned hard and his whole body went tense, a bow arched and ready to let fly. She tasted salt on her tongue.

"Wait." His voice was so guttural it barely sounded like him. "Don't move."

He pulled himself from her mouth. Her tongue clung to the roof of her mouth, as if she could still taste his firmness and heat. He took a few steps to a set of drawers next to his bed—which meant she got a killer view of his ass flexing as he walked.

He came back with a condom, already in the midst of rolling it on.

If they really did this "marriage" thing, maybe they could skip the condoms, she thought randomly.

If?

It was probably too late for "if." She'd already convinced

Susan Baker that they were about to get married. A little research, a little paperwork, and it would be done.

She pushed away that surreal thought and welcomed him back to her side. Snagging his arm, she tumbled him onto the bed next to her. The feel of his naked body touching hers sent her into a happy trance. He was so warm, so solid, so alive, so strong. And so, so *hard*.

Muscle-wise and erection-wise.

Suddenly almost clumsy, they grabbed onto each other and rolled over and over, with first one of them on top, then the other. They could barely contain themselves, both of them just about jumping out of their skins with excitement. Gretel was giggling and shivering at the same time. She nipped at his shoulder. He sucked at the soft skin of her neck. She buried her face in his stomach. He swatted her on the ass.

Finally Zander took charge and pinned her down on the bed, face up.

"Like that," he commanded. "Just like that."

"Or what?" she teased.

"Or I'll take emergency measures."

"Oooh, scary." The look in his eyes made her shiver with wild anticipation. He tore his gaze from hers and looked down at where their bodies were about to join. He took his erection in his fist and guided it toward her sex.

One of her hands was now free, but she did as he asked and kept it where it was. Now that he was about to enter her body, she didn't want any distractions. She blocked out everything else; the feel of the comforter, the click of snow crystals against the windowpane, the smell of his sweat, or hers, the taste of salt still on her tongue.

Nothing else mattered in that moment except for the slow thick slide of his penis into her body. And then—the pulse of time in which they adjusted to each other, him panting over her body, arms tense as steel, eyes dark as midnight.

After that, she lost herself in the thrust and retreat of his hard cock, in the slide of sweaty skin on skin, in the pleasure that built and built and finally bubbled over in a warm burst of an orgasm that made her toes tingle. Shortly after that, almost as if he'd been holding off, Zander gave a sharp grunt and plunged deep, deeper, and then stilled, tremors shaking his taut body.

When he finally went limp, barely holding himself over her, she lifted her head and nipped at his nose.

He raised his head and did something that completely surprised her. He kissed her. It was slow, deep kiss, not passionate or lustful, just...real. A grounding kind of kiss. A "here we are together and isn't that lucky" kind of kiss.

She kissed him back, a smile quivering at her lips. No, Zander wasn't at all like any of the other men she'd known. And that was definitely a good thing.

CHAPTER TWENTY-ONE

Zander needed some recovery time after that wild experience with Gretel. Not just physically, but in all ways. Together, they'd gone to a place he wasn't really used to. It was more than sex. A lot more.

Was that because they were doing this "marriage with an asterisk" thing? Because he needed to keep in mind that just because they might fill out some paperwork, it didn't mean Gretel was going to stick around.

He took longer than necessary to dispose of his condom, just so he could get a grip on himself. *Keep it real*, he kept reminding himself. As long as he and Gretel both knew exactly what they were getting into—and not getting into—they should be fine. Right?

He hoped so, because damn, he wanted to do what they'd just done again, and again, and again. How long were the boys going to be gone?

He was actually calculating the hours when Gretel popped her head into the bathroom. "I'm a little hungry, are you?"

"For sure. There's some shrimp stir fry in the fridge, and

some leftover mac and cheese. There might be some old pizza too, but that's from last week, so—" He made a face. He did his best, but he wasn't much of a cook. One look in the refrigerator and she would know that she was now in bachelor-boy-world.

"Sounds perfect, I love shrimp," she said cheerfully and danced away. He knew she danced because he could see the magenta flash of her streaked hair flying behind her, and the flash of her pert little butt.

God, how could she be so...endearing? Appealing? Enchanting?

Enchanting? He really had to get a grip on himself.

After washing off and pulling on some sweats and a t-shirt, he joined her in the kitchen, where she was randomly punching buttons on the microwave, making lights flash on and off.

He reached over her and set the timer for one minute.

"Show-off," she grumbled as she zipped her hoodie all the way up. It had a fleece lining almost the exact shade of her hair.

"I don't know much, but I do know how to nuke cold food."

She rested her elbows on the counter and looked at him seriously. "We need to talk."

A shock went through him, sending his stomach plummeting. Had Gretel changed her mind? Had that spectacular sex been just *meh* to her? "Okay."

She registered his sudden wariness, and her eyes widened. "Oh no! It's nothing bad. Don't look so scared. I was just thinking that we need to work on our prenup."

"Our what?" The microwave dinged and he grabbed a pot holder.

"Our prenup. It's not really a prenup, per se, but it's a negotiation. Remember, I told you that if we did this, we'd have to work out all the details ahead of time? Well, we kind of ran out of 'ahead of time.'"

He pulled out the stir fry and set it down on a hot pad. "So we're doing this? For real?"

"Are you having second thoughts?" The same expression of wariness now appeared on her face. "Better say them now, before we go any further."

"Listen, I'm in, as long as you still are. I have a lot more to gain than you do, so it has to be up to you."

"That's not really true. I'll be paying off a debt and saving some butterflies. This has to be a one hundred percent mutual decision."

He took two forks from the silverware drawer and handed her one. When she gave it a quizzical look, he laughed. "Sorry, did you want a plate too? We get into the habit of avoiding dishes because no one likes washing them."

"No no, I'm good." She waved the fork at him before diving in. "But that does bring up one of the deal points. Household stuff."

He squinted her. "Deal points? What does your father do, exactly?"

"He's a real estate developer," she explained through a mouthful of food. "But he makes all kinds of deals. Investments, loans, all kinds of things. Marriages. He's big on marriages."

"Yeah, you said he'd been married four times?"

"Gemma is his fourth wife. They've been married three years, which is maybe about average for him."

"Is that how long he was married to your mother?" Her world was so different from his, but he found it fascinating.

"My mother is a slightly different case." She stopped talking while she chewed a bit of food. She kept her gaze on the pan, not meeting his eyes. "She was my father's mistress while he was married to his first wife, who was Bethany's mother. She kept pestering him to get a divorce, but then he didn't have to, because Eva died. Breast cancer. After that, he did marry my mother and we went to live with him. So he was with my mom more than three years, counting the time before they got married."

There was something going on here. She still wouldn't look at him while she told that story.

"How old were you then?"

"I was five. I wasn't really aware of much, but I can remember very clearly the looks the household staff gave us when we first moved in. Not just the staff, but everyone. His friends, his business partners, his country club buddies. Everyone except Bethany."

He licked sauce off his fork and tilted his head curiously. "Seems like Bethany would have the most reason to be upset."

"Yeah, she would. Her father cheated on her mother, then her mother died. Then Aimee shows up with a kid in tow, and suddenly she has a sister she never even knew about. And Aimee's lording it around the house as if she's the queen bee. Bethany had every right to hate me. But she didn't."

He couldn't stand it anymore, and reached for her chin to turn her face toward him. The expression in her eyes nearly broke his heart. He saw...shame.

"None of it was your fault," he said gently.

"Oh, I know. I mean, I've told myself that a thousand times. So has Bethany. So have various counselors and kindhearted people. It's one of those things that's just...there. In the background, like the sky being blue and snow being white. Gretel being wicked."

"The sky isn't always blue. Snow isn't always white. And I like when you're wicked."

Laughter brightened her pretty aqua eyes, chasing away the guilt. "That is a very good and very literal point. Trust an Alaskan guy to know about snow and sky."

He smiled and watched her take another bite from the dish. "I know why Bethany didn't hate you."

"I know why she didn't hate me, too. Because she's a generous, kind and loving person. Also because I used to follow her around like a pesky little puppy. I adored her. It's probably hard to hate someone who thinks you're the best thing since ice cream."

"Yeah, I bet that was part of it. But Gretel, don't you see how completely lovable and adorable you are?"

She laughed that off with a wave of her hand. "It's true, I am extremely charming. It took you long enough to notice."

"No, it didn't. And I'm not talking about charm. I'm talking about...heart. You care about people, which makes it easy for them to care about you."

The smile dropped from her face and she shook her head sadly. "See, that's the thing. I've led a very selfish life. I never had to pay my own way. I charged things on a credit card and never had to see the bill. I went wherever I wanted—or wherever someone invited me."

She pushed away from the counter and went to pour herself a glass of water. After a long sip, she went on.

"That's why I'm trying to do things differently now. I'm trying to help other people, like the Noonans. I never used to think I had anything useful to contribute. Just a pretty smile and decent fashion sense. A nice singing voice. Fun personality. Charm." She gave a jaunty shrug, but it didn't fool him. There was a lot of pain behind that gesture. "So basically what I'm saying is, expect me to be fairly useless if I move in."

Her wink didn't fool him either.

"Look, Gretel, I don't know what you were like before I met you. But you've been helping the Noonans ever since you got here. So maybe you should stop underestimating yourself. Except when it comes to hauling wood," he added, just to balance things out. "Not your specialty."

She giggled and nudged his leg with her knee. "I'm actually

getting pretty good at it, thanks to a certain amazing wood-working genius."

He lifted his eyebrows. "I just got promoted to genius. From grumpy pants. Not bad." But in that moment, he realized why people wanted to be around Gretel. It wasn't because of her fashion sense or her personality. It was because she made people feel good about themselves. That was why Bethany hadn't hated her. Gretel had probably appeared in her life like a drop of sunshine on a miserably sad and rainy day.

He knew it because he was feeling the same way right now. As if a sunbeam had taken human form and landed on his kitchen counter.

He cleared his throat. "Okay, then should we start on those deal points? Do I need to get a lawyer?"

A dazzle of turquoise as she swung her head to meet his eyes. "So this is it? We're decided?"

"Unless you want another round of 'are we compatible in bed,' yeah. We're decided. Depending on the negotiations, of course."

She interlaced her fingers and extended her arms, cracking her knuckles. "Then let the games begin."

They shifted to the big worktable in the other room. Shoving aside the homework Jason had forgotten and the Lego spaceship Petey had made, he placed a stack of notepaper and some sharpies in different colors on the middle of the table.

"I don't know much about prenups, is this the kind of thing we need?"

Gretel pulled up a chair across from him and sat crosslegged with her feet tucked under her. He'd noticed that she never just *sat* on a chair. She always found some creative way to inhabit it. She nodded approvingly at his supplies.

"Very professional. I'm sure this will work out perfectly. Okay, so let's start with the hard stuff. Money."

"I don't have any," he said promptly. "Well, until my parents' life insurance comes through. *If* it comes through. Until then, woodworking pays the bills."

"I have about three hundred and fifty-two dollars saved up from the Wicked Brew." The pride in her voice made him give a double take. "I know that doesn't sound like a lot, but it's the first money I've earned for myself and I'm pretty frickin' psyched about that."

"Okay. Deal point one. We each keep our own money. Neither of us takes any money from the other. I cover all the household bills just like I do now." He wrote down, "Separate Money," in big letters at the top of one of the sheets of paper.

She nodded, then tapped a finger on her chin. "What about other people's money?"

"What do you mean?"

"Well, the honeymoon fund is spoken for. It's all going to the butterflies. But my father could change his mind and decide to reactivate my credit cards. He doesn't usually stay mad for long."

He doodled with the sharpie as he thought it over. "I don't want his money, and I don't want anyone thinking that I'm in this for the dollars. I think we need to put that in the agreement. No Morrison moo-lah. If he gives you money, that's up to you."

"No." She shook her head. "It doesn't need to be in the agreement because I don't want his money either. I can't wait for the day when he says, Gretel, please, take this credit card, and I grab some scissors and cut it in half. I've actually had fantasies about that."

"Interesting fantasy life."

"You have no idea," she purred, giving him an incendiary look from under her lashes.

That led to a short period of intense making out that nearly led to sex on the worktable. But he couldn't quite bring himself to go that far with his brother's Lego spaceship standing guard.

So they pulled apart and got themselves under control, then continued.

"Let's just leave it that we keep our money separate," she said, still a little breathless.

"Two separate tiny piles." He wrestled back his arousal as he finished writing that deal point.

She raised a finger. "I do reserve the right to buy extra things for the house."

He frowned. "Like what extra things?"

"Like anything I think would improve things here."

Uh oh. That sounded like trouble. "Do I get a say in it?"

"Hmm. No prior approval, but you do have veto power." She made that sound very official and legalese.

"What does all that mean?"

"It means that I don't have to consult with you before I buy something for the house, but if you absolutely hate it, we can talk about that."

Sounded fair enough to him. "Are we talking about zebra rugs and purple bathroom paint or something? Like your wild outfits?"

"Possibly. Would that be a problem? Oh! That's something I need to add. My mother always kind of changed her look to suit her husband of the moment. I will not be changing my look." She emphasized the point by tapping the paper. "Write it down. Gretel's look shall not be interfered with."

Gravely, he wrote it down, word for word. Then he added, "Gretel is welcome to interfere with Zander's look."

She read it over his shoulder and burst out laughing. "Are you sure about that? Cause I was thinking you could really use a manicure, and—"

Quickly, he crossed off that entry. "I take it back."

"Big mistake, Ross. Big mistake. I could have you walking down a runway if you let me."

"Now you're just scaring me. I'll handle my own appearance.

Write it down. Use that neon orange Sharpie and add some exclamation points."

"What about your hair? Can I cut it?" She put her hands together in a pleading gesture. "Pretty please? Sugar on top?"

He pretended to deliberate. He liked the idea of her hands on his hair. And he'd had enough military style cuts to last a lifetime. It would be...interesting to see what Gretel came up with. "Sure. Unless you literally put sugar on top. That's where I draw the line."

"No sugar treatments." She tapped the page. "Write it down."

Item by item, they went through everything they could possibly think of that might pose a problem—big and little, serious and whimsical.

He committed to finishing the second bathroom that his parents had begun. She promised to ship her extra laptops and extensive collection of young adult novels from Connecticut for the boys—especially Petey, who loved to read. He agreed to ease up on the chore board. She informed him that she would continue to attend the AA meetings that meant so much to her. He promised to keep plenty of pistachios on hand. She offered to make smoothies in the mornings.

"What if we need our own space?" From her serious expression, he knew this issue was a big one for her. "We might get sick of each other."

Hard for him to imagine, but he knew that was a risk.

"We have a second-story loft that we don't use in the winter. I can open it up for you and haul some furniture up there. It already has a daybed and a bean bag chair, maybe a few other things." Truthfully, he hadn't been up there in a while. He considered it the boys' playroom, a place they didn't have to keep tidy.

But they rarely used it, so why not offer it to Gretel?

Her eyes lit up. "That sounds perfect. I'll have space for all my stitch-and-bitch projects. Can I decorate it however I want?"

"It's fine with me. But Gretel, the entire house will be yours. Including my," he hesitated, feeling awkward, "*the* bedroom. I don't want you to feel like a guest stuck up in the attic."

Looking touched, she set her hand over his. "That's really thoughtful, Zander. You really want to do this, don't you?"

Yeah. Damn, he really did. He turned his hand over and interlaced his fingers with hers. "Yup."

She leaned over the table and brushed her lips against his in a brief but stirring kiss. "Look, this situation is going to be unique. We have to make it work for *us*. Zander and Gretel. And all of our little flaws and eccentricities."

That made complete sense, when she put it that way. Lord knew he had his share of both. "Then let's put in a kind of catchall fail-safe."

"How do you mean?"

"There's no way we can predict all the things that are going to come up. When I first moved back home, I hadn't lived with my brothers since they were little. I didn't know what they liked or needed. I didn't know that Petey loved watching YouTube makeup tutorials or that Jason gets a rash every time he eats pickles."

"I've seen him eat pickles."

"Oh yeah, he eats them anyway, he doesn't care. The point is, there's probably a billion things I don't know about you, and you don't know about me. We can't plan for all of them, I don't have that much paper." Already, the stack of notepaper had diminished quite a bit. "So let's establish a kind of safe word."

Her eyelashes fluttered. "Oh my. This is going in a direction I didn't really expect."

"Not that kind. We can talk about that later, " he added in a sexy growl. "Right now, I'm talking about if something comes up that's not written down here, we say, "whipped cream" or something. And then we discuss whatever it is."

She tilted her head quizzically as she bounced a Sharpie off her thigh. "Why can't we just say, 'can I speak to you in private'? You've said it plenty of times already."

He gave a burst of laughter. "But that could mean anything. It could mean I just want to be alone with you."

"Hmm, is that what it meant all those other times?" The smile hovering on her delicious lips made his mouth water.

He shrugged. "I don't know. Maybe." He didn't want to think too deeply about that now. "I still think we need code words, like military operations."

"Oooh, secret code words!" She clapped her hands. "I love that idea. I mean, this whole marriage-with-an-asterisk is kind of a secret code word. So 'whipped cream' means...what again?"

"It doesn't have to be that. That just came to mind because..."

"Because?"

Because he'd love to lick it off her body. "I'll show you later."

She went a little pink. "That's sounds naughty. I like it. Let's go with it."

He drew in a steadying breath. These negotiations sure were hard. "I'm writing it down. 'Whipped cream' means there's something important we need to agree on about the household."

"Great. Okay, what else?"

"How about if there's something going on with one of the boys?"

"Yes. Very important. I nominate my favorite word, 'pistachio.' Rhymes with 'mustachio,' which is very masculine. Easy to remember."

Zander chuckled as he wrote it down in green Sharpie. He couldn't remember a conversation that had entertained him quite so much. "I like our ice cream sundae theme. Is it time for dessert yet? And when I say 'dessert' I really mean—"

She held up a hand to stop that line of thought. "Later. We have work to do. After this we have to print out the paperwork and round up some witnesses and a minister."

"Can the boys be witnesses?"

She glanced up and his heart twisted at her vulnerable expression. "You want the boys to be the witnesses? That makes it so ... real."

"It *is* real. Remember, we can't do it unless it's real. I'm taking this seriously, in case you hadn't noticed." He gathered her hands between his. She still held the Sharpie, but he ignored it. "Gretel Morrison, will you marry me? With an asterisk but still real?"

A wide smile spread across her face. "I think so. But have we put everything we can possibly think of into the prenup? What about a time frame? Like until Jason turns sixteen?"

"I don't want a time frame. All we have to do is say it's not working and we want out. I don't want you to feel stuck. If that brings down the wrath of Susan Baker, I don't care. We'll deal with that if it happens."

She bent over the paper and wrote, "Escape hatch."

"Is that the secret code word?"

"No, because what if we happen to be in a submarine at the time?"

He laughed. Had anyone ever had so much fun writing a prenup? "What then? Hot fudge? Butterscotch? Sprinkles?"

"Maybe we shouldn't use a code word because it would make ordering dessert a nightmare. Besides, we should only invoke the escape hatch if we're really serious about it and truly believe it's the best thing for us and especially for the boys."

"Damn, Gretel Morrison. So mature. Wanna get married?"

"Let's do it." She help up her hand for a high five. But just as he brought his palm against hers, she pulled it away at the last second, the way she'd done outside the Noonans' woodshed.

"I take back the 'mature' part," he grumbled. "What now?"

"We never decided on the right code word for sex."

"You want a code word for sex? We don't need one. All you have to do is look at me. That's really all it takes."

"Like this?" She gave him an exaggerated under-the-lashes glance loaded with sexual insinuation. A look like that could turn the oxygen in the air into straight fire.

"That works."

She rolled her eyes.

"That works too."

She burst out laughing. "Apparently it doesn't."

"What do you mean?"

Another glance from her dazzling eyes sent a bolt of heat straight to his dick. "I'm getting an eye ache from giving you these looks. And you're just sitting there like a lump."

"A lump, huh?" He stood and came around to the other side of the table. Taking her hand, he guided it to the lump in his pants. "That kind of lump?"

She fluttered her eyelashes and aimed another of her scorching looks at him.

This time he got the message. Loud and clear.

CHAPTER TWENTY-TWO

When Gretel printed out the paperwork, she also discovered that the boys couldn't be witnesses, because they weren't of legal age. Instead, they took a four-wheeler over to Zander's dog team buddy's house. He had an online minister's license and was happy to do the honors. Two of his friends who were there for what looked like a drinking weekend acted as witnesses.

Gretel and Zander filled out the paperwork and signed it. And that was it. They were married. With an asterisk.

As soon as it was official, they told the boys. They chose game night as the best moment for a Ross family announcement.

"Big news, guys," said Zander. "You guys know Gretel and I have been hanging out a lot. We decided to take the next step."

The boys looked at him blankly.

"We got married," Gretel elaborated. "Meet your new sister-in-law. Me."

"Yay," yelled Petey, scattering the Catan pieces every which way.

"Petey!" Jason grumbled. "Look what you did."

Petey was on his feet, performed a funny dance in which he punched the air and moved his legs like pistons.

Gretel busied herself with putting the game pieces back on the board as best she remembered them.

"You seem pretty happy about this," Zander said as he watched his youngest brother's wild gyrations.

"Gretel lets Eli have ice cream after school."

Gretel made a mental note to explain to Abby why sometimes kids needed extra ice cream.

"This doesn't mean you're going to get ice cream." Trust Zander to be the voice of reason. If ice cream sweetened the sister-in-law deal, why not?

"It won't?" Petey stopped dancing and glared at Gretel. "Why not?"

She put her hand up to block Zander's line of sight and gave Petey an exaggerated wink.

"I can see that, you know. What are you telling him?" Zander glowered at the two of them.

She dropped her hand. "Um, I was telling him that he really ought to try pistachio ice cream."

"Don't encourage him—Oh. *Oh.* Now?"

"Maybe in a few minutes."

"What are you guys talking about?" grumbled Jason. He always seemed to be in a bad mood lately.

"Married people stuff," Gretel told him lightly. "So Jason, are you okay with this?"

He shrugged in that morose thirteen-year-old way. "Makes no difference to me. It's not like you're my stepmother."

"That's true. But I do know how it feels to have to get used to a new person. When I was your age, I had to deal with my second stepfather. It didn't really go well because he wanted me to go to boarding school and I refused to wear a uniform."

"Fascinating. Can we finish the game now?"

Gretel bit her lip, trying to decide if the exuberance of Petey's welcome balanced out the hostility of Jason's. She couldn't tell if his attitude was personal to her or more general and aimed at the entire world.

"Jason," Zander said sharply. "Is there something you want to say?"

"Yes. If we're done with this game can I go do some deadlifts?"

Zander held his gaze. Reluctantly, Jason swung his head to meet Gretel's gaze. "Welcome to the family, Gretel. Don't know what you want with Z, though, he's a pain in the ass."

"*Jason.*"

Before Zander got too mad at his brother, Gretel intervened. "Aren't we all, Jason, aren't we all. Zander, I forgot to mention that I have no problem with salty language because that would be pretty hypocritical. You should have heard me when I was a pissed-off teenager being told I had to wear a navy blue neck tie and a black pleated skirt."

Slowly, Zander relaxed and jerked his head at Jason in a "go ahead" gesture. Jason ambled in the direction of the weight room, after a quick glance at Gretel. Was that appreciation in his eyes? Could she be so lucky?

"I'd really love some of that pistachio right about now," she told Zander.

They both glanced over at Petey, who'd flopped himself onto a beanbag chair and was playing a game on his iPad. "Petey, you good?"

He waved a hand at them, not even looking up from his game.

The two of them went into Zander's bedroom, passing the weight room, where the sound of thrash rock was bleeding from Jason's earbuds. As soon as the door was securely shut, Gretel confronted Zander.

"You never had stepparents, did you?"

"Nope."

"Well, I consider myself an expert. And I know I'm not their stepmother, but it's the same idea. Do *not* force them to act a certain way with me. We'll work out our own relationships, me and the boys. Darn it, we should have put this in the agreement."

That telltale muscle in his jaw was flexing. "I don't like Jason being rude to you."

"Honestly, I don't think it's about me. It didn't feel personal. I think it's something else."

"He's supposed to tell me if something's wrong." He sounded like a commander irritated by an unruly soldier.

"Maybe you should put that on the chore chart, Boss Ross."

"Cute. Maybe I should." He ran a hand through his hair, leaving it messy and sexy. "I wish he understood that you're doing this *for us*."

"Not entirely." She grinned at him. "The butterfly sanctuary was over the moon when I transferred the funds—with interest. It was amazing. And you should have heard my father on the phone when I told him. He actually offered me a brand new Tesla to call the whole thing off."

Shock rippled across Zander's face. "Fuck."

"Don't worry, I didn't take it."

"But do you want to?"

She stared at him for a long moment. She could see why he would ask that, but still, it hurt. "Haven't you paid attention to anything I've been saying? I don't want to depend on his money anymore. He uses it to control people and I'm done being a puppet."

He groaned. "I know. I know. Sorry. I just—I don't want to see you lose out on something because of me."

"Escape hatch, remember? If I want out, I'll say so." She took his hand in hers, feeling the strength in those long fingers. "So far, I think it's going pretty well. What do you think?"

He ran his thumb up her wrist, under her sleeve. Her pulse responded by speeding up.

"I thought there would be more ... whipped cream." His voice was a purr sliding along her nerve endings. "And not the code word kind."

"Hmm, well, I think we can fix that." She glanced at the door, through which either of the brothers could pop in at any moment. "Come here." She led him to the big walk-in closet, where his clothes hung on orderly hangers and hers were piled on a bureau until she could put them away.

He slid the door closed behind them, shutting out the light from the bedroom, except for a narrow band along the floor. She couldn't really see him anymore, but she could feel his presence, that strong, vital aura that was pure Zander Ross. Reaching for him, she bumped her face against his chest and felt his knee jab her thigh.

"Oops," she said, at the same time that he said, "Sorry."

"Don't move," he said. "And no one will get hurt."

"Ha ha." But she obliged and stayed still, while he fumbled his way around her body until his hands were firmly clamped around her shoulders. As always, something inside her relaxed under his touch. He turned her around so her back was towards him. Then he bent her over, nestling her upper body onto the pile of her clothes. The soft velvets and cashmeres of her sweaters and leggings embraced her in comfort and luxury. She sighed and wriggled as if preparing for a nap.

Except the heat rising inside her was not exactly compatible with a snooze.

As his hands shaped her ass, she felt her nipples go hard. Pressed against her velour hoodie, cushioned by cashmere, those sensitive peaks sent an electric current straight to her clit

He lightly swatted her ass and a rush of liquid gathered in her sex.

"What...why..."

"Just testing," he said. He drew her leggings down to expose her rear to the stifling air of the closet.

"Just *testing?*"

"Yeah." He swatted her again, this time touching bare skin. She reacted again, her nipples surging against the cloth below her. He followed that touch by caressing the tender skin, which tingled and pulsed.

"And?" she gasped. "Are you done testing?"

"Not quite." He slid his hand between her legs, found her clit and flicked his thumbnail against it. She moaned deeply into the pile of cashmere. Fondling the pulsing nub between his fingers, he worked that moan into a cry that wrenched from her throat.

Another finger came inside her, hooking deep to find a spot toward the front of her body, a spot that sent piercing pleasure through her system. She bucked as he stroked and caressed, squeezing her clit until she wanted to scream, until juice flowed across his fingers, until her inner thighs trembled with need, until her back arched and her ass pushed against him.

Then the finger inside left her, to be replaced with the thick length of his cock. As part of the marriage agreement, they'd both gotten tested. Without the need for that kind of protection, and with Gretel already on birth control, they'd chosen to do without condoms.

Great decision, she decided as her inner channel embraced his arousal. She was so wet and slippery that he slid inside easily, like a water slide. When he was fully seated inside her, he pressed a hand on her lower back and somehow that changed the angle in a way that sent hot fire exploding through her.

She let fly a string of babbling words, burying them in the pile of clothing, as he slowly fucked her from behind.

The darkness added to the experience, since all her other senses filled the gap. Zander's panting breath, the smell of mothballs and cashmere, the light swirl of air against her exposed skin. And most of all, the sensations igniting in her clit and deep in her core with every move he made.

He didn't draw it out this time. From the urgency of his strokes she knew that he couldn't. He was barely hanging onto his control, and every deep thrust put him closer to losing it.

She was right there with him on that edge, quivering like a ripe berry about to fall off the bush. She wanted to fall, needed to fall, but the orgasm was just out of reach. His magic fingers, that was what she needed, the way he stroked her clit, his body rough against hers, that friction...

And then everything went to pieces as she exploded into a wild orgasm that ripped through her body like a tornado. While she was still gripped by those blissful spasms, he gave a strangled cry and a jet of hot liquid pulsed into her. They vibrated as one, joined in the same circuit of electric pleasure.

He settled his body over hers, cradling her in warmth while she shuddered out the last remnants of the orgasm. They cuddled together with his cheek against hers, their breaths mingling. The stale air of the closet surrounded them with stillness.

"Gotta say, I never thought getting married would mean having sex in a closet," he mumbled.

She gave a shaky laugh. "Are you complaining?"

"Fuck no. That was fucking incredible."

"I've never heard you swear so much," she teased. "And you were giving Jason a hard time about that."

"Yeah, well, I try to keep that side of me in the closet."

"Ha ha."

He helped her up and they both fixed their clothing before they stepped out of the closet.

"I think I'm going to talk to Jason," she said as she headed for the bathroom.

"Good luck with that. Jason doesn't talk. If you really want to talk to someone, try Petey."

"But Petey's not the one I'm worried about. Thirteen is a terrible age. I just want Jason to know he has one more person in his corner."

At the door of the bathroom, she turned and realized he was right behind her. He'd unwittingly followed her across the room as they talked. She made an impudent face at him. "I need my privacy now, if you don't mind."

"Right. Of course." He stepped back, looking startled that he'd almost walked into the bathroom with her.

She got it. That feeling of connection between them was a powerful thing. Breaking it even for a moment made her feel...empty.

CHAPTER TWENTY-THREE

When Gretel had first formulated the marriage plan, she hadn't thought about how it would *feel*. She'd only thought about how it would *help*.

She definitely hadn't thought that it would mean much to her. Marriage was a state her mother flitted in and out of, like changing from day wear to evening wear. For her father, it was a way to present himself to the world, which was why his wives got younger and younger. Gemma was only about ten years older than Bethany.

But it turned out that being "married" to Zander was...fun, even with the asterisk. She loved knowing that she had an ally who she could turn to. Zander always took her seriously. He had to, after all. It was in the agreement. All she had to do was say "whipped cream," and he'd stop everything and they'd go off and have an argument. Sometimes she'd win, sometimes he would, but most of the time they worked out some kind of compromise that satisfied both of them. Or neither of them.

In which case they usually found that some time in bed helped them move on from the issue, whatever it was.

It turned out that married life was busy. The boys always needed something—rides, food, Band-Aids, something. And then there was the winter-in-Alaska factor. Everything took longer because of the weather conditions. Driving to town could take as long as an hour if they had to shovel out the Suburban, which meant they all had to get up earlier so they could have breakfast.

She got into a routine with Zander in which she fed Niko and made breakfast smoothies while he got the morning fire going and made lunch for the boys. He either drove the carpool and did errands in town, or he spent the day in his workshop. Sometimes he took his snowshoes and went searching for more antlers in the snow.

Danny D got sick of the winter weather and went home to Molokai, so Gretel picked up more shifts at the Wicked Brew. She'd gotten such a big response to her call for local acts to perform at the coffee shop that she changed her plans and turned the event into a talent show. Everyone loved that idea, so she made up flyers and posted them around town.

Local Talent Competition! Come cheer on your friends and neighbors at the Wicked Brew. Free coffee and Fifteen cent cookies! Winner gets free coffee for a month!

Zander helped her set up the sound system—honestly, the man had skills in so many different areas. When the night came, she was thrilled at the turnout. Ten acts had signed up. They ranged from singers to comics to a fire dancer and a spoken-word poet.

When the fire dancer performed, everyone trooped outside and stood in the snowy parking lot. She lit the tiny jets embedded in a hula hoop and spun fire until sparks flew through the dark winter air.

Everyone cheered and stomped their feet, though they might have just being trying to keep warm.

The musical acts were pretty good, mostly of the folk singer-songwriter variety. Toni from the Olde Salt brought her marimba, which filled the space with its resonant, rhythmic tones.

Harris Badger played a song on his fiddle, something so mournful it brought the audience close to tears. It evoked lonely nights at sea, cold wind across the ocean, lost love and pining for yesterday.

Maya, standing with Gretel near the coffee counter, clapped for him proudly. He gestured for her to get up and perform with him, but she refused.

"What do you play?" Gretel asked her, surprised. Maya had never mentioned a talent for music.

"I used to sing with him," she said. "But I'm the police chief now and that ain't happening."

"What? Why not? Are you worried it would destroy your intimidating reputation? Because it wouldn't. You're too intimidating for that."

"That's not exactly it." Maya sipped from her latte. At first Gretel thought she wasn't going to say anything more, but then she confessed, "I get bad stage fright. I've been known to freeze as soon as everyone looks at me. It's not fun."

"What about when you're on the job? Solving crimes and laying down the law?"

Maya shrugged. "It's all about the uniform. I put that on and I'm Officer Badger, not the introverted Maya who gets hives when performing."

"Chief Badger," Gretel reminded her.

"Right. Thanks."

"I like performing, but I know people who don't. I've heard the trick is to imagine the audience naked."

Maya looked at her with horror. "You think I want to see this crew naked? No, thank you. Well, a couple exceptions, maybe. Looks like you snagged one of those exceptions."

Gretel clicked her coffee mug against Maya's. "No argument

from me. But Zander's not the only hottie here. I see quite a few others."

"Yes, and you never know when I might have to arrest them."

They laughed and clicked their mugs together again.

"How do you feel about neurosurgeons?" Gretel asked. "My friend Ian Finnegan—"

"You mean the one with the crush on you? The one who limped back to Anchorage after you broke his heart?"

"That's a huge exaggeration."

"I heard he's got an obsessed patient after him. You want me to get in the middle of a man and his biggest fan?"

"Well, you do carry a weapon—"

"This talent show was a good idea," Maya interrupted as she surveyed the crowded cafe. Clearly she wasn't interested in Gretel's dating suggestions. "The winter can be long and lonely here. Anything that gets people together in a positive way has got to help. Oh no. What's Old Crow doing?"

The weathered old fisherman was making his way to the mic.

"He told me he's a storyteller."

"Oh, no doubt."

Old Crow launched into a local legend about a native tribe that had disappeared into a glacier in Lost Souls Wilderness. "Some say it's just a tall tale, but my mother saw them leave with her own eyes when she was a child. They prepared for years, the elders say. Their leader had a vision one night, that the only safe place for his people was a new place. One with a sky made of ice and rivers of crystal."

Gretel was so wrapped up in the story that she jumped when Bethany tapped her on the shoulder.

"Can I talk to you for a sec?" her sister whispered.

They stepped into the back corridor so they wouldn't disturb the rapt audience. One look at Bethany's face and Gretel's stomach dropped. She didn't look at all happy.

Gretel crossed her arms in a preemptive defensive gesture. "What's up?"

"You and Zander got married? Actually married? What is going on with you, Gretel? Daddy's freaking out. So is Aimee, which is freaking Daddy out even more."

"I don't know why they're worried about me getting married, when they've done it a total of seven times between the two of them."

"Okay, forget about them." Bethany's clear brown eyes were filled with concern. "You're my footloose, free-spirit little sister. I've never once heard you talk about wanting to get married."

"Well..." Gretel wetted her lips. No one's opinion mattered to her more than Bethany's. "People change."

"That much? That quickly? Are you okay?"

"Do I seem not-okay?"

Her sister scrutinized her with an extended doctor's-eye head-to-toe survey. "You seem okay," she admitted. "On the outside."

"The inside is fine too. I know it may seem crazy, but we have our reasons for getting married. It's what we both want, so you don't have to worry." She hesitated before plunging onwards. "Do you like Zander?"

She held her breath waiting for the answer. It shouldn't matter; Bethany barely knew Zander, after all. But she'd always looked up to her big sister.

"From what I've seen, sure. Nate says he's a great guy. This is about you, not him. Why do you want to tie yourself down? I don't get it. This isn't you. I mean, are you in love with Zander? Is that it?"

Good God. Her sister really knew how to cut to the quick. Was she in love with Zander? She honestly had no idea how to answer that question. And she couldn't lie to Bethany. "I'm not sure," she muttered.

"Isn't it the kind of thing you should know before you get married?"

The hint of criticism burned. "Hey! Who are you to talk? You and Nate faked a relationship before you got together! And I supported you. I always support you."

Bethany threw up her hands. "You did. But that was different. He was helping me out of a bind."

"Then it's the same."

"So you're trying to help Zander, is that it? Something about his brothers? Gretel, I know you have the kindest heart in the world, but that's going too far. You should be flitting off to Bali by now, or lying on a beach in Hawaii. Your mother—"

"Don't bring up my mother. I know the drill. She'll buy the tickets, she'll pay for everything, all I have to do is smile for the camera or for her rich friends or—" Gretel stumbled over the lump in her throat. "You think you know me, Bethany. But maybe you don't know everything."

Something flinched across Bethany's face, an expression of shock or regret or—Gretel couldn't really tell because her eyes were blurring.

"But I appreciate your concern," she finished. Turning away, she headed for the tiny bathroom.

"Gretel!" Bethany called after her. But she didn't stop, because she couldn't bear any more of that big-sister criticism.

SHE TOLD Zander about that conversation while they were curled up in his bed. The rising wind keened and beat against the windows, but in the cocoon of the bed, Gretel felt safe and warm and astonishingly content.

"I don't blame your family for being worried," he told her. "My parents would be too."

"I understand that. I do. It's just...I wish my own sister could have a little more faith in me. I did think about this. We're not just reckless crazy kids." She turned onto her side and lifted herself up on one elbow. "Are we?"

"I don't know. I don't think so. Would reckless crazy kids have a multi-point agreement written in Sharpie?"

That got her laughing. "Probably not."

"Is there something I can do to help? Want me to talk to your mom?"

"No. She'll just get hysterical on you and you won't know how to handle it. You're such a guy's guy. You'd crumble in a hot second."

He reached over and tugged her on top of him, then adjusted the blankets snugly around her. "I can handle her. I'll grow my beard out and wear an old blood-stained hunting jacket and forget to shower for a month. I'll bring her a hunk of raw venison. Either she'll love me or she'll run away screaming."

Gretel giggled against the warm skin of his chest. "I would honestly pay you good money if you would do that. The expression on her face would be worth every penny."

"That's a whole other negotiation. Right now I'm focused on this one." He cupped her ass and slid her up and down his hardening shaft.

"I'm open to that negotiation. What are your terms?"

"How about two orgasms for you?"

"In exchange for what?"

"An orgasm for me?"

She snickered as she moved her hips in sync with his hands. "You're not really up on the whole negotiation thing, are you?"

"I have my own techniques. I figure if I give you everything you want, you'll give me everything I want. It's been working so far."

"So true." She shifted her position, dragging her sex across his erection, then settling its swollen tip at her entrance. "Know what I want right now?"

"I can guess."

He guessed right. So very right.

CHAPTER TWENTY-FOUR

It didn't take Gretel long to see that Jason wasn't going to tell Zander if something was wrong. But she'd managed to get some smiles and laughs out of the boy, so she set her sights on the next stage—getting him to open up.

She figured the best approach was to join him in his natural habitat—the snow. She asked him to show her his ski run workout. As soon as they were gliding down the trail, Jason turned into a different person. All of his snarkiness vanished and he turned into a confident, joyful kid.

They skied for a while in comfortable silence broken only by Jason pointing out a flock of chickadees chittering on a spruce tree, or Gretel asking where he got his skis. He went on a long rant about how hard it was to get good equipment in Lost Harbor, and how frustrating it was that at thirteen he wasn't allowed to work as a deckhand yet, so he'd done yardwork all last summer to earn enough for a new pair of skis.

"What about when you're on the ski team? Can they hook you up with the quality gear?"

"Sort of. It's really more Coach Stern who gets the good deals."

She caught a note of hero worship in that wistful statement. It was enough to get her curious. Zander had told her about his theory that Stern and Sterner were the "other options" mentioned by Susan Baker. But nothing further had developed, so maybe their marriage-with-an-asterisk had done the trick.

"It must be great having such incredible ski coaches. Are you excited for next year?"

Jason herringboned up a short hill, then waited for her at the top. She wasn't nearly as good on her skis, and slid back a few times until she finally managed to crest the hill. He wasn't even breathing hard, but instead of mocking her he gave her a sweet smile. "I'm used to this hill."

In that moment, she saw the true Jason, the sweet boy trying to balance puberty, grief, and everything else in a teenage boy's life.

Maybe she should just plunge right in.

"Jason, is everything okay with you and Zander? You know Zander, he just won't talk about it. He's...old-school, you know. Are you angry with him?"

"No! I mean...maybe. No."

Okay, that was clear as mud. "Is it because of me?"

"No! You're...nice. Arrgh." He jabbed his ski pole into a snow bank with a growl—reminding her of the grumpy side of his older brother. "It's nothing."

Ah-ha. So there was something.

They skied around a fallen log slumbering under the snow. "Well, it's not nothing, but I understand if you don't want to tell me."

He held onto a tense silence as they skied along the trail. She could practically feel the emotion wanting to burst out of him.

"A lot of people don't know this, but I'm incredibly good at keeping secrets. If there's something you want to get off your chest, I promise I will never tell anyone."

"It's not a big deal," he muttered. "I just—I want to ski. That's all. And Zander ..."

She ducked under an overhanging branch. "Zander doesn't have a problem with you skiing, does he?"

"No."

She waited. *Just be patient. He wants to talk.*

"Zander wouldn't understand. He'd be...hurt."

"Hurt? Because you want to ski?" None of this was making sense. "Maybe you should give him a chance. Tell him how important it is to you."

"There's no point!" he burst out. "He thinks I'm just a kid. Just a little brother on his chore chart."

"Oh Jason, I really don't think—"

"All he wants is the Ross family to stick together. That's all that matters to him. And he left the Marines to take care of us and—"

"Oh my God." Gretel stopped in her tracks and clapped a hand over her mouth, her ski pole dangling to one side. The pieces all clicked into place like a gear shift in motion. "It was *you*."

"What?" Jason slid to a stop and angled his skis around to face her. "What do you mean, it was me?"

She stepped her skis closer to him and fixed him with a dead-serious look. "Jason, answer me honestly. Do you want to go live with Coach Stern and Sterner?"

He shot her an agonized glance. "How do you know about that? Does Zander know?"

"He suspects. But he talked to them and they didn't say—"

He shook his head. "That's the thing. It was my idea, not theirs. I thought it would help my skiing. But they said I'd have to get Zander's permission and I know he'll say no. He's all about "the Ross brothers." But it's not like I want to leave the family or anything. I just want to be closer to school and get all the training I can and—"

Sympathetically, Gretel reached for his arm and squeezed it. "It's okay. Really."

"No, it isn't, I know he'll be upset and think I'm breaking up the Ross brothers platoon or whatever. He'll take it personally. I already told Coach Stern to forget about it. I just wish *I* could forget about it," he ended in a wistful grumble.

Gretel wanted more than anything to give the poor boy a hug. But he'd probably feel awkward about that, so she spared him. "Listen, Zander is a grownup. He can handle it."

"But he sacrificed everything to come and take care of us. I can't just leave." He knocked his ski pole against a branch, bringing down a shower of brilliant snow crystals.

"So...you think he can handle boot camp and deployment and everything else involved in the military, but he can't handle his brother wanting to chase his destiny?"

Jason twisted up his face. "I don't know about all that destiny shi—stuff."

She snorted. "And you think I can't handle the word 'shit'? Dude. What if I talk to Zander? Or we talk to him together? Would that help?"

He lifted his eyes to hers, revealing a glimmer of hope. "You would do that?"

"Of course. The coaches said you have to get Zander's permission, right? That means you're going to have to talk to him. But I can pave the way. I can try, anyway."

"He'd listen to you." Jason looked a lot happier all of a sudden. "He's different with you. He smiles more. And he's lightened up on the chore chart."

"Yeah, that chart..." She made a face, and they laughed

together. Relief radiated from his young face, all bony cheek-bones and a trace of acne.

What was the best way to handle this? Jason was right; Zander would be hurt. Maybe it would be better if she broke the news, not Jason. He could swear freely that way.

"I'll talk to him first," she offered. "And we'll go from there."

"You think he'll listen?" He reoriented his skis to continue down the trail.

She followed after him. "It might take a lot of pistachios, but I think so."

He frowned over his shoulder at her. "Did you say pistachios?"

"Long story."

"IT WAS HIS *IDEA*? THAT LITTLE—" Zander wheeled away from Gretel and snapped his mouth shut before he said something he really regretted. "Sneak."

"No. Zander. You can't think of it like that."

Gretel had knocked on the door of his workshop and sat herself on one of the handcrafted bar stools he was restoring. He'd been happy to see her brighten his workspace with her sparkly silver dress and argyle leg warmers.

Until she'd dropped her bombshell.

"How am I supposed to think of it? He's thirteen and he wants to go live with strangers."

"He wants to ski. It's not about *you*. It's about him. I think…" She paused, causing him to turn around and cock his head at her.

"Go on. Might as well spit it all out."

"I'm just guessing here, but I think he feels normal when he's skiing. Like his life wasn't ripped apart by a boating accident. He completely transformed while we were out in the woods. He was happy, confident, grounded. That kid loves to ski. He's passionate about it."

"I know that, which is why I spend half my paychecks on ski boots and poles and—"

"Zander." Calm and firm, her voice caught him off guard. This wasn't the lighthearted Gretel, or the sensual Gretel or the magnet-for-a-snowbank Gretel; this was the wise Gretel, the one who had seen all kinds of misbehavior in her lifetime. "This. Isn't. About. You. He loves you and he's terrified of hurting your feelings."

Those words shot through him like a bolt of lightning. Jason, terrified? Of hurting him? "Go on," he managed.

"He doesn't want to leave the family. You are still his family. But he wants to give himself every chance to be a ski superstar. He's really serious. Like, a lot more serious than you think."

Zander made himself look back over the past couple of years. All the hours Jason had spent in the weight room. The lawns he'd mowed for extra money. The way he'd light up as soon as he fastened his bindings.

"Fuck," he said finally. "I fucked up."

"Oh Zander, no."

"Yes." He'd let his ego get in the way of Jason's future. Big fucking fuckup.

She was shaking her head, wanting to protest some more, but he stopped her with a gesture.

"Here's the thing. When I came back here, I was all about 'protecting the family.' Like a Marine would. Armed and ready. Then it turned out that wasn't what the boys needed. They needed someone to do the laundry and remind them about their homework. Just everyday stuff. So I got that part down. But there's a part I missed." He tapped his chest in the region of his heart. "I wasn't paying enough attention."

Gretel impulsively threw her arms around him. "Well, join

the club because I screwed up too," she said. "This whole "marriage" was to stop Jason from leaving. I feel like an idiot."

"No." He brushed her hair away from her face. "You're the one helping to fix it. Jason actually *talked* to you. You don't know how huge that is."

He could see in her eyes that she was still upset. He couldn't have that, not when she'd just shone a giant spotlight on what was going on with his brother.

"Do I have to haul you into the bedroom and show you how glad I am that you're here?"

Finally, that Gretel spark reappeared. "Bedroom? Who needs a bedroom when there's a perfectly good space right here?"

"You mean a space filled with power tools and dangerous chemicals?"

"Baby, you're the only power tool I need," she purred.

"And you're more dangerous than any chemical in this room."

He snuck his hand under her dress and stroked her through her underwear. Her breath hitched. "You know, we can't just solve every problem by having sex."

"Of course not." He found his way under her panties and into the sweet silky nest of her curls. Juicy heat met his fingers and within seconds they were slick with her arousal. "But there's no harm in trying. Come on, spread those legs apart. A little more. Oh yeah." Now he could fit his whole hand against her sex, which meant he could rub against her clit with his wrist while he sent a finger deep inside.

Before long—before he'd had nearly enough—she was shuddering against him, her climax sending a rush of heat over his fingers.

And that would have been enough—he loved feeling her come apart—but she unzipped his pants and wrapped her arms around his neck and hoisted herself up. Stumbling across the workshop, he found his way to the one piece of wall that didn't have any shelves or half-repaired furniture. He pinned her against it and speared her with his swollen cock until they both erupted into an intense orgasm.

They were getting spoiled with those orgasms. But he wasn't complaining.

CHAPTER TWENTY-FIVE

The conversation with Jason was difficult, but it would have been a lot worse without Gretel. She let them do most of the talking, but when things got heated, she found a way to bring them back to earth.

"So you're a hundred percent sure this is what you want?" Zander finally asked, once he'd gotten the bitter taste out of his mouth.

"I want to try it." Jason fiddled with the Alyeska lift pass he refused to remove from his jacket. "If I get too homesick I can always come back. Right?"

"Jesus, of course you can. This is your house just as much as mine." How could his brother even doubt that? Maybe he'd been too much of the hardass platoon leader and not enough of the empowering older brother.

"Do you think Petey will be okay without me?" Jason shoved back his tumble of black curls.

"I don't know. Once he finds out he has to do all of your chores on top of his, he might be a little pissed. I'm kidding,"

Zander added quickly. "Actually I was thinking of ditching the chore chart."

"What? Now that I'm leaving? That's some bullshit."

Zander hid his wince. Hearing Jason say it like that, like it was a done deal—he had to admit, that hurt. For three years, his singular goal had been to keep the Ross family together. This felt like such a failure.

But it's what Jason wants, he kept telling himself. *Support him. Don't hold him back.*

Gretel cleared her throat. "I actually had an idea about Petey."

He cocked his head at her. You never knew what kind of ideas Gretel would come up with. If it wasn't getting married out of the blue or holding a talent show at the Wicked Brew, it was painting a mural in the attic or teaching Petey how to dip candles. She was full of ideas from off-the-wall to stroke-of-genius.

"I'm almost afraid to ask," he murmured.

She planted her hands on her hips and looked at Jason for help. "Now is that fair?"

"Definitely," his brother agreed with a grin.

"No gratitude, no loyalty," she grumbled. "My idea—though you don't even really deserve to hear it with this kind of attitude —is to accept one of my mother's vacation offers. Jason, you don't know this but she's constantly trying to lure me away with airplane tickets to exotic locations. But they're all tropical so you wouldn't be interested. No snow. Although I suppose you could jet-ski—"

"Don't tempt him," Zander warned. "He has to keep his grades up if he wants to ski."

"Good point. Close your ears, Jason."

Jason grinned and did nothing of the sort. Now that this conversation had happened, a load seemed to be gone from his shoulders. Maybe he'd do the dishes without complaining now—for the short time that he was still around.

"Go on about the tropical locations, Gretel," Zander urged. "You're welcome to take a vacation, so long as you know that means you lose the winter challenge. I better have a front row seat at your performance."

She stuck out her tongue at him. "Oh no. A break is not the same thing as leaving. Besides, you'd come on vacation with me! And so would Petey."

He blinked at her. He hadn't expected that. "But—I can't—I haven't—"

"Yes, I know, you haven't left Lost Harbor since you came back. But think about it. Petey is going to be sad with Jason gone. This will cheer him up and make him feel special too. Jason has all this ski stuff to look forward to, and now Petey will have something too. We'll get a little change of scene, almost like a honeymoon-with-an-asterisk." She gave him a quick wink, just for him. "My mother will get her wish for a mother-daughter vacation."

"Uh...with an asterisk."

"The best kind of asterisk. A man!" She threw her arms around him, and Jason rolled his eyes. "Please say yes. We can go just for a long weekend so Petey doesn't miss too much school."

"Do you know how long it takes to fly anywhere from here? It doesn't make sense to go for such a short time. We'd spend the whole time in the air."

"Okay, a week. We'll talk to Petey's teachers and bring his homework with us. I know the drill. My mother used to take me out of school whenever she wanted to go anywhere."

That didn't surprise him. He'd noticed a few gaps in Gretel's education—like the entire math part.

"But what about everything else, my work, I'm behind on those bar stools, and Mrs. Holt wants me to come sort through her collection of antiques and—" At Gretel's glance, he caught himself. Jesus Christ, he was only twenty-seven and he sounded like an old man. Why was he throwing out objections to a tropical vacation? "I'll figure it out."

There was no reason he couldn't go on a quick honeymoon-with-an-asterisk with his new wife-with-an-asterisk. Except that he'd gotten so used to duty and responsibility that he wasn't sure he knew how to let loose on vacation anymore.

"I thought of something else," he told Gretel when they were alone that night. She sat on the edge of his bed pulling off her leg warmers. "I thought you didn't want to take funds from your parents anymore?"

"From my *father*. He's the one who cut me off."

"So it's okay to take money from your mother?"

"I'm not taking money from her. I'm allowing her to give us a wedding present." With an impish wink, she snatched up her phone and waved it at him. "She'll be super-excited. I'm just waiting for your enthusiastic consent."

"I'll show you enthusiastic consent." And he jumped on the bed and tumbled her over onto her back.

Her phone went flying and all his reservations right along with it. If he wanted to be with Gretel, he couldn't refuse to leave Alaska. If he wanted to be with Gretel, he had to go with the fun-loving flow.

Did he want to be with Gretel?

More and more, he couldn't imagine life without her.

THE NEXT DAY, Zander met with Coach Stern and Sterner at their home.

They showed him around the spacious house, with its five

upstairs bedrooms and three bathrooms. The entire basement area fitted out as a training room. The Ross weight room could have fit in one corner of the space.

"Pretty nice setup. So would Jason eat with you guys too?"

"Of course. We usually have a full dinner table, what with ski team members and players we're fostering."

"He's...allergic to pineapple." His throat closed up as he said it. Taking care of Jason involved so many little details like that. He hadn't thought that he would miss that sort of thing. But he did.

"We know," Sandy Stern told him gently. "It's in his medical information, from his signup. Zander, please understand that he's not leaving your family. You still need to be involved, every step of the way. For one thing..." She hesitated, glancing at her husband, who nodded. "We can provide room and board, but his expenses are going to grow the further along he gets in his ski training. I'm afraid that will be a little out of reach for us."

"I understand. No problem. I got it."

He had no idea *how*, but he would. The hell if he'd let Jason down.

"We can work together on finding a sponsor, but he'll need to win a few races first. And he'll need you for moral support and cheering section and all of that. We always encourage as much family involvement as possible. That's why we insisted that he get your permission before we so much as breathed a word about this."

He found himself frowning. "So why did—" Abruptly, he stopped. Maybe they didn't know that Childrens Services had gotten involved. If so, he had no intention of telling them. He liked them just fine. He knew they'd take excellent care of Jason. But they had that upscale, never-struggled look that meant he couldn't relate to them.

So how had Susan Baker gotten wind of this? He might never know, and it didn't matter. He called her himself as soon as he and the Sterns had come to an agreement.

"Hi, it's Zander Ross. You said to call you if anything changed. Something has. Jason is going to move in with his ski coaches, Doug and Sandy Stern, while he pursues his Olympic dreams."

"I'll note that in the file. I'll be keeping an eye on them, of course."

"Good. So will I."

"Then we find ourselves on the same side."

He gritted his teeth. "Lady, I am always on the side of what's best for my brothers. If Jason doesn't like living with the Sterns, he can come back. If he loves it there, I guess I'll just be cheering him on. I'm not some kind of...prison warden."

Despite what his brothers occasionally claimed.

"Well, fine. Neither am I."

"Okay. So are we good?"

"We're good enough. Carry on. You're doing a better job than many, so there's that."

Man. She sure was hard to please.

Jason moved his things over to the Sterns' house a week later. It hurt to see him go, even though Jason kept saying that he'd be back for the weekend, and back for their traditional Easter snowball fight, and back whenever they wanted to go sledding.

Petey and Zander helped him load a few duffel bags' worth of ski gear and clothing into the truck, while Gretel holed herself up in the attic loft, where she was working on a top-secret surprise for Jason. Not even Zander knew what it was. But he was curious, as they all were, even Jason who was playing it cool.

Finally she came racing out of the house in her bare feet, carrying a full garbage bag in her arms. As soon as her feet touched the snow, she yelped and hopped back inside. The Ross brothers exchanged amused glances. A moment later she marched back outside in unlaced, clunky snow boots.

Under his breath, Zander said to Jason, "You're sure you want to miss all this free entertainment?"

"Actually, it's a lot harder to leave now that Gretel's here. Except that now I don't have to worry about you."

Zander's eyebrows climbed up his forehead, but he didn't have a chance to follow up on that "worry" comment because Gretel had made it across the yard to the truck.

"Ta da!" With a flourish, she handed the garbage bag to Jason.

"I'm pretty sure the Sterns have their own garbage." Jason took the bag gingerly.

"Ha ha. It was the only bag I could find on short notice. Open it!"

He found the opening of the bag and peered inside. Slowly he pulled out something warm and fluffy and—

"Mom's quilt," Jason said in wonder. "The one Niko tore apart when he was a puppy."

"First and only quilt she ever made." Zander frowned at Gretel. "Where did you find it? I figured it was in a rag bag somewhere."

"I found it in the loft, inside a trunk. I saw Jason's name on it." She showed them a corner of the quilt, where the name Jason was written in faded orange ink. "I've been taking it to stitch-and-bitch so they could help me fix it up." She pointed to a few inset pieces of fabric that served as patches. It was easy to tell which fabric had come from Gretel; the patchwork pieces were filled with vivid color and patterns—wolves and snowmen and skiers.

Jason had gone silent as he stared at the quilt.

Uh oh—was he upset that Gretel had reworked something

Mom had made? Zander shot Gretel a worried glance, but she was still watching Jason.

"I grew up living between houses," she told him softly. "I never had just one place. So I always brought stuff with me that felt like home. I had a Lion King blanket that ought to be a dish rag by now. Anyway, I thought you might like something like that, but if you want to just leave it here, that's fine."

"No. I like it." Jason lifted his head and met her eyes. "It's cool."

"Wonderful." Her radiant smile could have melted all the snow in a ten-foot radius. "Just don't look too closely at the stitching."

She opened her arms to give Jason a hug and amazingly, his prickly little brother allowed it. Not just allowed it, but let it continue.

"For a proper hug, you have to count to three," Gretel said as she pulled away. "It's science. Actually, it's not, but I've found it to be true. See you soon, Jason! Come by the Wicked Brew anytime. Skiers drink for free. Actually they don't, but it'll be on me." She beamed at him and stepped back.

Jason stuffed the quilt back into the garbage bag and stowed it carefully in the truck next to Petey, who squawked in protest until he realized he could snuggle up against it.

After everyone had loaded in, Zander backed down the driveway. Jason and Petey were already squabbling over the way Petey's knees were poking into Jason's back. Maybe they had to squeeze in one last fight before Jason left.

Zander tuned them out and kept his focus on Gretel, who stayed behind because there wasn't enough room in the truck. She was waving and hopping up and down and making skiing motions and God knew what else.

And all he could think was how much harder this would be if he didn't have Gretel to come home to.

Was this marriage-with-an-asterisk getting out of hand? Was there a way he could set some boundaries for himself? An emotional red line that he refused to cross? Was something like that even possible when it came to Gretel Zsa Zsa Whitney Morrison?

CHAPTER TWENTY-SIX

Most honeymoons probably didn't include a mother and a little brother, but somehow it worked out better than they could have imagined.

Aimee had been dragging Petey to every tourist activity she could find. Petey didn't seem to mind, and it worked out great for Zander and Gretel. They'd spent most of that time naked in bed.

Aimee and Petey would come back with t-shirts and sunburns and photos and Zander and Gretel would pretend they'd been at the beach.

Finally they'd decided they'd better *actually* go to the beach sometime before their flight home.

"It's hot out here," Gretel grumbled to Zander as they set up an umbrella on the beach outside the Waikiki resort where they were staying. The ocean sent soft rippling waves toward them—nothing like the crashers in Lost Harbor. The surfers were doing their thing at the other end of the beach, which was less protected. But they'd decided to stay close to the hotel in case...

Well, in case they thought of something better to do than sunbathe.

Which kept happening on a regular basis.

"Suck it up, buttercup. If we don't get some sun your mom is going to get suspicious." Zander piled sand around the base of the umbrella so it would stay upright. He was intent on making sure it was the most properly set-up umbrella on the entire beach—such a Zander thing to do. The way his muscles flexed in his bare arms while he worked on it took away a lot of her annoyance.

"I guess it's worth it to see you in your board shorts."

He scorched her with a glance up and down her bikini-clad body. "Same, girl. Same." He tested the umbrella pole and found it sturdy enough.

Before they'd gotten on the plane, Gretel had fretted that traveling together might burst their bubble. Not everyone traveled well together, after all. But so far, so good. More than good.

"It's weird to see my mother with Petey." Gretel brushed sand off the seat of her lounge chair and draped a towel over it. "I can't tell you how many times she took me somewhere, then started flirting with some dude and I'd just wander off and entertain myself. I hope she doesn't do that with Petey."

"I gave him my cell phone. He'll call us if there's trouble." He stretched out on a short chaise lounge, legs braced apart, feet buried in the sand, and adjusted his sunglasses on his face. Gretel drank in the long lines of his body and the smooth curves of his muscles.

"You're so relaxed. This is so unlike you."

"We're on vacation," he answered drowsily. "Aren't you supposed to relax on vacation?"

"Theoretically, yes. But my mother is here. And I...don't feel relaxed." With a grumble, she lay on her towel and propped her feet up on the chaise. She'd spent an entire cruise through the Greek islands in basically this position. Why hadn't she felt restless then? "I'm worried about the Wicked Brew."

"What about it?"

"I think Danny's going to sell it. He might even have a buyer already, and I'm afraid whoever takes over won't care about the locals. They'll turn it into a tourist trap."

"I didn't know you cared so much about that place."

"Well, I didn't know either. I guess I've gotten kind of attached to it. Did I tell you about Storyteller Sunday? I got inspired by Old Crow and all his tall tales about the disappearing glacier tribe. So I told him to spread the word among his friends and now we're going to make it a regular thing. I was even thinking that I should record some of these stories and put them on YouTube. Oh! And more people have been calling about performing on open mic night. Someone even called from Anchorage because he'd heard the Wicked Brew is a good place to try out new material. When people call they ask for me, not Danny, because he doesn't care about any of this stuff. What if he sells the business to someone who wants to tear it down? I wouldn't be surprised because it's kind of a wreck. The door to the bathroom doesn't close right and—"

A soft sound interrupted her—almost like a snore.

She nudged him with her toe and he didn't respond. Well, at least someone was able to relax. Pretty funny that it was Zander and not her.

He was supposed to be the hardworking, serious one. So why had she been antsy to get back to Lost Harbor ever since they'd arrived? Except for the hours and hours she and Zander had spent in bed. That was the only time she'd been able to fully enjoy herself.

Right now, her stitch-and-bitch group was gathering at Harris Badger's house—she hated missing that because he was going to make his special BBQ shrimp. Tomorrow was the AA meeting at the church. Those meetings kept her grounded, even though she never said much herself. A group of marimba players was set to perform at the Wicked Brew and no one had even posted it on the Facebook page.

And then there was Eli's birthday. She'd promised to bring him a present from Hawaii, but that didn't quite make up for missing his big day. And of course she wanted to know how Jason was doing at the Sterns' house. What if texts weren't coming through here on this dot in the middle of the ocean?

Maybe they should just go back to Alaska and their normal life. They could take a vacation sometime when there was less going on.

My God. What was happening to her? This was so unlike her.

A spray of cold water splashed onto her legs and she sat up with a start. Petey stood next to her chaise lounge, his sunburned face alight with mischief.

"Look what I did." He showed off his fingernails, which were painted hot pink. Aimee, in sunglasses and a sarong, came sauntering after him.

"Well, look at that. You finally got your nail polish. How does it feel?"

"Weird. I don't really like it."

"Now you know."

Aimee reached them, tall and stunning, with the diva attitude of someone who'd always made her way in life by her looks and wits. She tilted up her sunglasses and surveyed the snoring Zander. Her eyes, so much like Gretel's, glimmered against the carefully tended tan of her face. "You wore him out, I suppose."

Gretel shaded her eyes and looked up at her mother. "He's relaxing. Leave him alone."

"Don't be so touchy. Honestly. It's a good thing Petey is along so I don't get glared at all day long."

Petey missed that comment, since he was already hurtling at top speed toward the water.

"I'm not glaring at you. I'm squinting into the sun. Must you take everything so personally?"

Aimee deftly changed the subject, as she always did when she was coming out on the losing end. "I quite like Petey. It's almost like having a grandson without that unpleasant "grand" part."

"Technically, is there a name for your relationship? He's the brother of your son-in-law. Your nephew-in-law?"

"Technically, he's not even that. I don't yet acknowledge this marriage, Gretel. The least you could do is give me a wedding with guests and champagne. Instead you snuck it in like a thief in the night."

"Well, you can argue with the State of Alaska about it. According to them, we're married. Officially certified and everything."

Aimee pushed out her lips in a pout. They looked puffier than the last time Gretel had seen her. More collagen? "Who cares about that? Just tell me you have a prenup and that it favors you." Gracefully, she lowered herself onto the straw mat and took a tube of sunscreen from her tote bag.

"You'll be happy to know that we put quite a bit of time into our prenup. It was really fun, actually. We learned a lot about each other. Also, it's in colored Sharpies, so it's awesome."

Aimee went pale under her sunglasses. "You really should have sent it to me. I know all the ins and outs of a solid prenup."

Gretel stretched her arms over her head and rested them on the back of her chaise. This might be the first conversation with her mother in which she didn't feel at a disadvantage. There was literally nothing Aimee could pull that would change anything about Gretel's newly married state. Not financially, not logistically, not emotionally.

"I can send it to you. As long as the dog hasn't eaten it while we've been gone."

Another shudder from Aimee. "Darling, I'm really quite worried about this situation." She lowered her voice. "Not that he isn't handsome. I certainly see the appeal. He has a kind of rugged, smoldering sex appeal—"

"Okay, you can stop now. You're making me very uncomfortable."

Aimee carried on as if Gretel hadn't spoken. "But why couldn't you just go to bed with him? No need to take it this far. My only comfort is that it's clearly just so you could claim your honeymoon fund."

Gretel shrugged, unbothered. Her mother narrowed her eyes at her.

"Maybe it's more. You probably feel sorry for him. That must be it! Parents dead in a tragic accident, left alone to raise his two brothers in some frozen monstrosity of a town. You always were such a bleeding heart, wanting to adopt every stray that came along. Remember that one-legged puppy you brought home?"

"He had three legs! One eye."

Aimee waved that off with an elegant flourish. "He tugged at those heartstrings of yours. I wouldn't be at all surprised if they're getting another workout right now. Cue the sad violins and the wounded hero and the—"

"Mom! Stop it." Gretel cast an agonized glance at Zander, making sure he was still asleep, before she continued in a fierce whisper. "I don't feel sorry for him. I admire him. I respect him. Did you ever think that maybe I have real feelings for him?"

"Like...love?" Aimee said the word as if the feel of it on her tongue was unfamiliar. "If so, big mistake, darling. Love can really cloud your judgment. It would certainly explain a lot. But do you honestly intend to stay in that tiny dump of a town for the rest of your life? That's a complete fantasy. And he can't leave, can he, not for years? You're going to waste away at the ends of the earth—"

"Mom! Stop freaking out on me." Had she really thought that she was now immune from her mother's opinions? How wrong she was. "I beg you."

"How can I help it now that I know what we're dealing with here? Love. Good lord."

"I didn't say that!" Gretel thought about diving headfirst into the sand, but that wouldn't help anything. She needed to throw her mother off the scent. She needed a shiny object. A squirrel.

"You don't need to, I see it plastered all over your face." Aimee twirled a finger in Gretel's direction. "This is so much more alarming than—"

"A wedding!"

"Excuse me?"

"You said you wanted a wedding with guests and so forth. Maybe we should talk about that. Like, what do you have in mind, a destination wedding? Or maybe Daddy's place? The Plaza Hotel? Who do you want to invite? Any celebrities? Your entire contact list or just the creme de le creme?"

Pure desperation, that's what this was. But it worked.

"The Plaza ... I hadn't thought about that. I always dreamed of having a wedding there, but none of my husbands wanted a society wedding. Oh! Did you know that Cornelia Van Der Horsen threw a wedding for her daughter in Thailand? She built custom cabanas for all the guests and draped them with the most fabulous sari fabric, the entire event was to absolutely to die for."

Gretel was so relieved that her distraction had worked that she threw herself into her mother's insane fantasy. "Okay, well, I think cabanas in Thailand sounds perfect, because Zander could do all the construction himself and—"

"Sure, make me swing a hammer at my own wedding," came Zander's sleepy voice. He rose up on his elbows and smiled at the two of them. "Swear to God, you go to sleep for a minute and wake up with a new construction project."

Gretel tried to mouth to him that none of this was real, but the message was too complicated to convey that way. He ignored her and kept his shades trained on her mother.

Aimee was smiling at him with the most favorable expression she'd shown yet. "I have the perfect designer in mind for your tux."

"Good to know," he said amiably. "I'll leave it all up to you."

"Smart boy," she said approvingly.

"Zander, we're just kicking around crazy ideas here." Gretel had no idea how to put this genie back in the bottle. She shook sunscreen onto her hand so hard it splattered across her thighs. "You don't have to take any of this seriously."

"But darling—"

"I think it's a good idea," Zander said—surprising her so much she dropped the bottle of SPF 50.

"Excuse me?"

"Aimee wants it, and you're her only daughter. It's understandable."

Gretel glanced at her mother, who was gazing at Zander as if he was the second coming of Calvin Klein. "I'm glad someone understands." She blew a kiss towards Zander.

"But—" Gretel curled her toes into the sand, as if anchoring herself against a strong wind. Everything seemed to be shifting around her. Zander and her mother, allies? Was that the strangest thing ever, or what?

Zander reached for her hand, enclosing it in his, and that one touch brought her back to reality. He was doing this for her, she realized. For the sake of their relationship with her mother. And it was working. Aimee couldn't stop beaming at him, not even when Petey raced back to their umbrella, dripping wet and panting.

"Zander, you have to come body surf. It's so much fun," he shouted.

"Okay, but hang on." Zander grabbed one of his hands and stared at his nail polish. "Hot pink? Where did that come from?"

"It's Pink Flamingo. And we need to get some polish remover because it doesn't feel good at all. Come on!"

LATER, in bed, Gretel cupped Zander's face in her hands. "That was really sweet of you, to play along with my mom about a wedding. But we don't have to do that. It's not in our agreement."

He scanned her face with his deep green eyes that always seemed to see so much. "I wouldn't mind."

"You wouldn't?"

He shook his head, watching her carefully. As if he was looking for something. "Would you?"

"I don't know." She ran her tongue between her lips. "Mom loves big splashy events like that. All of her weddings were incredibly elaborate. She went through wedding planners like candy, I think she must have fired at least six of them. She could have been a wedding planner herself if she hadn't preferred modeling and marrying."

Zander gave her a quiet smile. "She's a force of nature."

"She is. The whirlwind kind. Whereas you—you're like the eye of the storm. So calm, like nothing bothers you. Is that it? Like, it doesn't matter one way or the other if you agree to a big wedding?"

He shrugged one big shoulder, causing the sheet to slide down a bit. "It matters. She's your mother. I want her to be happy. I know how much you love her."

"I do," Gretel whispered. "I really do. Even though she's crazy half the time, and she doesn't understand me at all, I do love her."

"I know." His deep voice purred against her nerve endings.

But how did he know? How was it that Zander seemed to "get" her on a level no one else did?

She remembered her mother's comments about "love" and her worry that Gretel might be making bad decisions based on being in love with Zander. It wasn't true, was it? When her mother had said that, she'd wanted to deny it, but hadn't been able to.

Why not?

Did she love Zander?

Screw it. She didn't want to think about that possibility. It was too unnerving. Instead she scooted down his body and nestled her face into his warm belly. She felt the muscles twitch under her touch, and his penis stir. She didn't move for a moment as she adjusted to the humid heat under the sheet, and to the ocean salt still clinging to his skin, despite his shower.

His hand came onto her head and he played with her hair, massaging her scalp with his long fingers. Before coming to Hawaii she'd dyed it again, giving herself some indigo along with the magenta. Her mother always hated when she put clashing colors in her hair.

"You're a natural blond, Gretel Zsa Zsa Whitney Morrison," she always said. "Why do you want to escape your own hair color?"

Because escape was what she did. It was her default mode.

But more and more, she wasn't sure escape was what she wanted when it came to Zander.

She sighed with pleasure as he worked his fingers through her hair. "I'm going to open a hair salon and you're going to be my shampoo boy," she murmured.

"Is that right?"

"And Petey can do the mani-pedis."

He laughed, his belly rising and falling under her cheek. "You're the craziest girl, did anyone ever tell you that?"

Crazy...

She turned her head and licked his shaft, one long stroke of her tongue against the hardening flesh. It reacted with a pulse and a kick.

Crazy in love. The thought flashed through her mind. And vanished just as fast because it was just a song, just a phrase, and she wasn't sure she knew what love was.

But she knew what desire was. As she filled her mouth with his erection, arousal shuddered through her—hot and familiar, something she understood, something she could surrender to. Something that could chase all those other thoughts—love, weddings—to the back of her mind.

CHAPTER TWENTY-SEVEN

Vacation by the numbers: six full days in Hawaii. Seven nights snuggling in bed with Gretel. Four surfing lessons for Petey. Six times Gretel sipped on a Mai Tai, then passed it off to him to finish. Twenty-six times the two of them snuck back to the hotel room for some "honeymoon time." Five times Aimee offered to take Petey home to Connecticut with her.

That, of course, was where he drew the line. Jason moving into town was one thing. Ten-year-old Petey was staying right where he was.

By the time the three of them collapsed into their seats on the airplane heading home, they were sunburned, sand-blasted, and sick of the flavor coconut.

Gretel curled her hand in Zander's and rested her head on his shoulder. "Is it my imagination, or was that vacation more exhausting than shoveling out from a three-foot snowstorm?"

"I loved it," Petey announced as he took out his iPad, where all his favorite games lived. "Aimee says she's going to let me go to New York with her."

"In a few years, maybe." God, would Aimee even be part of

their lives in a few years? Zander didn't want to count on that. But overall he thought the trip had gone well. Aimee didn't seem to hate him, at least. If she hated him, would she have kept talking about weddings?

Every time she did, Zander had held his breath, waiting for the truth to hit Gretel.

With Jason gone, they had no compelling reason to stay in this "marriage-with-an-asterisk." The threat from Children's Services was gone. He hadn't heard anything from Susan Baker since Jason had left. No one was trying to take Petey away. Sure, Gretel's presence made them a more "traditional-looking" family. But unless Petey started failing all his classes and getting into fist-fights with shop owners, they'd be fine.

As for Gretel's reason for their "marriage," she'd already fulfilled her pledge to the butterfly sanctuary. The other purpose —to get her mother off her back—was a complete failure. It had done the opposite. Aimee was all set to throw them a wedding and show Petey the world.

Had Gretel realized yet that their entire rationale for being together was gone?

Unless...

There was that conversation he'd half overheard, as he was coming awake from his nap on the beach. Gretel and her mother had been arguing, and he'd slowly realized that they were fighting about him. As he swam toward consciousness, words flowed past him. "Feel sorry ... frozen monstrosity... real feelings...love...cloud your judgment...plastered all over your face...wedding..."

By the word "wedding," he'd been fully focussed on what Aimee was saying. He'd stepped in to rescue Gretel, because he could sense her desperation. But what about the part that had come before?

The part where Aimee accused Gretel of being in love with him?

She hadn't said "yes." But she hadn't exactly said "no" either. Instead, she'd shifted the subject and damn, he really wanted to know more.

Because the way he felt when Gretel was around—it was different from anything he'd experienced before.

But then there was the other part of what Aimee had said. "Tiny dump of a town...waste away at the ends of the earth..."

She had a very good point.

Was Gretel really going to be happy staying in Lost Harbor? He couldn't leave, not while he was raising Petey.

And that was another thing.

He liked being a father—or at least a father-like figure. Before he'd taken on the care of his brothers, he never would have imagined it. But it was true. He wouldn't mind more kids at some point. His own. Was Gretel ready for that amount of commitment? When she had the whole world out there waiting for her?

He inhaled the fresh scent of her hair—damn, it smelled like coconut just like everything else—and adjusted his position so her head was nestled into the divot between his shoulder and his chest. She sighed in her sleep.

Here was a wild and crazy idea: what if he told her how he felt? *I think I might love you. I think this could be real. I think I need you. I think I want to drop the damn asterisk.*

Better not rush into that. He didn't want to scare her off.

When they finally reached Lost Harbor—two flight changes later—they discovered that another foot of snow had fallen. Nate picked them up at the airport and caught them up on everything they'd missed while they were gone.

The power had gone out for six hours during the blizzard, and the Nightly Catch's pipes had burst. Boris Clancy's pet chicken had gotten trapped in a stove pipe and he'd had to dismantle his entire venting system to get her out. The Lost Harbor Puffins hockey team had finally won a game, their first of the winter season. They'd celebrated by getting drunk and erecting a giant blow-up puffin on top of the Olde Salt. In the process, two of the players had slipped off the roof and were now out for the season.

"There's a reason we're called the Lost Harbor Losers," Nate admitted. "A very good reason."

"Pretty sure there's a couple good reasons," murmured Zander.

Nate flipped him a finger, then spoke to Gretel in the backseat. "Ian Finnegan's back in town. He was asking for you. I told him to stop by the Wicked Brew."

"Oh cool!" Gretel clapped her hands. "It'll be nice to see him."

"Who's Ian Finnegan?" Zander had never heard that name before, and he knew most people in Lost Harbor at least by name.

"He's a neurosurgeon who occasionally comes to the Misty Bay Hospital to check up on the brains of Lost Harbor," Gretel told him.

"That doesn't take long." Petey cracked up at his own joke.

Zander ignored him; he was too busy trying to figure out what this neurosurgeon meant to Gretel. Why would she even know a neurosurgeon? "Friend of yours?" he asked her.

"Yes. Sort of. There was a double-date situation. And then my dad showed up and I got sent to town for champagne and things kind of spiraled from there."

Spiraled? Was that code for something? Did he have to worry about this Ian Finnegan? Even though he and Gretel were married?

That asterisk was becoming more and more of a problem.

CHAPTER TWENTY-EIGHT

Gretel had never been so happy to be home. The flight into the tiny Lost Harbor airport had been breathtaking. They'd circled over a layer of ice fog that filled Misty Bay like whipped cream. On one side of the bay, the peaks of Lost Souls Wilderness flirted with the cloud cover, rising in majestic crags of snow-covered rock against a pale gray sky. On the other, the homes of Lost Harbor clung together, a cozy brigade taking on the elements.

Even the new foot of snow didn't bother her. After they waded through the snow to the arctic entry and grabbed shovels, she and Petey each took a snow scoop and made a race out of it. By the time the pathway to the front door was cleared, her arms were aching but she was exhilarated by the pure champagne of the crisp air—so different from the humid atmosphere of Hawaii.

She loved Hawaii, of course. And the beach. And traveling. She still loved all of those things. But even more, she loved having something to come home to.

While she and Petey were shoveling, Zander made a fire in the woodstove and got some chili cooking. It was the perfect meal after all that snow shoveling, and they huddled close to the fire while they wolfed it down. Niko, who'd spent the last week with the Noonans, was just as blissfully content to be home as she was.

Zander sorted through the mail that had arrived while they'd been gone. "Jesus, Jason's trip to State is going to cost a fricking fortune. The school won't cover it because he's not an official member of the team yet." He set it aside, and opened up another one.

His face tightened as he scanned it, but he refused to say anything about it, other than it came from his parents' life insurance company.

After dinner, Gretel dug out her nail polish remover and helped Petey get the last traces of Pink Flamingo off his nails. "Want to try a different color?" she asked him.

"Nah. I just wanted to see what it felt like. I thought it would feel like magic." He waved his hand in a bippity-boop gesture.

"Well, I guess you could say makeup is a kind of magic. But not that kind."

Zander was watching them with a lazy smile. "Anyone up for a game of pickup sticks?"

"Yess!" Petey ran off to grab their set of pickup sticks.

Zander grabbed the opportunity and swiveled her close to him for a kiss. "Welcome home, Gretel Zsa Zsa Whitney Morrison," he murmured after they'd emerged, panting, from a kiss that seemed to reach deep into her soul. Talk about magic.

"Welcome home," was just about the most romantic thing he could have said. Short of the "L" word. But that word wasn't part of their vocabulary.

THE WICKED BREW had missed her badly. Everyone told her that—the customers, the other baristas, even Danny D. She had to admit that it felt good that her one-week absence had left such a hole.

She felt terrible about the performances she'd missed, the storytellers and the marimba group that no one had bothered to promote in her absence.

"Never leave again," one of the baristas whispered to her. "Danny D might seriously lose it next time."

"Has he said anything more about selling the Wicked Brew?"

"Every time he gets pissed off. So, yeah. A few times a day."

Crap. Just when she'd started to carve out a place for herself, it was probably going to disappear.

Midway through the morning, Ian Finnegan came in for a coffee. She danced out from behind the bar to give him a hug.

"How are you, my favorite brainiac?" she teased him after she'd finished the hug. Even with his nerd-heaven glasses and generally awkward manner, he was a very good-looking guy.

"Strange. Bethany probably told you about my stalker."

"She did." Gretel squeezed his arm sympathetically. "What's the story?"

"I operated on her daughter, who has a rare form of epilepsy, and now she thinks we're meant to be together."

"I assume you disagree?"

"Vehemently."

"You know I flunked vocabulary."

He went on as if he hadn't heard her, in that single-minded way of his. He must be really upset about the stalker situation. "I had to take out a restraining order. It's been a nightmare. She stole my phone and went through my photos. It just keeps getting worse. It's nice to come to Lost Harbor and get a break from it."

"How about a mocha latte to take your mind off it?"

He smiled at her with such sweetness that she started racking her brain for someone to set him up with. Maya Badger? No, she'd already nixed that. Toni the bartender? Trixie Tran, who ran the ice cream shop in the summer?

Well, she'd work on it.

After making Ian his mocha latte, she chatted with him for a few more minutes, making him laugh with her suggestions for possible dates. By the time he left, he was looking much more cheerful. Her job was done.

And then—her phone rang.

As soon as she saw her father's photo flash on the screen, she knew it was trouble. Did she have to answer? She was at work, after all. Any minute now, someone would come in and want a coffee.

She let it go to voicemail.

But right away, he called again. Daddy despised voice mail and never left messages.

Crap, it must be important. She hadn't spoken to him much since he cut her off financially last fall. Not because she was angry, but because she'd seized on it as a chance to take command of her own life and she didn't want Lloyd Morrison, with all his power and wealth, interfering with that.

She hadn't even spoken to him at Christmas. He and Gemma had gone to St. Barts and the time zones had never lined up.

When he called a third time, she finally gave in. After telling Danny D that she was going to take her break, she took the phone into the storage room in the back. The intense aroma of the sacks of coffee beans reminded her of when she'd dragged Zander back here and basically proposed to him.

The memory made her smile.

The smile didn't last long.

"I just got off the phone with your mother. *A wedding*, Gretel? You want me to pay for your *wedding*?"

"No! Oh God, I should have called you about that. Just ignore her. You don't have to pay for anything."

"She said you're serious about this boy."

"Well, he's not a boy. And we did get married already, so that's pretty ser—"

"It's ridiculous, and that's all it is. It's a childish rebellion. Completely absurd."

Gretel inhaled more coffee bean aroma, counting on it to ground her against the blast of her father's scorn. Her hands were starting to sweat. "I guess that's your opinion. But there's nothing you can do about it. Like I told Mom, it's already official. Stamped in gold by the State of Alaska. Signed by me, Zander, and two random dog mushers."

"Ah yes. Zander Ross. I've researched your quote husband."

A sick feeling gathered in her stomach. "You can leave off the quote. He's my husband."

"You didn't learn much about him before you decided to hitch your future to him, did you?"

"If you mean did I hire a private investigator like you probably did, no. But I didn't need to. I know him."

"Did you know that he's in debt because he spent money he didn't yet have? That's feckless."

In debt. Zander had never mentioned that. He'd only talked about the life insurance that still hadn't come through.

"I'm sure it's because of his parents' insurance." She closed her eyes in immediate regret. Just like that, she'd stepped onto his turf. She should have stayed away from this entire topic.

"He'd better hope that comes through."

That sounded almost like a threat. "What are you talking about?"

"Without those funds, I don't see how he can get rid of his debt while paying for his brother's ski expenses."

"How do you know about—" She snapped her mouth shut. Dumb question. If her father had hired a private investigator, he knew everything.

But maybe that was a good thing. If Zander's biggest flaw was that he'd gone into debt to take care of his brothers, then he was pretty freaking flawless.

"If you've dug up that information, then you also know that Zander served in the military, that he resigned to come home and take care of his brothers. That he's a *good person*. Isn't that the most important thing? Isn't that what you want in a son-in-law?"

Her father snorted as if she'd said something ridiculous. "I thought this was one of your hair-up-your-ass schemes and that you would have moved on by now. But your mother thinks it's more than that. She's talking weddings and the Plaza and Thailand and God knows what else. So I'm drawing a line. For your own good."

"Daddy, you really don't seem to get it. It's not up to you anymore. I made my choice. And I'm *choosing* to stick with it. I'm an adult, I have the right to do that, even if you don't like my choice!"

There, that felt good. The ground steadied under her feet. She didn't care about Zander's alleged debt. He hadn't mentioned it, but he'd been crystal clear from the beginning that their money had to be separate. That wasn't a character flaw, that was doing the best he could with a tough situation. That was Zander in a nutshell.

"You care about this family, is that what I'm hearing? The Ross family? You've taken them on like a bunch of stray puppies, like Aimee says?"

"Of course I care about them. But they're not strays and that's extremely insulting—"

"If you care about them, then I have good news for you."

Gretel leaned against the storage shelf. There went firm ground again, slip-sliding away, disoriented her all over again. "What are you talking about?"

"Jason Ross. The skier. Quite a future he has, if he can afford to get there."

Gretel bit down so hard on her cheek that it hurt. Here it came. The carrot. Or the stick. Or both.

"I'll be his sponsor. I'll pay all his expenses until he's able to cover himself. For as long as he needs the support, I'll give it. That includes gold-plated health insurance for the whole family, travel expenses for the whole family, all of his gear. And when I say 'gear' I mean top-of-the-line, nothing but the absolute best. I'll cover private coaching when that becomes a requirement, private tutoring, living expenses on the road, room and board, whatever the fuck he needs. Blank check. No questions asked. Like a magic carpet ride to the Olympics."

Gretel's imagination reeled at what that kind of sponsorship could do for Jason. The difference between an athlete who made it and an athlete who languished could easily be the level of funding they enjoyed. Rich kids had an advantage in that respect, or kids who caught the eye of a wealthy patron. Here in Lost Harbor, Jason's opportunities to catch someone's eye were limited.

With Lloyd Morrison's support, there were no limits except Jason's own talent and commitment.

And from what she'd seen, he wasn't lacking in either of those departments.

"The catch?" she managed. Lloyd Morrison never gave anything away. There was always a quid pro quo. He always wanted his pound of flesh.

"Don't play dumb, Gretel. I want you to leave this insult of a marriage. My daughter, married to some blue-collar military dropout. It's humiliating. You get a divorce, or better yet, an annulment, and you put Lost Harbor in your rear-view mirror. For good."

The phone threatened to slip through Gretel's sweaty fingers. "What does that mean, for good? Bethany lives here."

"So she can come to Connecticut if she wants to see you."

"I'm not going back to—" she began heatedly.

"Fine. No strings on what you do after you leave Lost Harbor. Two conditions only: you get that divorce right away and you leave Alaska."

She wetted her lips. "How long..." She didn't quite have the heart to finish.

"My guy tells me Jason has some big expenses coming up. There's a state competition that his family will have to pay for. If I want to get the ball rolling in time for that, I'll need an immediate decision if you want to help Jason."

She swallowed hard. Her throat ached from tension. Her purpose for "marriage" with Zander had been to help the family. How could she say no to something that would help them so greatly?

"Gretel?"

"Let me think about it," she croaked, and hung up the phone.

She leaned back against the shelving and gripped the unfinished edge of one wooden shelf. A splinter tore into her palm. Shoddy workmanship.

Zander would never build shelves with splinters sticking out of them.

She pulled her hand away and gazed at the wound. It brought back a quick memory of Zander helping Petey with a splinter he'd gotten from picking up a log. Petey had hollered like someone undergoing surgery with no anesthesia, but Zander had been so patient with the tweezers she brought him from her makeup kit.

Afterwards, she'd sanitized the bloody tweezers and left them in the bathroom. At least there would be something there of hers after she left.

Tears rolled down her face, but only partly because of the pain in her palm. She'd married Zander to help the family. How could she justify staying married to him when it would *hurt* the family?

It wasn't just the sponsorship. It was the other veiled threats about Zander's debt. Lloyd Morrison had no moral qualms about interfering with things like that. She didn't know if it was possible for him to call in whatever loan Zander had taken out. But if she didn't agree to his offer, he might try. If that didn't work, something else would. Her father could be vindictive and vengeful when he didn't get his way.

Just look at how he'd cut Gretel off in order to hurt Bethany. Everyone knew that Bethany was a responsible, caring person who would never abandon her younger sister. Just like that, Gretel had been dumped onto Bethany. Which was one more reason why Gretel had worked so hard to become self-sufficient. She didn't want to be a burden to her beloved older sister.

Now her choices were down to two: do as her father wanted and skip town, after dumping Zander. Or stay and cost Jason a ski sponsorship and possibly plunge Zander into financial peril.

The thought of leaving made her heart ache. She didn't want to leave, but staying would be selfish. Or she could be unselfish and leave. Wasn't that the lesson she was trying to learn? How to put other people first?

Face it. Her father had won, as he always did. She had only one real choice.

The only question was how to do it quickly and cleanly while causing the least amount of hurt possible to Zander and Petey and Jason. Jason would be fine—better than fine because he'd be getting an exciting new ski sponsorship very soon. Petey was such a cool kid, such a one-of-a-kind, funny, curious-about-the-world kind of boy. He'd be fine, too.

And Zander...well, he'd never said that he loved her. He

looked at her with passion in his eyes, and he touched her as if he truly cherished her. But he'd never said any words of love—neither of them had. It wasn't part of their deal. He'd be okay, especially when all his financial worries vanished. Maybe this was the best thing that could happen to the Ross family.

As for herself? That was a lost cause. Her heart was already breaking.

She drew in a deep breath and called her father back.

"Let's negotiate," she said, thankful that her voice sounded relatively steady.

"You want to negotiate with me?" His amusement made her stiffen. *Don't let him roll you, Gretel. Get more out of him.*

"Yes. I'll do what you want if you sweeten the deal. That life insurance policy you mentioned? Make sure they get that money. It's theirs, after all."

"How would I—?"

"I don't care!" she interrupted. "You're Lloyd Morrison. You can make it happen. That's my offer. Take it or leave it."

A pause, then, "We have a deal."

CHAPTER TWENTY-NINE

Gretel was in a mood that Zander had never seen before. Skittish, almost edgy, nervous. When he picked up one of her palms to check, he found it sweaty and worse than that, injured. "Sweetheart, this is going to get infected. Look at how it's swelling."

"It's fine." She snatched her hand away from him. "It's just a splinter."

"You're not getting gangrene from a splinter on my watch." He made her sit down under a bright light while he extracted the last remains of the splinter. When he finished, he was shocked by the tears shining on her face, because she hadn't made a single sound while he was working.

"Did I hurt you?" he asked, gently brushing the moisture from her cheek.

She shook her head, but he didn't quite believe her. So he lifted her in his arms and carried her to his bedroom and tried to distract her with all the tools at his disposal. Mostly his tongue, which went on a mission to find the most sensitive spots on her body. The inner crook of her elbow. Her right nipple. The exquisitely soft curve of her inner thigh. And of course the biggest prize, the ripe plum of her clit.

By the time she came in wild, thrashing spasms, he felt pretty good about himself. But her tears were still flowing.

Maybe instead of an orgasm, she needed some comfort. Just in case, he wrapped her in his arms, tucked his long legs around her slim ones, and murmured sweet words in her ear—how beautiful she was, how wild and at the same time, candy-sweet.

But the only thing that stopped her tears was sleep.

THE NEXT MORNING, Zander woke up to the sound of his alarm. Unusual, because he generally woke earlier than that, already running down his checklist of tasks for the day. Blame all the sex.

He flung his arm over to Gretel's side of the bed, but she was already gone.

Also unusual, since she was more of the sleep-in type. But then he remembered that she had an early shift at the Wicked Brew. She must have tiptoed out of the room so as not to disturb him.

His hand touched her pillow. He rolled over and buried his face in it, inhaling the faint whiff of her scent. If he couldn't have Gretel first thing in the morning, he'd have to make do with her fragrance.

Outside the window, thick snowflakes were falling through the pristine sapphire light of the winter dawn. He swung his legs out of the bed, feet touching the cold floor. Hopefully Gretel had taken his rig instead of that old Frontier of the Noonans'. He didn't trust that thing in new snow.

Just in case Gretel hadn't left yet, he decided to send her a text. His phone told him it was after eight. That meant Petey had already been picked up for school. Gretel had handled the whole morning routine.

Hope you took the Tacoma, sweetcheeks. It's better in the snow.

He got no answer, which probably meant that she was already driving. One of the conditions of their agreement was that she never text while driving—he'd thrown that in there for safety's sake.

Someone had to look out for her.

Out in the living room, a robust fire was crackling in the woodstove. Gretel had really gotten the hang of fire starting, he'd give her that.

And not just the literal kind.

Chuckling, he crouched down to close the damper so the house wouldn't get too hot. The scent of coffee stole through the air—Gretel must have already made a pot, and left some for him.

She must be feeling better. He hoped so, though he still had no idea what had been bothering her last night. She'd fallen into a deep sleep and hadn't stirred even when he'd shifted her head onto her own pillow and adjusted the covers around her. He'd stroked her hair for a while, those silky tinted strands sliding through his fingers like water. Then he'd dropped a kiss on her temple.

"Dream sweet, my love," he'd murmured. The word "love" had slipped off his tongue so naturally, so easily, so perfectly.

He got to his feet and strode into the kitchen. He had so much to do today. He wanted to reorganize his workshop to make space for a new project—a tiny house a young couple wanted some help with. He was on after-school carpool duty. He was also working on a present for Petey's birthday—a treasure chest for all his games. It was best to work on it while he was in school so there was no chance he'd burst in and ruin the surprise.

In the kitchen, he reached onto the shelf and pulled down his favorite mug, the one he used every day. Jason had given it to him on that first terrible Christmas after the accident. Its handle was in the shape of a wolf's head. Clever design, really.

But today something was different. A piece of paper was curled inside. He pulled it out and read it while he filled the mug with coffee.

"Dear Zander. I'm invoking the escape hatch. I can't explain why, just please know that it's for the best. Maybe it's just the way I am—always the wanderer. I'm sorry. I want you to know that it's nothing that you did. You were a wonderful "husband" and I will never forget you, or any of you wild Ross brothers. I left a note for Petey too, but he might still be sad. Give him lots of hugs from me. He needs hugs. Jason too, if he'll let you, but I'm not worried about him. I put the divorce paperwork in the silverware drawer so Niko wouldn't eat it."

For a long moment, Zander didn't move. His feet were rooted to the floor, his entire body in suspended animation. It wasn't until he felt Niko's cold nose snuffling at his hand that he broke out of his stupor.

Mechanically, he filled Niko's food bowl and splashed some water in his dish.

Gretel was gone.

Now that he'd read her note, he noticed other things. Her knitting project, which she always left on the armchair right next to the wood-stove, was gone. In the arctic entry, there were empty hooks where her coats had hung. Her zebra-print boots were gone, and so where the more sensible snow boots. Even the air felt different. Empty. Flat.

Her snowshoes still hung on the rack he'd built. Wherever she was going, she didn't intend to snowshoe.

He strode into the bedroom and yanked open the closet. Most of her clothes were gone, but not all of them. Maybe she hadn't had enough time to pack everything while he was sleeping. Maybe she was traveling light.

Traveling light was her specialty, after all. She'd taken charge of all their packing for Hawaii and they'd managed the trip with nothing but carry-ons.

A deep lance of pain hit him right in the gut. He gripped the edge of the bureau and doubled over.

The bureau. He'd taken Gretel from behind right here in the dark. The hot images swam back to him, taunting him with their erotic edge. *Gretel was gone*, and they'd never be naked and wild together again. Last night had been the last time, ever.

And then it hit him.

She'd known that she was leaving. Of course she had—that was why she'd been crying last night. He'd thought he could comfort her with sex, or with cuddling—what a fool he'd been. She'd never had any intention of staying. This was all a game to her. An adventure. A whim.

That escape hatch was something she'd planned to use from the very beginning.

A rush of cold fury replaced the pain. That felt better than the hurt. Anger, he could handle. He pulled on some clothes, barely aware of what he was putting on his body. She couldn't have gotten far yet, and she wasn't going to get away with this. Sneaking off while he was sleeping. Not giving him a chance to say anything. Fuck that.

He slammed the door behind him as he stalked to his Tacoma truck. She'd driven the Noonans' truck after all. At least she hadn't stolen his rig for her hit-and-run.

Stop this. Gretel isn't a thief.

But his anger shouted over his common sense. He was going

to catch up with her and he was going to tell her to her face what he thought of her actions.

Despite his anger, he kept a careful eye on the woods alongside the road. The plow truck hadn't been up here yet and the light covering of new snow made the road surface slippery. He might be pissed at Gretel, but he didn't want her to drive off the road.

But he saw no signs of anything amiss—no abandoned rigs or tire tracks heading for the woods.

So he allowed his anger to take full rein. Gretel had used him. She'd breezed into his life and made him fall for her, then breezed right out again without even the courtesy of a face-to-face conversation. Even worse, she'd walked away from his little brothers after showering them with affection and attention. It would have been better if she'd never come here.

No, it wouldn't. Again, he blotted out any hint of common sense. Jaw set, knuckles white, fury coursing through him, he reached the intersection with the main road. From here, he could either drive through town or take a bypass route that would take him to the highway heading away from Lost Harbor. Which way had Gretel gone?

She wouldn't leave without stopping in at the Wicked Brew.

Swinging the wheel hard, he took the turn toward town. Yup, there was that old Nissan Frontier, parked outside the Wicked Brew. Adrenaline raced through him. *She was still here.* He was going to see her one more time. And man, was he going to let her have it.

He jerked his Tacoma to a stop right outside the front door. Even the sight of that stupid cup with those stupid creatures carved into the steam pissed him off. Gretel had considered it important to say goodbye to this cafe, but not to him? That was just fucked up.

CHAPTER THIRTY

Ignoring the "Closed" sign, he stormed into the Wicked Brew, then stopped in his tracks. Something weird was going on. First of all, the place was empty. Why would the Wicked Brew be closed at this hour? Second, the only light came from the back hallway.

He stood still for a moment as his eyes adjusted to the dimness. "Gretel?" he called. "Is anyone here?"

A crashing sound came from the back, then Gretel appeared in the archway that led to the area where the storage room and bathroom were located.

He scrutinized her closely in the low light. She had a strange look about her—almost shaken. Maybe she was surprised to see him. *Of course* she was surprised to see him.

"Zander." Her voice came out low and unsteady. "What are you doing here? Did you get my note?"

"Yes, I got your note. Nice touch, leaving it in my favorite mug. 'Would you like a breakup with that coffee?'"

She wetted her lips with her tongue—the gesture that always drove him mad. "I'm sorry. But it's for the best."

"What happened to the whipped cream?"

"Excuse me?"

"Whipped cream! We're supposed to discuss important things and agree on them. It's right there in our ironclad prenup."

"Okay. Fine. We'll discuss it. Let's make an appointment maybe later this afternoon or—"

"Fuck no. How do I know you won't just hit the road? You obviously don't respect our agreement. You would be halfway to Grandview by now if you hadn't stopped to actually say goodbye, in person, to the Wicked Brew."

"Zander, please." She put her hands together in a prayer position. "I do respect our agreement. You're my husband and I...I love you. Only you. You're the only man I love. The only one." Her voice rose to a louder pitch as she went on.

Thunderstruck, he glared at her. "What the fuck, Gretel? One minute you're leaving, the next you're—" He scrubbed both hands through his hair. "You're just playing games. All of this is like...a comedy sketch to you. Like it's not real. But *I'm real*. So is Petey. And Jason. And you're just walking away like it doesn't matter. Fuck that, Gretel."

Her eyes gleamed with tears. Fake tears, probably. How could he trust them? How could he trust anything she said?

"Just go, Zander. Please. I'll text you later." She jerked her head toward the door, her eyes wide and pleading.

He *should* go. What was the point of staying? But...

Something didn't feel right. Gretel wasn't acting like herself. He'd seen many sides of Gretel since he'd met her, but he'd never seen her so skittish. Her eyes kept darting away from his and she kept wiping her hands on her apron.

Nervous. She was extremely nervous. And it wasn't because of him. Something else was going on.

Instead of leaving, he took a step forward. "Were you serious when you said you love me?"

She flushed, which made him realize she hadn't had any color in her face until just now. "Just go. It doesn't matter now. Please, just leave."

"No. You said it. I want to know why. I want to know if it's true or if you're just saying it and why you expect me to just leave when you told me you love me and—"

"You should listen to her!" A female voice rang out from behind Gretel. Gretel flinched and shot Zander one more desperate look as she jerked her head toward the front door. "You should have gotten the hell out!"

Gretel stumbled forward, with a woman right behind her, shoving her from behind, as if she—

Oh my God. She had a gun to Gretel's back.

Zander went cold and clear. Full alert. What exactly were they dealing with here? He analyzed the situation the way he'd been trained. The woman, who looked to be in her late thirties, was armed and hostile, with a manic look about her. Meth head, maybe? Her hair was a greasy tangle. She wore a dirty blue parka and a turtleneck with a stain on it. As they came closer, she pointed the gun at him and he saw that it was a Ruger LCR, a smallish six-shot revolver.

She aimed the Ruger at Gretel again, but surveyed Zander with curiosity. "Are you really her husband?"

"Yes," he said calmly, all trace of passion and anger erased from his voice. "I'm her husband. Is this a robbery? Because I'll give you everything you want. Just let her go. My truck is right outside. We can drive to the bank and I'll clean out my accounts for you. Just let her go."

"I don't need money." The woman spit at Gretel's head. Gretel flinched as the saliva struck her, as if she was antici- pating a bullet. Now that she'd come farther into the room, he noticed a bruise on her forehead. The woman must have hit her.

Zander clenched his fists against a wild surge of fury. He

needed to keep his cool here. This stranger was on the edge and almost anything could push her over.

"What do you want, then?" he asked her.

"I want my man. She stole him." She pushed the revolver deeper into Gretel's back.

Gretel winced again, then quickly tried to mask it. "I keep telling her that I'm married to you, so I couldn't have stolen her man."

"I saw photos of you in his phone. And then I saw you here with him. You hugged him for a long time. Such a *slut* you are."

"No no, that was just friendship. You know what? Ian told me about you. He said he operated on your child. How is she doing?"

"You shouldn't talk about her." The woman drew her hand back to hit Gretel again, but Zander jumped in to interrupt. He couldn't bear to watch Gretel get struck right in front of him.

"Hang on a second, I have the right to know what's going on. If my wife's having an affair, someone should fill me in on it."

The woman's gaze tilted toward him, wild and bloodshot. But at least she wasn't hitting Gretel.

Her hand wobbled—she was getting tired of holding up the gun. Maybe he could use that to his advantage.

"Does someone want to explain this whole thing to me?" he demanded, keeping the woman's attention on him. "You. What's your name?"

"Elizabeth. Most people call me Lizzie, but not him. He calls me Elizabeth."

"And who's 'him.' Is it Ian Finnegan?"

"You know him?" Her voice filled with hero worship.

"I wish I did, but I don't. Maybe you should tell me about him." Establish a bond. That was the key. Anything to keep her from lashing out at Gretel. "Maybe I'll go beat him up myself. Where is he?"

That got a strong reaction out of her. She swung the Ruger away from Gretel and toward Zander. *Good.* Not that he liked having a gun pointed at him, but he liked it even less pointed at Gretel.

"Don't touch him. It's not his fault. It's hers." The revolver swung back toward Gretel, but in the meantime Gretel had inched away enough so that the three of them were points in a triangle. A misshapen triangle, with him a few steps farther away. But Gretel had created enough distance so that the woman couldn't keep the gun on both of them. Smart move, so long as it didn't piss her off..

"Tell me what she did," Zander demanded, dragging her attention back to him. "I'm her husband, I deserve to know."

"I want to shoot." The Ruger swung back and forth between the two of them, as if she couldn't decide which one to aim at.

"That's a very, very bad idea," Zander warned her. "You'll go to prison if you pull that trigger. It'll be really hard to see Ian in prison. And what about your child? If she just had surgery, she needs you."

"You don't know anything!" she screamed and turned the Ruger on him.

Zander put his hands in the air and, by some miracle, kept his voice even. "You're right. I don't. That's why I'm asking. Please tell me what's going on. If I can help, I will. I promise."

"It's her! He wants her! I saw the photos! She's pretty and rich and spoiled, I know her type, she's the kind of girl everyone wants and her life is perfect and *he* wants her too and I hate her! She doesn't deserve to live!" With a cry of anguish, she wheeled back around toward Gretel and Zander saw in a flash that she *was* going to shoot. But her hand was shaking so much that she needed both of them, and that gave Zander his only chance.

Before she'd even rotated fully toward Gretel, Zander

launched himself into the air toward her. He aimed for her closest arm, hoping to knock the revolver from her grasp.

She fired just as he slammed into her. He knocked her arm enough so the shot went wide, but not wide enough. Gretel cried out and stumbled backwards into the coffee counter. She clapped a hand to her upper arm—where the bullet must have struck her. Worst of all, the woman still had possession of the Ruger.

The two of them, he and the shooter, hit the floor with a thud. He heard her shout something angry, but couldn't make it out.

"Go, Gretel," he yelled. "Call 911! Call your sister, call Maya!"

The woman underneath him was kicking and thrashing, a bucking bronco trying to get him off her. She was a tall woman, heavy-set, with the chaotic strength of someone driven by hate and fury. She fired another shot, but it went into the wall. He had to get that gun away from her, but it was just out of his reach.

Gretel staggered into his field of vision. Shit—she was trying to help him, he realized. She wasn't running, she was coming toward them. Jesus. Was she trying to get shot again?

"Stay back!" he yelled at her.

He couldn't see if she obeyed him, because he was focused on the gun. He pinned the woman's legs under him and crawled across her body toward the weapon. In her hand, the black Ruger was turning, wobbly but determined, until it pointed in Gretel's direction.

One last microsecond was all he had. He flung his body forward in a desperate move to put himself between Gretel and the gun.

Something seared into his ribs.

And then blackness swallowed him up.

CHAPTER THIRTY-ONE

Gretel screamed as the gun went off again. By some miracle, Zander managed to deflect another shot. But now he was unconscious and slumped on top of the crazy stalker, who was fighting to get free.

Even though her right arm throbbed like a swarm of bees, adrenaline kept her going. She made it to the pile of Zander-squashing-the-Stalker and kicked the gun as hard as she could. Her zebra-print boots also had a pretty substantial heel and a sharp toe, but even so, it took two hard kicks to get the gun out of Elizabeth's hand.

Gretel pounced on it and grabbed it with both of her wildly shaking hands. "I don't know how to use this!" she yelled as she aimed it at the stalker. "But it can't be that hard and you're right in front of me!"

The woman hissed at her, but try as she might, she still wasn't able to free herself from the weight of Zander's big body. Even unconscious, he was saving her.

"Stay there," Gretel told her, sidestepping around them. She had to get help for Zander. That was the only thing that mattered. But she had no idea where her phone was, and she couldn't let go of the gun. Her arm was bleeding badly and her vision was blurring around the edges.

Keeping the gun trained on the woman, or near her, anyway, she backed toward the front door. Of course she couldn't pull the trigger because she might hit Zander. But this stalker-chick wasn't all there, so hopefully she wouldn't realize that in time.

When she reached the front door, she pushed it open with one hand, her gun hand still aimed at Lizzie/Elizabeth.

"Help!" she yelled over her shoulder, into the outdoors, in the loudest and clearest voice she could manage—as if she were singing above a crowded club. She didn't look away from the woman as she shouted, so she had no idea if anyone was out there. *Come on, Lost Harbor. Come through for me.* "Call 911! We need help! Call the police! Call an ambulance! A man has been shot! Help!"

She kept yelling and shouting even as the world blurred around her and the cold from outside crept under her clothes and gripped her with icy claws. Didn't matter. She wasn't going to stop until someone came and took care of Zander. She'd stay out here all night if she had to. Or until that woman came after her like some zombie who wouldn't stay down.

She didn't stop calling for help until a Lost Harbor police car pulled up—she heard the sirens and the red-and-blue flashers going off behind her.

She heard Maya Badger's familiar voice and the sound of footfalls. "Gretel? Are you okay? You're bleeding!" Maya was right behind her now, but Gretel was too spent to do anything besides let her arm fall to her side.

"Where's that ambulance?" Maya yelled to someone behind her. "We need it *now*." Then lower, softer, right in her ear, "Gretel. Give me the gun. I got this. You can let go now. Is there another gun inside?"

"No. Zander," she whispered as she loosened her fingers enough for the gun to be taken away. "Take care of Zander."

And then Bethany was there, wrapping her in a blanket, and Maya was charging inside the coffee shop and all that adrenaline was vaporizing from her body. She let Bethany whisk her toward the ambulance, where Nate and another EMT were busy pulling a gurney out of the back.

But she wouldn't rest until she knew if Zander was okay. Before Bethany could push her into the ambulance, she clutched at her sister.

"Bethany. Find out if Zander..." She couldn't complete the thought. It was too horrible to contemplate.

"You have to rest, Gretel. You're in shock. We're going to take you to the hospital."

She summoned the last bit of her strength. "No. I can wait. Zander's hurt worse."

"Let your sister check you out," Nate called from next to the gurney, which he and the other paramedics were wheeling toward the Wicked Brew. "I'll get an update on Zander. I'll be right back."

Gretel nodded. Bethany helped her onto the van's tailgate and unpeeled the bloody sweater from her body. "Jesus, Gretel. You have a serious wound here, but it could have been so much worse."

"Yeah. Zander knocked her arm—" Her throat closed up.

"Shhh," Bethany soothed her. "Keep breathing. We got this."

But did they? She didn't even know where the bullet had hit Zander. She shook her head, trying to articulate her fear into words, but nothing came out.

Bethany wrapped a bandage around her arm. "This is just temporary to stop the bleeding. You still have to go to the hospital. What's this bruise here?" She touched her forehead, but Gretel shook her off. None of that mattered now.

Nate reappeared at a jog, eyes grave. "He's alive, Gretel. He'll be okay. But he's going to need surgery and we need to get him to the ER right away."

"I'll take Gretel in my car," said Bethany. "I can get her there faster."

"Sounds good. I gotta get back in there." He ran back in the direction of the coffee shop.

Gretel let Bethany guide her toward her car. She wanted to stay and see Zander with her own eyes. But that was silly. There was nothing more she could do. He needed doctors and surgeons. He needed gold-plated health care. Time off work to heal. Enough money to allow him that time.

Whether Zander knew it or not, he needed her to leave.

None of what had just happened changed anything.

———

AT THE HOSPITAL, Bethany re-bandaged Gretel's arm and checked her over for other injuries. Her big sister kept a blanket wrapped around her and brought her some hot chocolate and fussed over her. All that tender care finally stopped the shivering.

Ian came rushing in at some point, horrified to hear that his stalker had attacked Gretel. "I'm so terribly sorry, Gretel. I came down here to get away from her. I never imagined she would leave Anchorage."

"She seemed to think I'm a threat to her. Where did she get that idea?"

Ian took off his glasses to clean the condensation off them. He must have just come in from outside. "I made a reference to a woman I was attached to, but I never used your name. I was hoping to inspire her to move on. I couldn't conceive of her taking it even further."

Gretel nodded wearily. "You can't predict something like

that. It's not your fault, Ian. Where is she now?" She addressed that question to Maya—Police Chief Badger—who had just walked in.

"She's in custody, heavily sedated. Her husband is on his way."

"She has a *husband*?" Gretel exchanged a shocked glance with Ian. "She never mentioned that while she was berating me for stealing her man." Her hand stole to the bruise on her temple, where a dull ache pulsed.

"He says she's been struggling with emotional issues for years, and their daughter's health crisis sent her into a tailspin. She became obsessed with Ian as some kind of white knight savior." She hesitated. "Given that history, I'm not sure how the DA will want to handle this case."

"I don't care," Gretel told the police chief. She'd be gone and all this would be just a terrible memory. "But Zander's hurt even worse than me, so he should have a say in what happens. And she should never, ever be able to get her hands on a gun again."

Maya's stern expression softened with a wry smile. "We'll do what we can. Gretel, I gotta say, you handled the situation like a pro. If Zander comes through like they say, it'll be thanks to you."

"*If?*" Gretel shoved aside the blanket and jumped off the hospital bed. "What do you mean, *if?*"

Maya grabbed her by the shoulders. "I misspoke, Gretel. Listen to me. He's going to be fine. I swear to God, he's okay. What I meant was if he comes through with no lasting damage. I'm so sorry. That was terrible. I checked in with the surgical team before I came in here and they said it's looking really good. I probably should have mentioned that when I first walked in."

Gretel couldn't get her heart rate to slow down. It was hopping like a jack rabbit all over the place. "Police Chief Badger, I love you, but you really, really need to work on your tact."

"No arguments here." Maya gave her a long hug. "Take care, Gretel. The whole town's rooting for you."

Gretel bit her lip, tears springing to her eyes. Bethany noticed, and as soon as Maya was gone, she guided her back to the hospital bed with a gentle touch. "Are these post-trauma tears or is something else wrong, kiddo?"

Gretel tried to answer, found more tears welling up, and shook her head.

"Is it Zander? He'll be okay. Nate went to get the kids out of school so they can be here when he comes out of surgery. They can wait in here with you if—"

"No." Gretel grabbed her sister's hand. She couldn't see the boys. She couldn't let them see her. She had to get out of town, immediately. "I need to go."

"Go? What are you talking about? I'm not letting you leave until all your vitals are stable and—"

"Bethany. I'm begging. I need to leave before the boys get here. I'm going back to Mom's in Connecticut."

It was as good a place as any to recover from a gunshot wound. Then she'd figure out what came next.

"Gretel!" cried Bethany. "Why? You're not thinking clearly. You're in shock."

"I'm thinking one hundred percent clearly. I was on my way out of town when that crazy stalker came into the coffee shop. I'm leaving Lost Harbor, Bethany. I was going to tell you when I got further down the road."

"But...I don't understand." The dismay on her sister's face nearly tore her heart in two. "I thought you liked it here. Zander, the boys, the Wicked Brew, the town, all the eccentrics..."

"I love it here!" Gretel couldn't keep the truth from bursting out. "But I have my reasons and they're good ones, and it's *for* the boys, so you just have to trust me."

If she told Bethany everything, her sister might try to talk her out of it, and right now Gretel didn't have the strength to argue. She had to save her energy for the road trip.

"Will you trust me?" she managed.

Bethany gave her a slow nod. And maybe for the first time, Gretel saw something in Bethany's eyes that she'd always unconsciously longed for—the respect given to an equal. Not to a baby sister, but to a grown woman.

"Will you tell me eventually?" Bethany asked her.

"I will. I promise. Now will you help me make a quick escape?"

Bethany swung into doctor mode and gathered up some bandages and acetaminophen and antibiotic ointment in case of infection. She got Gretel discharged, then ushered her out a side door so there would be no chance of running into the boys. She drove her back to the Wicked Brew, where Gretel's truck was waiting.

"How about I take you to the airport instead, and Nate and I will return the Noonan's truck to them?"

"Technically, it's my truck, because they gave it to me. But since I'm not about to drive it to Connecticut—sure. Tell them I'm going to write them a long letter really soon." Tears leaked from her eyes again as she thought about Abby and Earl and the kids. She was going to miss them like crazy.

Bethany grabbed her bags from the truck and they headed for the airport. Gretel's arm still throbbed, which gave her an idea.

"Bethany, what if you tell everyone that I was so shaken up by the attack that I went home to my mother's to recover? Could you do that? I just don't want to hurt anyone's feelings by leaving like this."

"Aw, sweetie. You have such a soft heart. Are you really sure about this?"

Gretel gave her a look.

After that, Bethany stopped questioning her. They got to the airport just in time for Gretel to grab the next flight out.

And just like that, the wintry peaks and frozen shoreline of Lost Harbor dropped away and she was back in her usual habitat —in transit from one place to another.

It had all happened so fast that she hadn't even gotten to see Zander one last time.

CHAPTER THIRTY-TWO

"You're a damn hero, Zander Ross."

Great words to wake up to. Unfortunately, they didn't come from the pretty lips of Gretel Morrison. They came from Nate Prudhoe, who stood next to his hospital bed with Jason on one side, Petey on the other. Both the boys looked scared shitless.

Good God. They'd nearly lost another "parent."

He managed a grin and a "shaka" sign; he and Petey had learned it in Hawaii. "Who said you could skip school?"

"Everyone," said Jason.

"Does it hurt?" asked Petey, eyeing his bandaged middle with fascination.

"Fu—" Nimbly, he turned 'fuck yes' into, "For sure." At least his brain didn't seem the worse for being shot. "How's Gretel?"

"She's good. A bullet grazed her arm and she's in shock, but it could have been so much worse. She told us how you knocked away the gun. She says you saved her life at least once, maybe twice. Quick thinking, Zander. You did the Marines proud. Like I said, you're a hero."

What a relief. His body relaxed bit by bit. "Last thing I remember, I was trying to stop another shot."

"You did. And then you collapsed on top of her, so you got the last laugh. Gretel managed to get the gun away from the assailant and call for help. Fact is, she probably saved you too."

"I told her to run, but she didn't."

A funny expression came over Nate's face. "She was very determined to make sure you were okay before she accepted so much as a Band-Aid. Pretty damn gutsy."

His heart swelled under his casing of bandages. "Where is she? Still being treated?"

"Bethany's on her way, she'll know more."

There was something Nate wasn't saying. Zander squinted at him, and found his image wavering in and out. "So what's the damage?"

"The bullet grazed your right lung and did lots of soft tissue damage. The surgeons repaired the wound, but there will be some recovery time. Expect at least a couple of months."

He nodded stoically. He'd been wounded once in Afghanistan. Recovery always felt like it took forever. He wasn't looking forward to battling the VA for coverage, either. There was a good chance he'd walk out of this hospital with a hefty bill and no way to make money until he was back on his feet.

"We'll help," Jason announced.

Petey gave an exuberant nod of agreement. "I'll do all the dishes!"

"I'm going to move back in so I can take care of you," said Jason.

Zander frowned at Jason, touched, but not enough to go along with that. "You will not. You'll stay right where you are and focus on your skiing. Petey, you're welcome to do all the dishes you want, but there's no need. My arms seem to be fine." He raised them in the air, hiding the wince of pain that caused.

Nate cleared his throat. "Actually, Bethany and I were going to suggest that Petey stay with us until you can drive comfortably. The Noonans offered too, but Earl has to get back to the Slope and Abby still has her hands full."

Zander cut his gaze to Petey. "What do you think, bud? Want to stay in the Hilltop mansion for a bit?"

"Yeah!" Petey pumped his arm. But then he frowned. "What about Gretel? Can't she drive the carpool?"

One glance at Nate's face, and Zander knew that Gretel had left. She'd slipped through the escape hatch and was gone. The incident in the Wicked Brew hadn't changed her mind. Her saying those words—"I love you"—hadn't changed anything. Maybe they weren't even true.

But even though he was still woozy from surgery, he remembered exactly how her face had looked as she said them. They were true. She did love him.

And yet still, she was gone.

He cleared his throat. "Gretel's ... uh..." He couldn't say it. Maybe the anesthesia was messing him up. Yeah, that had to be it.

Nate stepped into the silence. "Gretel was really shaken up by what happened in the coffee shop. She decided to go to her mother's to recuperate."

"Her *mother*?" Petey scowled. "She doesn't even live here. She lives in the Lower Forty-eight."

"Right. That's where Gretel went." Nate met Zander's gaze with a shrug, as if it was a mystery to him too.

"When's she coming back?" Jason demanded. He looked more upset by this news than Zander would have expected, all things considered.

"I honestly have no idea." Exhaustion dragged at him like an anchor. He tried to fill his lungs with oxygen, but immediately felt the sutures strain. "But we're going to be fine, boys. The Ross brothers rule, right?"

"Yeah, but Ross sisters are good too." Petey folded his arms across his chest.

How was he supposed to deal with this insurrection on top of surgery? Not to mention heartbreak? Right now he couldn't tell the difference between the pain in his heart and that in his wounded organs. It all blended together into a general sense of misery.

Luckily, Nate stepped in at that point and told the boys that Zander needed to rest. Yeah, he needed rest. He also needed Gretel. But he'd have to learn to live without her, which might be even harder than learning how to breathe again.

THE DOCTORS RELEASED him a few days later. Soon afterwards, he got a bill from Misty Bay Regional Hospital. He opened it with a sense of dread, but instead of the horrifically high amount he'd been expecting, he discovered that he owed zero.

Maybe the VA had come through without him having to push for it.

He set the bill aside and didn't think more about it, until he got word from Jason that his expenses for his trip to State had been taken care of.

"By who? The Sterns?"

"No. They said I have a sponsor now. They don't know who it is either. It's someone who wants to be anonymous."

An anonymous sponsor? That sounded odd. He called up Coach Stern and asked if they'd ever encountered an anonymous sponsor before.

"Only if it's a private citizen. Businesses always want the credit, and usually every sponsor does. But it sometimes happens, if there's a reason to keep their connection to the athlete confidential."

"I don't like it. I want to know who's behind this. Is there any way to find out?"

"There might be. Let me do some research."

A few days later Coach Stern called back with a bombshell. "The bank account that was set up to take care of Jason's expenses can be traced back to the Morrison Development Corporation. I assume that Gretel had something to do with it. Have you asked her?"

Speechless, Zander ended the call and tossed his phone on the kitchen counter. The house was so empty these days, with Gretel and both the boys gone. Susan Leafborn, a physical therapist—he thought of her as the good Susan—came to his house every day. Who was paying for that, come to think of it? He'd assumed it was the VA, but maybe not.

A knock sounded on his front door. If it was the good Susan, he'd ask her who was footing the bill. If it was the bad Susan, well, he was all out of brothers anyway. Not much she could do to hurt him now.

Darius Boone, the fire chief, stood on the front stoop. He was such a big dude that he blocked the entire view of the property. "How ya doing, Zander? I hear your recovery's going well."

"Feels slow, but I can't complain. What's up?"

"Can I come in? Got something to discuss with you."

Zander ushered him inside. He couldn't imagine what the fire chief could possibly have to discuss with him. Darius Boone was relatively new in town, having assumed the top spot in the mostly volunteer fire department about a year ago.

The fire chief stood in the middle of the living room and

surveyed the space. "Nice design. High ceilings, always a plus for me."

"Thanks. My grandfather started it, and my parents took it from there. There's still a lot to be done."

"Isn't there always." The big man straddled one of the bar stools. "Thanks for giving me a segue."

Zander frowned in confusion and propped his elbows on the kitchen island. "This is about my parents?"

"Sort of. I wanted to give you a heads up about something. Ever since I started in the job here, I've been going back and forth with Worldwide Insurance, the company that ended up with your parents' life insurance policy. Apparently it got sold a few times. It's not uncommon."

"Yeah, I know the company. They're assholes. They won't honor my parents' policy. But why are they pestering you?"

Darius folded his arms across his wide chest. They'd played hockey together once; the man was a beast on the ice. "Basically, they've been trying to say that your parents' accident was their fault. The fire department was the first agency on the scene. So they took the report that we filed and they've been trying to twist what it says. But I have to sign off on it—either me or my predecessor. She wouldn't, and in fact she gave me a head's up about this situation when I took over."

"Jesus. No one ever told me about this."

"Yeah, it's kind of a sensitive area. As an official agency, we can't look like we're colluding with the filer. It could damage your case."

Zander snorted, noticing as he did so that it didn't hurt as much as it would have a couple weeks ago. "When I think about all the time I wasted on the phone with them, sending emails. Those fuckers are never going to give me that money, are they?"

"Well, that's the thing. Recently I got something in the mail from a new company saying they'd bought the policy.

Completely different tune. They said all they need is my signature on the report—which is a very accurate report stating the crash was due to weather conditions and not human error—and within days they'll disburse the funds."

Zander blinked at the fire chief. With his rugged physique and stubbled jaw, he fit in easily with the men of Lost Harbor. It was easy to forget that he'd moved here from Texas.

"That sounds like a good thing."

"Yeah. It's a long time coming. I've sent probably fifty emails since I've been on this job, trying to get them to do the decent thing and pay up."

"I guess it worked, huh?"

Darius shook his head. "No, it wasn't me. It's this new company. That's why I wanted to give you a heads up, in case something sketchy is going on. I can't imagine what, but then, I'm not an insurance agent shark."

"What's the company?"

Darius dug into his pocket and pulled out a business-size envelope. He handed it to Zander. The name of the company meant nothing to Zander, but he realized in a flash that it didn't matter.

Somehow, Gretel was responsible for this. Jason's sponsorship, his hospital bill, his insurance money. All of it was thanks to Gretel. He just knew it.

Darius slid off the stool, preparing to leave. "I'm sure that money'll come in handy. I'm happy for you, Zander."

He didn't care about the money. He needed to know what the hell was going on here.

"Thanks for doing all that, fighting the insurance company. You didn't have to. You didn't know me from a sea slug."

Darius focused his dark eyes on him. "Not at first. But I learn quick. If you need anything, don't think twice. I got your back."

Zander nodded. Actually, there was something. "Can you

give me a ride into town? I'm not supposed to drive yet, and I have to find Bethany Morrison."

If anyone knew what was going on, it was Bethany. If it took playing the wounded hero card to get the truth out of her, that's what he'd do.

CHAPTER THIRTY-THREE

As her "All Better Now" party at the Greenshores Country Club dragged on, Gretel's smiles were becoming harder and harder to force. The party was her mother's idea, of course, but her father and Gemma had stopped by too. Her recovery was just an excuse for the gathering, since she didn't know most of the people here. They knew each other, though, and had lots to talk about—inside gossip, mergers, acquisitions, and so forth.

The only thing she really had to say, she'd already said. It was "no" when her mother pleaded with her to move back permanently. "No" when her father offered to finagle her an internship at a fashion magazine. "No" to everything that involved staying on the East Coast and taking their money.

Technically, "No, thank you," since she'd taken care to be polite and firm while she was stating her intentions. Her adult comportment seemed to take them off guard.

Both her parents kept sending her wary glances as she lingered near the stage where a swing band was playing, and an emcee had introduced her earlier. Maybe they were afraid she'd jump onstage and perform. Or maybe they were confused by her lack of interest in the freely flowing champagne.

Her heart might be broken into little bits, but that didn't mean she was going to slide back into her old ways.

The opposite, actually. She was going to treasure every morsel of pain and growth that she'd gone through since arriving in Lost Harbor. No one could take that away from her. She'd even located an AA meeting in this upscale corner of Connecticut. It had been a lifeline for the past few weeks. She'd recovered from the bullet wound just fine; recovering from Zander was another matter.

The day the signed divorce paperwork had arrived in the mail she'd cried until her tears ran out.

Her eyes misted over as she listened to the band play the Elvis classic, "A Little Less Conversation." She'd sung that to Zander one night, the first night they'd gotten together, and he'd made that goofy Elvis move. She missed him so much.

A full month later, and she still thought about Zander all the time.

She'd finally explained everything to Bethany. Her big sister had been furious with their father for all his manipulations. But she'd agreed to give her regular reports on how the Ross brothers were doing.

That helped, a tiny bit, but not nearly enough. Missing them felt like flesh being carved out of her body. It felt permanent—as if that hole would never be filled.

Which explained the problem with her disappearing smiles. She tried again, since her mother was looking her way across the crowd of guests in their resort wear. Nope, not happening.

The emcee appeared onstage and tapped the mic. "Ladies and gentlemen, a few announcements. First, let's have a big hand for Aimee, who planned this beautiful event ..."

Gretel's attention faded as he thanked the band, then moved

on to some club announcements. Could she leave yet without being rude? How long had she been at this party? At least a week, it felt like. Time dragged here in Greenwich, which was ironic since there were so many people and so many different things to do. Tennis, golf, swimming, brunch, lunch, Pilates, shopping, dinner parties, on and on.

In Lost Harbor, things moved according to the season and the weather. The pace gave her time to soak in the beauty of tiny moments she would have otherwise missed. Snow crystals glittering as they drifted down from a tree branch. A flock of chickadees changing direction in midair. Ice mist suspended over a low spot in the woods.

In Lost Harbor the connections she'd made felt deeper, more real...wait. She snapped back to attention, because it wasn't just her brain thinking "Lost Harbor." Someone had said it out loud.

The emcee. He was reading something from a piece of paper.

"Direct from Lost Harbor, Alaska, these are today's Bush Lines," he was saying. "Zander Ross, along with his two brothers, would like to announce that Gretel Morrison overcame all hurdles and expectations by staying through the worst of the winter. She would have stayed even longer except her generosity and selflessness inspired her to leave. We would also like to say that we don't want her to leave, and in fact we reject any kind of deal that requires her to leave."

Gretel's jaw fell open. A murmur of confusion spread through the crowd of party guests. *Zander.* Was he here? Where had that paper come from?

She whirled around. Desperate for the sight of the tall, rough, magnificent man who held her heart in the palm of his hands.

And there he was, just inside the French doors that led to the terrace, with Jason and Petey at his side. He was watching for her, eyes alight, his face softened by a slight smile.

She flew across the room, elbowing people out of the way as

she went. She was afraid to blink, as if he might disappear back into her fantasies if she did. But no—he was real and solid and warm and wonderful and he didn't even flinch as he caught her into his arms and squeezed her tight.

"Zander! You're here! You're really here! How's your—oh my God, your lung, are you okay? Can you breath?" Too late, she remembered his wound.

"You're all the air I need," he murmured in her ear. "First time I've been able to breathe right since you left."

"I'm sorry, it was for you guys—"

"I know. Bethany told me. I knew you wouldn't just run away. I should have trusted my gut."

"I missed you so much! I still can't believe you're here." Still wrapped in his arms, she touched his back, his shoulder blades, his neck.

His chest vibrated with his laughter. "Not for long, hopefully. I'm here to bring you home, if you'll come." He loosened his grip and she tilted her face up to meet his gaze. "I love you, Gretel. I'm yours, every bit of me, body and soul. I want you back in my arms, in my bed, in my heart. You're my everything, my sun, my stars, my fire on a cold night. My Northern Lights. Please come home. We need you. I need you."

His passionate words felt like honey poured directly into her heart.

"But...there's reasons...financial reasons..."

"I know those reasons. I reject them. Jason does too. We all talked about it, as a family, and we'd rather give up the money, the sponsorship, all of it. We want you, Gretel. *I* want you. Only you." Those last words growled into her ear with hot wicked intentions that shivered down her spine. "Unless there are other reasons..."

"No. No, that's it. I just wanted what's best for you all—"

"*You're* what's best. It isn't even close."

She shot a quick glance at Jason and Petey, who were mostly looking at anything except the two of them. Typical boys, embarrassed by such blatant emotion. Well, they'd just have to get used to it. Because she loved this open, heartfelt side of Zander. Showing him how much she loved him back would be pure joy.

"What about the divorce?" It was already official; her father had pulled some strings to make it happen that fast. He was going to be furious that all his machinations had been for nothing.

Off to the side, she caught sight of her father, who stood next her mother. Aimee was whispering something to him that caused his red-faced glare to recede.

Gretel caught his eye. He shrugged in resignation, as if to say, "I tried. You're on your own now." Her glance shifted to Aimee, who tipped her glass of champagne toward her. *Thank you, Mom.*

"I'm not worried about the divorce," Zander was saying. "We'll get married again when we're good and ready. I just want to be with you." All of Zander's deep and soulful heart shone from his eyes.

"Okay. Okay. Yes. Let's go home." She buried her face in his neck and sobbed with happiness. He held her like that for a long time, then relaxed his embrace so they could join his brothers.

Sniffing back her tears, she offered her hands to Petey and Jason, and all four of them stood in a tight circle that felt exactly like home.

She cuddled against Zander, feeling his thumping heartbeat through his clothes. Nice clothes, she realized. Black trousers, a well-cut green twill shirt she'd never seen him wear. Both the boys wore new jeans and nice sweaters. He'd bought them all new outfits and flown his two brothers all the way to Connecticut to prove to her how much she meant to them.

She loved this man from the bottom of her heart, forevermore. "Who needs a wedding? I guess we can just be wicked together," she told him.

"It's a deal."

OPEN MIC NIGHT at the coffee shop; always one of Gretel's favorite events. Especially now that the cafe belonged to her. Danny D had finally decided to sell, for real.

In the most amazing turn of events, Zander had bought it with part of the life insurance money. An investment in their future, he'd told her. And also a drop in the bucket of his new fortune.

Yup, ironically enough, he was now the wealthy one of the two of them, and there was nothing Lloyd Morrison could do about it. The life insurance had paid the Ross family two million dollars, more than enough to cover all of Jason's future ski expenses and invest in a coffee shop.

It had been Zander's idea to buy it, and his idea to rename it to Gretel's Cafe. *Her* place to make her own, to transform as she wanted. She already had so many ideas. For one, she planned to travel the world and seek out coffee farms that produced only the most delicious beans. She also intended to insist on sustainable growing methods and farms that guaranteed a share of the profits to the local workers.

Her Robin Hood instincts finally had free rein.

Besides, the only way to make sure the farms were up to these standards was to see for herself, and that meant she could still satisfy her wanderlust. Her love of travel hadn't disappeared just because she'd fallen in love with Zander. She still wanted to see the world. But she also loved having a home to return to.

Most of all, she loved having Zander to return to.

Gretel's Cafe brought in a steady income, and with her plans for expansion, would do even better. Maybe someday her bank account would even match Zander's.

Aimee, for one, was extremely happy about Zander's new status as acceptably well-off. Gretel's father was coming around too. Whenever she and Zander got married again, they'd both be invited to the wedding.

So would Susan Baker, who'd connected them with a kickass lawyer. Zander's guardianship of both boys was now official, although Jason was still living with Stern and Sterner until the end of the school year. As soon as he came back, the whole family was going fishing. Gretel couldn't wait.

The space buzzed with chatter. Spring was coming to Lost Harbor and people were discussing their gardens, and how many of their chickens had survived the winter, and how much work their boats needed, and how bad "breakup" was going to be.

"Breakup" was what Alaskans called the time when all the ice began melting and everything turned to mud. Gretel didn't care for the term, since it made her think of Zander and the time they'd spent apart. She never liked thinking about that time.

She leaned against Zander's hard chest. He was completely healed now, and back to working magic with wood. In fact, he'd carved her new sign for her.

Gretel's Cafe, it read in beautiful curlicue swirls. The two words sat on a sled that was being pulled through the snow by a laughing girl who looked a lot like Gretel.

The man was an artist with his wicked, beautiful hands.

"Are you ready for this?" she murmured to him, tilting her head to gaze up at that beloved face.

"Ready for what?"

"There's something I owe you."

"Honey, you don't owe me a thing. Except maybe a kiss just because you love me."

"I do love you." She stood on tiptoe and brushed a kiss onto his chin. "But apparently you've forgotten our first ever deal."

He gazed down at her with lifted eyebrows. "Are we getting married again?"

"We could. I do want to talk to you about that, and about a few other related things. But I have to do my duty first."

"Duty, huh? You sound like me."

"I guess it rubbed off." After one more kiss, this one met by his warm, loving lips, she pulled herself away and stepped to the mic.

"Welcome, everyone, to Open Mic night at Gretel's Cafe! I'm so happy to see you all—familiar faces and a few of you who have finally chipped your way out of your winter ice caves and made it into town. I've always heard that strange things happen around Lost Souls Wilderness, and we have living proof right here." The crowd laughed good-naturedly. The Lost Harborites were good sports. "Now, I usually leave the performing to everyone else, but tonight I'm going to claim some time. A while ago a certain wood-worker challenged me to stay here for the entire winter. I didn't quite make it, due to a few twists of fate."

Zander was shaking his head at her with a broad smile, letting her know she wasn't required to do this.

"Since I lost that challenge, I'm here now to pay up. Harris, would you mind? Darius, come on up here."

She'd enlisted her stitch-and-bitch bestie to accompany her on his fiddle. The fire chief, it turned out, was a master of the bass. He'd brought it out of retirement to help her fulfill her bet.

Wearing a black cowboy hat that made him look hot as hell—just because she loved Zander didn't mean she couldn't appre-ciate a fire chief in a cowboy hat— Darius took his place on stage behind her. He carried the bass as if it weighed less than Harris's fiddle.

"Let's smoke this," he said. He grinned at Harris, who nodded and struck the first note. Together, they launched into the tune the three of them had been practicing for the last week—her favorite Elvis song, "A Little Less Conversation."

Except she'd completely changed the words.

Gretel took hold of the mic. "Lost Harbor, Alaska, this is for you. My required ode to your winter greatness."

She waited for the right beat to hit, then launched into the song.

> *"A little less snow tonight, a little more sunshine,*
> *   please.*
> *All this endless shoveling ain't satisfactioning me.*
> *A little more beach and a little less windchill,*
> *A little less frostbite and a little more chlorophyll*
> *Close your doors, put a log on the fire and baby*
> *   satisfy me.*
> *Satisfy me, Alaska.*
>
> *Baby close your eyes and listen to the blizzard*
> *And shiver in the winter gale*
> *Its a subzero night, I'll show you how to survive it,*
> *Come inside and you know we can't fail.*
> *Come on baby I'm tired of freezing*
> *Grab the calendar and please stop teasing*
> *Come on, Spring,*
> *Come on, Spring,*
> *Don't procrastinate,*
> *Don't be so damn late,*
> *Lost Harbor's tired of waiting around.*
> *A little less snow tonight, a little more sunshine*
> *   please.*
> *Satisfy me, Alaska, Come on, come on."*

THE CROWD WAS LAUGHING and applauding by the time she finished, but she really only noticed Zander's reaction. He was cracking up, just the way she loved to see. Not that she didn't adore his serious side too. But knowing that she'd lightened his heart and brought a smile to his lips gave her a special joy.

He strode onto the stage and swept her off her feet into a movie-worthy dip.

"Oh, I'll satisfy you," he whispered. "Always."

"I accept that challenge."

"No negotiation?"

"Nah."

He smiled into her eyes and they sealed that deal in the best possible way. With their hearts and souls...by way of a wicked kiss.

THANK you so much for reading! You can find all the Lost Harbor books here. Want to be the first to hear about new books, sales, and exclusive giveaways? Join Jennifer's mailing list and receive a free story as a welcome gift.

ABOUT THE AUTHOR

Jennifer Bernard is a *USA Today* bestselling author of contemporary romance. Her books have been called "an irresistible reading experience" full of "quick wit and sizzling love scenes." A graduate of Harvard and former news promo producer, she left big city life in Los Angeles for true love in Alaska, where she now lives with her husband and stepdaughters. She still hasn't adjusted to the cold, so most often she can be found cuddling with her laptop and a cup of tea. No stranger to book success, she also writes erotic novellas under a naughty secret name that she's happy to share with the curious. You can learn more about Jennifer and her books at JenniferBernard.net. Make sure to sign up for her newsletter for new releases, fresh exclusive content, sales alerts and giveaways.

Connect with Jennifer online:
JenniferBernard.net
Jen@JenniferBernard.net

Lost Harbor, Alaska

Mine Until Moonrise

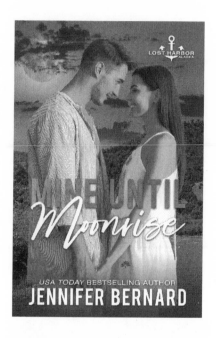

Yours Since Yesterday ~ Book 2

Seduced by Snowfall ∼ Book 3

The Rockwell Legacy

The Rebel ∼ Book 1

The Rogue ∼ Book 2

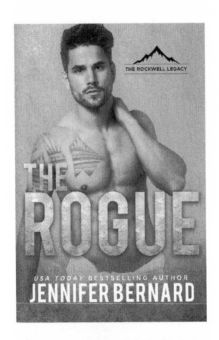

The Renegade ~ Book 3

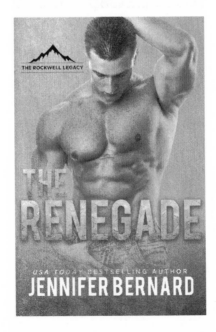

The Runaway ~ Book 4

The Rock ~ Book 5

The Bachelor Firemen of San Gabriel Series

Love Between the Bases Series